DOUBLE VISION—
OR A FACE FROM THE PAST?

Rounding a corner, she nearly collided with a frowning gentleman who was riding the other way.

John Underwood!

Panicking, she jerked her horse from the path. Acorn sideswiped a holly bush and recoiled, nearly unseating her. Fighting both the horse and her pounding heart, she doused her fear with a cold bucket of reality.

John was dead. He had been dead for six months. It was James's forbidding expression that had momentarily confused her.

"Welcome home, my lord." Somehow she kept her voice calm, even through the boil of new emotions. . . .

A
Clandestine
Courtship

by

Allison Lane

A SIGNET BOOK

SIGNET
Published by the Penguin Group
Penguin Putnam Inc., 375 Hudson Street,
New York, New York 10014, U.S.A.
Penguin Books Ltd, 27 Wrights Lane,
London W8 5TZ, England
Penguin Books Australia Ltd, Ringwood,
Victoria, Australia
Penguin Books Canada Ltd, 10 Alcorn Avenue,
Toronto, Ontario, Canada M4V 3B2
Penguin Books (N.Z.) Ld, 182-190 Wairau Road,
Auckland 10, New Zealand

Penguin Books Ltd, Registered Offices:
Harmondsworth, Middlesex, England

First published by Signet, an imprint of Dutton NAL,
a member of Penguin Putnam Inc.

First Printing, January, 1999
10 9 8 7 6 5 4 3 2 1

Chapter One

"Finally!"

Smiling, Mary Northrup laid the letter aside. Justin was coming home. At last she could send out invitations to the welcome party that would reintroduce him to the neighborhood after a seven-year absence. And the timing couldn't be better. Her mourning period would end tomorrow.

But now that the reunion was imminent, she had mixed feelings about seeing him again. His return would throw her life into upheaval, and not just because she was the old baron's widow rather than the current baron's wife. Her diminished importance extended further than that. She had supervised both the house and the estate virtually unfettered since her marriage. Despite knowing for a year that it couldn't continue, she was no more prepared to give it up now than she'd been the day Frederick had died.

Perhaps it was time to find that dream cottage. Losing control of Northfield Manor would be frustrating enough. Turning over her staff would be worse. She had selected and trained most of them. Many were friends, though there was never a question of who was in charge. Even if Justin kept her on for now, her authority could not last. He must eventually marry. She did not want to watch others meddling with *her* people and *her* home. The dower house was too close, so she needed to move clear away. Besides, she would never be fully accepted by local society anyway.

But that was for the future.

Her immediate problem was coping with Justin. He had been fifteen when she'd wed his brother and had resented her presence, ignoring her efforts to befriend him. They had passed a quarrelsome fortnight before he'd returned to school. His next visit home had been cut brutally short when he'd stormed off to buy colors following a week of ferocious arguments with Frederick.

It had been a relief at the time, for she had not known how to deal with him, but his transfer two years later to a regiment sailing to India had shocked everyone. He had not returned to Northfield before leaving. The news had arrived by post, devastating his young sisters, who had been anxiously anticipating an expected leave. Not once in the five years since, had he explained his decision. In fact, his letters had been remarkably reticent on many points, containing none of his thoughts and no hint of his character.

Now he was back. And at three-and-twenty, he was too old for mothering, too old to require a guardian, too old to need consent for anything he chose to do. So she had no idea what to expect. Even this latest missive contained little information beyond his arrival date. He had not disclosed his intentions.

I have sold my commission and will take up my new duties, he had written in his only reference to Frederick's death. Did his lack of condolences arise from antipathy toward his brother, or did he still distrust her? What was he like now?

Her greatest fear was that he would resemble Frederick. Not in looks, which she knew were different, but in interests and character.

She shivered, though a resemblance could work to her advantage. Frederick had hated the country, leaving her in charge of the estate while he lived in London. It was an arrangement that had suited them both, and one that might suit Justin as well.

But he wished to take up his duties, which implied a desire to assume management of Northfield.

Or did it? Perhaps he was referring to Parliament. The barony gave him a seat in the Lords, and a political career would keep him in London. Many of his youthful arguments had revealed an interest in current affairs and the future of the nation. Had that been a passing fancy, or had his years in India increased his concerns?

Stop this! Such thinking was useless, revealing a cowardly refusal to face reality. He could just as easily be referring to his duty to marry and provide for the succession. After all, Frederick had wed within a month of achieving the title. It might be a family tradition.

And even if Justin hated estate work and postponed any thought of matrimony, he would hardly leave her in charge. Few men accepted women in positions of authority. Frederick had done so out of laziness, but an army officer who had earned two field promotions was not lazy. And Justin might be worse than his brother in other ways.

Again she shivered.

Turning over control of the estate would be tricky. He knew little about the Manor or its tenants. Though they had corresponded regularly, she had never described Frederick's business or mentioned her hand in running it. He was probably unaware of her role.

Just as she knew nothing of his interests. He had not responded to news of his childhood neighbors. His letters had been friendly, but bland, touching only on the mundane. And even that could have been a facade. No gentleman would admit faults such as indiscriminate womanizing, unethical or illegal activities, brutality, uncaring selfishness, or any other failing, particularly to a lady whom he knew only by sight. So what was he really like? Saint or sinner? Caring or brutal? Industrious or incompetent?

The answers were important, for she had to plan how to approach him. A smooth transition required that she teach him the estate's problems, peculiarities, and limitations. And she must do so without implying that he was ignorant or suffering any other shortcoming. Men did not like criticism—even when warranted—and their anger terrified her.

Sighing, she read the letter again, hoping to find evidence that Justin was milder than Frederick. But nothing had changed. Setting her fears aside, she rued her vivid imagination. It conjured too many potential disasters, and fretting over the future was pointless. She would discover the truth soon enough. Even if he turned out to be a brutal misogynist, she would have to accept it. For better or worse, her life was now under his control.

And she could not seek that cottage just yet. She had one last duty to the Northrups, one Justin would support. No gentleman wanted two aging sisters on his hands, so she must find husbands for Amelia and Caroline. Frederick's death had interrupted the task, but she could postpone it no longer. Time was flying.

The girls were her only real family. Both of her parents were dead, and her brother was a destitute curate in Cornwall. She probably had several distant relations, but she wouldn't know how to find them. Her father had not stayed in touch.

Footsteps pounded along the hall.

"Trimble says pst-fin-rvd Justin red-cm home," exclaimed Caroline, bursting into the drawing room. As happened all too often, she was talking so fast that only a few words emerged ungarbled.

"Is he back in England then?" asked Amelia, quietly joining them. Amelia did everything quietly, having long ago adopted the relaxed movements and serene disposition that helped keep Caroline coherent.

"He is." Mary was grateful that her sisters-in-law had interrupted her useless fretting. The butler set a tea tray before her. "Thank you, Trimble." She poured. "Justin will remain in London for a few days to deal with the legalities of his accession, but he expects to arrive here in a fortnight."

"What legalities?" asked Caroline carefully. Tea always slowed her speech. The concentration that kept her cup steady controlled her spirits as well.

"Among other things, he will be meeting with Frederick's solicitor and man of business."

"He will learn nothing new." Caroline set her cup on a table.

"Everything will be new to him," Amelia reminded her. "He has been gone for many years. I doubt he knew much about Father's finances and nothing about Frederick's."

"Fredik lost r dowries."

"Easy, Caro," murmured Amelia, pointing to the abandoned cup. Caroline retrieved it. "We can do nothing about that now. At least we still have a home. You should give thanks every day that it is entailed."

"Even if it is shabby beyond belief," muttered Caroline.

Which was true, Mary admitted. She needn't look to be aware of the threadbare spot in the carpet, the fraying seats on the chairs, and the peeling wallcoverings near the windows. But there was little they could do about it.

She relaxed as Caroline sipped her tea. She never knew what to expect. Some days the girl was nearly uncontrollable—though bad days were occurring less often as she matured. In contrast, Amelia was the most restful lady of her acquaintance—and the sweetest. She rarely made demands for herself, devoting her time to helping Caroline and easing the lives of their tenants. She deserved a husband and family of her own—which made the squandered dowries even more tragic and Mary's efforts more urgent.

Caroline was equally deserving, for despite her excitability, she shared Amelia's common sense. And she was a sparkling beauty who drew every eye. As her self-control strengthened, her vivacity charmed more often than it repelled, giving them hope that the problem would ultimately resolve itself.

"We will host a welcome party as soon as Justin returns," said Mary. "He will need to meet everyone, for they will recall him only as a child."

"Wonderful!" Caroline jumped up to dance about the room. "Let's give a ball—he must marry now that he snw baron." Her twirling accelerated until she bumped dizzily into the fireplace.

Mary cringed, wishing she had eased into the subject. Was Justin aware of Caro's affliction? He had spent most of his time in school before joining the military, and she had omitted mention of it in her letters, not wanting to burden him with problems he could not address from India. "Sit next to me, Caro," she begged. "I need your good sense just now."

Caro gulped air, clenching her fists until she could walk across the room and take a seat.

"Can we afford something so grand?" asked Amelia.

Mary frowned. "I doubt it. Even a modest ball would involve upwards of two hundred guests. Those who traveled any distance would have to stay the night. But too many linens need replacing, and we haven't enough servants to handle the extra work. Then there is the expense of musicians, food—"

Caroline's face fell.

Mary continued. "I was thinking of a dinner for our neighbors, followed by cards, but perhaps we could include informal dancing. Now that my mourning is over, no one could accuse us of frivolity. You have been very patient with me."

"It has been no hardship," claimed Amelia before Caroline could protest. "Lady Carworth escorted us to most gatherings."

Caroline nearly snorted, for Lady Carworth disliked her excitability. Taking a deep breath, she spoke slowly. "Informal dancing will be quite enjoyable, so whom shall we invite?"

"The Carworths, Squire Church, the Redfields," said Mary.

"The vicar, the doctor, Miss Hardaway, Miss Sharpe," added Amelia.

Caroline made a face.

"The Grangers."

"Colonel Davis."

"Weren't the Adams boys once Justin's particular friends?"

Discussion eventually produced a list of fifty and an agreement that they were honoring both Justin's arrival and Mary's emergence from mourning.

"Can we seat so many for dinner?" asked Amelia.

Mary frowned. "Cook will need help, and we will have to find more footmen, but it should work."

"Perhaps Lady Carworth will loan us some footmen."

Mary suppressed a grimace. The lady would agree. It would enhance her reputation for generosity while drawing attention to the Northrup failings."

"I wonder if Lord Ridgeway will arrive by then." Caroline was again holding her teacup.

"I am surprised that he has not inspected his seat before now," said Amelia. "It has been six months since he acceded to the title."

"He is visiting those properties near his own estate first," Mary reminded them.

"But how long can that take?"

Forever, if that was what he wanted, but Mary wasn't about to embark on that topic. His movements were of no interest. "If he arrives before the party, we will invite him, but I doubt he will do so. According to the *Times*, he is spending the Season in London."

"Poor man. He must have been horrified to learn of his

brother's death. How could anyone murder a lord on Christmas Day?"

Mary ignored Caroline's observation, unwilling to discuss—yet again—Shropshire's ongoing scandal.

The murder of the ninth earl of Ridgeway still dominated every conversation from the Lusty Maiden's taproom to the most exclusive drawing rooms. The lurid tale tumbled forth hourly, daily, weekly, with no sign of waning interest. But despite the lip service paid to civilized outrage, every voice conveyed satisfaction, for Ridgeway had been the most hated man in the shire.

Shuddering, she pushed thoughts of the murder aside. The new earl had always been very different from his brother. That should not have changed, for he had been a grown man when he had last visited Ridgeway.

Perhaps he would be interested in Amelia. Acceding to the title left him in need of a wife. His sojourn in London proved that he knew it, but he had not yet met with success. The Season was nearly over, without an announcement.

Amelia would make a perfect countess. She was sweet, kind, well-trained, and competent. The earl's fortune was vast enough so that her lack of dowry should pose no problem. With luck, he would visit Ridgeway Court soon.

Mary bit back a sigh over the problem of finding matches for her sisters. Amelia was already twenty, and Caroline eighteen. Despite her own dissatisfaction with marriage, she did not want them to dwindle into spinsters. Showing them to advantage was another reason for this gathering. Hopefully, Caroline could control her excitement long enough to impress at least one gentleman.

James Underwood, tenth Earl of Ridgeway, motioned his friends to fall back so he could enjoy a moment of solitude. Not that he was bored by their conversation. He had deliberately sought their company to provide a distraction from his thoughts.

But for the moment he needed to be alone. His face was out of control, revealing his most private feelings. Let them think he was anxious for the first glimpse of his boyhood home. Let them conclude that he was moody and unpredictable. Their beliefs didn't matter as long as they never discerned the truth: He dreaded this visit.

What was he doing here?

Ten years ago he had escaped along this very road, vowing never to return. Grief, shock, fury, and a pain he had tried to deny had accompanied him. It had taken years to banish those emotions, but he had done it, building a life he enjoyed and establishing a reputation he could be proud of. Setting the past behind him had removed its influence over his future. Or so he had thought.

Until John's murder.

His first reaction had been rage. Not at the death—he and John had been too estranged—but because it forced him to break that vow and return home.

He choked.

Home. The word no longer applied to Ridgeway Court—if it ever had. Long before his actual departure, he had ceased belonging there. In the years since, he had called many places home—rooms in Paris, a palazzo in Naples, the house in Bombay—but his true home now lay in Lincolnshire. His estate might be smaller than Ridgeway, but it welcomed him as the Court never would. So he would be the first Underwood in centuries to live elsewhere. Certainly the first Ridgeway.

But before he could return to the comfort of home, he had to inspect the family seat. It was not a task he could delegate to others. His steward was busy at the Haven. His man of business was trying to make sense of the Ridgeway financial affairs. His secretary was investigating rumors of John's misdeeds in London. They were the only men he wholly trusted. So he must do this himself. And he could put it off no longer.

He had already visited the other Ridgeway properties. After correcting their problems, he had spent two months in London, pretending to search for a bride. Both activities had revealed horrifying accounts of John's misuse of power. Even discounting half the gossip, he had to accept that John's behavior had worsened in the last ten years. Every person he met looked at him askance, every eye holding the same question: Was he like John?

He had convinced most of them that he was not. Accomplishing that had given his London sojourn a purpose, but he could stay there no longer. The Season was drawing to a close, the most desperate matchmaker was plotting his downfall, and he had heard that Ridgeway's tenants were in dire straits.

So he could no longer postpone this visit. Further delay would hurt innocent people and expose his fears and irresponsibility to the world. But facing the ghosts from his past would be difficult, which was why he had invited Harry and Edwin to accompany him.

They were not close friends—he had met Harry while inspecting a small estate in Kent four months ago and had met Edwin when he'd arrived in London—so they could not discern his thoughts. Nor would they see through his public facade. But they would provide company.

Or so he had thought. If his face was slipping before he even reached Ridgeway land, how was he to protect his secrets and hide his shame?

Somehow, he would manage it, he assured himself, shifting in the saddle as the road twisted uphill into the forest. And it should not be difficult. He had deliberately chosen companions who rarely questioned surface appearances.

At nine-and-twenty, Harry Crenshaw had made a name for himself as a carefree rakehell. He was a younger son whose fortune allowed him to enjoy life with willing women, good wine, and intriguing wagers—such as whether a man could stand on one foot for a quarter hour after drinking a bottle of brandy. Few knew Harry's serious side—his work to abolish the use of climbing boys and his support of mothers widowed by the war. James had stumbled across the information quite by accident and had never mentioned it. But Harry's own secrets would keep him from prying.

Sir Edwin Stokes was Harry's opposite. Though only six-and-twenty, he eschewed ballrooms and boudoirs in favor of books and music. While not serious enough to be considered a scholar, Edwin was fascinated by the Romans and was convinced that significant remains were buried on his estate. He planned to search for them once he returned home. In the meantime, his preoccupation blinded him to other men's concerns.

Even when he talked and laughed with friends, a portion of his mind remained with the Romans.

James nodded in satisfaction. A rake and a dreamer. Neither would pay attention to his moods. And the entertainment they provided would allow him to mask any unseemly emotions this confrontation with the past might raise.

"Is it true that you know Napoleon?" asked Edwin when James paused to allow their mounts to catch up.

"We have met, but I can hardly claim to know the man. I was in France during the Peace of Amiens ten years ago," he added, seeing the question trembling on Harry's lips.

Paris had been his first stop after leaving England—and the beginning of a Grand Tour few of his friends had managed. The remnants of the old aristocracy had welcomed the English flocking across the Channel, suppressing their doubts and hiding their woes behind determined celebration. The gaiety had pulled him out of his own pain and turned his eyes to the future.

France had offered delightful diversions, though even a cursory examination had convinced him that the peace would not last; Napoleon had been using the interlude to consolidate his power, resupply his army, and enflame the populace into supporting new campaigns. But the memories could still make him smile. From there, he had traveled to Austria, Italy, Egypt, and finally to India, where he had acquired a fortune that made his inheritance seem paltry.

"How were the Parisian ladies?" asked Harry slyly.

"Sophisticated, but just as willing as that serving girl you ogled in the taproom last night."

"I do enjoy a lusty wench, and she was certainly lusty." Harry let out an exaggerated sigh, then burst into laughter at Edwin's flushed face.

Though Edwin never openly criticized other men's liaisons, he was a bit of a prude who blushed like a schoolgirl when embarrassed. It was not a reaction he could hide, for he was cursed with the pale, transparent complexion common among redheads, so it provided endless entertainment for his fellows.

"We are nearly there," said James unnecessarily, to protect Edwin's feelings. The lad was good-natured about his affliction, but James disliked jokes at anyone's expense. He had been the victim of teasing too often to ignore the pain that usually accompanied it. His brother had been a master at using subtle barbs to undermine an opponent's nerve or tarnish his reputation.

"Did you visit Rome in your travels?" asked Edwin.

"No, but I was in Naples for several months." He saw the question on Harry's lips, licked his own in appreciation, then described the Roman sites he had visited. Even Harry asked thoughtful questions, immersing them in antiquity and diverting his mind from his last day at the Court.

His description of the catacombs enthralled his companions as they passed the gates to Northfield Manor. His visits to Avellino and Benevento—where he had admired the Roman theater and the exquisite artistry of Trajan's Arch—carried them beyond a dozen tenant farms.

But his reprieve couldn't last forever. They rounded a corner and crossed a bridge. Ridgeway dust now swirled around his horses's hooves and billowed behind the carriage wheels.

Memories swept over him, making his hands tremble. Panic clawed at his chest, worse than he had expected, gripping him with an airless tension that would not dissipate. Evil eyes bored into his back.

He cursed under his breath, for his reaction made no sense. It was the people he had fled, not the place. And the people were gone. What evil could remain now?

The park gates stood open, offering an unlikely welcome, but the house was hidden behind its hill. Secretive. Furtive. Like so many of its masters. That had certainly been true of John. What would he find here?

He shivered.

Harry was again waxing poetic over the tavern wench, but James no longer cared. Memories of his brother lodged a lump in his throat. This was why he had procrastinated. He could not face Ridgeway without also coming to terms with his feelings for John Underwood, ninth Earl of Ridgeway, and his elder brother by ten minutes.

Their relationship had always defied description. He had wanted to believe that their shared blood was more than an accident of birth and that *family* meant something. Twins were supposed to be closer than normal brothers, able to read each other's thoughts, willing to support each other against any threat. So he had made excuses, offered forgiveness, and ignored even blatant treachery for more than twenty years. When that failed, he had left, repudiating both blood and family.

Fool!

His unswerving trust had blinded him until it was too late. Now he was faced with cleaning up the wreckage John had left behind and with trying to understand what had gone wrong. The first step was to figure out why John had died.

What had he done to incite murder?

James closed his eyes in a futile attempt to quell a mounting headache. The question had too many answers. He had finally accepted John's venality ten years earlier. Their shared blood tied him to a man he could never respect, tarnishing his own image and drawing suspicion onto his head that would never dissipate.

But despite that, he could not allow John's killer to escape. So how was he to discover which vice had triggered the final attack? And how many new transgressions would he uncover at the Court? They would be legion—which was another reason he had postponed this visit; he had not been ready to face the worst.

John had never visited his other estates, so his orders there had merely inflicted general hardship as he milked the properties of every shilling. But his motives at Ridgeway would have gone far beyond his quest for wealth.

James shivered. He had already seen evidence in London that John had used the power of his position to avenge perceived slights. Had he expended his fury at his twin by striking out at anyone James had cared for? It wasn't an idle fear, for John had threatened to do just that.

Edwin was retaliating against Harry's sexual braggadocio with a discourse on Roman viaducts that had Harry gnashing his teeth, but James hardly heard it. Traversing this road, seeing these hills, and hearing the stream boil over a rocky fall recalled every horror of his last visit.

He forced the memories away by scrupulously examining every tree and shrub in his path, but the battle to forget only increased his feeling of doom. He dreaded this return, dreaded facing the depth of John's anger and the ashes of his revenge, dreaded meeting tenants who would blame him for calling disaster onto their heads.

But he had no choice. He was now the earl, responsible for the welfare of Ridgeway and all its people. He could evade his duty no longer.

Rounding the hill, he led the way to the house.

Chapter Two

Mary turned her horse along the shortcut through Ridge-way's woods. She needed to visit one of the tenants, but first she must recover the poise her encounter with Mrs. Bridwell had shattered.

Her reaction had been stupid, she admitted as Acorn picked his way across a stream. The vicar's wife never failed to find fault with her, and today had been no exception. She should not have let the spiteful words destroy her composure, for they meant nothing.

But they had caught her at a bad time. Between preparing for Justin's arrival and fretting over her future, she was exhausted. Instead of turning the criticism aside with her usual bland comment, she had bolted, loath to reveal the tears pooling in her eyes.

She had overreacted. Today's complaint was an old one—her habit of riding about the countryside unescorted. And the transgression was irrelevant anyway, for the woman only used it as a bridge to censure her other behavior and deride her low birth: A *lady* would travel by carriage with a footman in attendance; a *lady* would not dream of supervising estate workers, inspecting repairs, meeting with bankers, or issuing orders to the steward; and—horrors!—a *lady* would never foster doubts about her virtue.

Obviously the woman had never been to London.

Mary grinned and relaxed.

She had not visited London, either, seldom traveling beyond the market town of Ridgefield. But anyone who read the city papers would know that *virtue* was loosely interpreted in aristocratic circles.

Mrs. Bridwell's opinion was annoying, but nothing would change it, and though Mary was her favorite target, she rarely had a good word for anyone. Perhaps she was envious that Mary had wed into the aristocracy. Or maybe she was naturally catty—she certainly lapped up the rumors, even those proven to be false. Or her pique might arise from guilt. Mary still carried out parish duties Mrs. Bridwell ignored. Everyone knew it, looking askance at the woman. They also knew that Mary's un-ladylike habits had been dictated by necessity.

Not that she considered running the estate and raising Frederick's siblings to be hardships. As a vicar's daughter, she was accustomed to work and felt uncomfortable with nothing to do. Nor was she used to taking servants along on every errand. Besides, the estate could ill afford to hire a groom whose sole job would be to ride with her all day.

She shrugged. Let Mrs. Bridwell condemn her. Riding alone was a minor offense.

Rounding a corner, she nearly collided with a frowning gentleman who was riding the other way.

John Underwood!

Panicking, she jerked her horse from the path. Acorn side-swiped a holly bush and recoiled, nearly unseating her. Fighting both the horse and her pounding heart, she doused her fear with a cold bucket of reality.

John was dead. He had been dead for six months. It was James's forbidding expression that had momentarily confused her.

"Welcome home, my lord." Somehow she kept her voice calm through the boil of new emotions.

James escaped the house, seeking the sanctuary of the woods where he could think. Memories were clouding his judgment, making it impossible to tell whether the frigid atmosphere arose from his own fears or from staff antipathy. He had to decide quickly, for the answer would determine what changes were necessary.

His usual approach was not working. As with his other estates, he had arrived without warning. John's servants ranged from good to bad to venal. Appearing unexpectedly prevented them from assuming a false facade, giving him a better chance to judge their competence and attitudes. It also kept anyone from hiding evidence of malfeasance, allowing him to quickly separate the wheat from the chaff.

But not at Ridgeway. By the time he'd reached the Court, he had been in no condition to judge anything. Memories, voices, pain, and disillusionment had swirled through his head. Guilt had overwhelmed his senses, making him short-tempered. So it was hardly surprising that the servants had appeared sullen. Even the clearer head of morning improved nothing. They seemed to hate him deeply, passionately, and irrevocably, but that made no sense. He knew none of them.

John had turned off the entire staff after gaining the title— hardly surprising, for many of the old servants had carried tales of his childhood misdeeds to the earl. The new staff had been smaller—another way to increase John's revenues—and poorly paid. He doubted any of them had seen service before Ridgeway. Yet none of that explained their hostility.

He hated repeating John's actions by turning everyone off, but he must have servants he could trust and who would perform their duties with at least a modicum of competence. These had been doing a very bad job, starting with the housekeeper.

The manor was filthy. Cleaning had been sporadic at best, and a cursory glance through the accounts showed wholesale pilfering. The butler's accounts were also short. The lower servants were surly, and the sight of the stables nearly made him weep. They had once been the glory of the estate. Now he cringed at consigning his cattle to such deplorable conditions.

Yet he was hesitant about making changes. More was going on than service or lack of it. The servants' faces also reflected fear. Already they were whispering about ghosts, so prudence demanded he move slowly. Was the poor performance aimed at John, and the hatred at John's likeness?

His own ghosts tormented him, driving his friends' chatter into the background. He had expected the pain and guilt that still haunted him ten years after his last meeting with John. But he had not expected to feel his father's presence so clearly.

The eighth earl had been capricious—kind and supportive one day, furiously vindictive the next. He had also been weak and lazy, paying little heed to justice or honor. When someone complained about a twin's behavior, he had found it easier to punish the nearest son than to figure out who was at fault. So James had paid for many a prank he had not played. John had been a master at staying out of sight.

But he wasn't ready to deal with the past. His immediate problem was the staff, which required a clear mind. According to his valet, many of the servants suspected him of either killing John or arranging for his death. Some also blamed him for his father's death.

That was what had sent him on this lone ride. He had never connected their last argument with the fit that had killed him. The idea added a new layer of guilt to his usual burden. Could it be true?

He had rarely protested those unjust charges, having learned that argument merely increased his punishment. But that final accusation had been too base. He had sworn on his honor as a gentleman that it was false. He had even named the people who could prove he had been in Ridgefield at the time. Clearly, the culprit was John.

But his father had not believed him. The earl had favored John ever since the boy had nearly succumbed to a fever at age three. John's convulsions had terrified everyone in the household and had left the earl loath to punish him for years afterward lest he bring on a new attack. The earl's fondest dream had been that his heir would be worthy of the title. Since he did not want that dream shattered, James made an easy scapegoat who could keep his illusions intact.

James shivered, then realized that the pounding was not in his head. A horse was approaching. He pulled back to a trot as a lady swept around the corner, nearly colliding with him.

His breath caught.

Mary Layton. More beautiful than ever. He had forgotten how sunlight made her blonde hair sparkle and how those bottomless blue eyes could drown him. She had always been shapely, but maturity had improved her. Not even her unfashionable riding habit could disguise that glorious bosom.

His gut clenched with lust.

He was opening his mouth to greet her when she recoiled in

shock. Emotions flitted across her face too fast for him to identify, but she finally settled on icy disdain.

"Welcome home, my lord."

Years of practice hid his pain. He had never believed that she loved John, but he could find no other explanation for her iciness. No one had ever cared for both brothers, so her former friendship must have been a ploy to hide her liaisons. But his purpose was to mend fences wherever possible.

"So you still live here, Miss Layton."

"Lady Northrup."

His brows rose. Why had she accepted the baron? The man was old enough to be her father and the most boring lord in Shropshire—unless John's attentions had left her with child. Northrup might have wed her to avert scandal. He had never seemed magnanimous, but stranger things had happened.

"Congratulations," he offered, to stop his useless speculation.

"Thank you," she said dryly. "I take it you have not kept up with local news."

"Hardly. Everyone knows why I left. Who would have dared keep me informed?"

"You overestimate the local gossips. Or underestimate them. A dozen theories were proposed to explain your unexpected departure."

"Such as?"

"One claimed you fled retribution for killing your father—and offered several suggestions for how and why you did so. Another vowed you had lost a fight with John over the future of the estate. A third swore you were avoiding arrest for ravishing Meg Price and poisoning Cotter's horse. A fourth insisted that you fled your creditors. There were others, and many people believe more than one."

He could feel the blood drain from his face. "Which do you prefer?"

"The estate story. Father was saddened when John refused to accept the reforms you had been urging. I doubt you gave up the fight easily. And he must have been upset that your father did not cut you out of his will. John would have begrudged you

even a pennypiece." The color returned to her face as she relaxed.

"You might say that. He threw me out." It was not a scene he
wished to remember. Nor did he want to dwell on the ease with
which she referred to John. "So tell me the local news. What
has happened in the years I was away?"

"Besides John's murder?"

He nodded.

"We have a new vicar—Mr. Bridwell. He was installed eight
years ago, following my father's death. The blacksmith retired
about the same time, moving to Birmingham to live with his
daughter. The new smith is not as talented, but he does an adequate job. Old Barnes died six years ago. His son now runs the
inn. The men swear his ale is better than anything his father
served, thanks to his wife, whose father runs the Golden Spar-
row in Bartles Corner."

"Any improvement must be welcome. Barnes served the
worst ale in the shire."

"So they say. Tate died ten months ago."

"The miller?"

She nodded. "No one has yet replaced him, for John died before he had a chance to see to it." She straightened. "I haven't
time to chat just now. If you wish to hear the latest gossip, join
us for dinner Friday. Everyone will be there. We are celebrating Justin's return from India."

"I have two London friends with me."

"They will also be welcome. Amelia and Caroline are ready
to make their bows and could use some London acquaintances." She launched into praise for their accomplishments.

But he was hardly listening. Now that she was relaxed, the
memories surged. He had been infatuated with her that last
summer, though their flirtation had not been serious. At three-
and-twenty he had not been ready to settle down. But her laughing face had stayed with him for years, invading his
dreams—not surprising, for comely women often did so. Yet he
had never been able to explain why his groin saluted every time
he thought of her. Ten years later, it still reacted.

He shifted in the saddle.

She had seemed special—young, innocent, caring, and beautiful. They had shared many ideas—according dignity to the lower classes, finding employment for weavers who had lost their livelihoods to the mills, paying men enough so their children would not have to slave in manufactories for pennies, educating the tenants so they could understand and accept the advances in agriculture. . . .

Not all the ideas had been practical, and his time in India had proved that life could have been much worse for the lower classes. But her enthusiasm had been catching. Her aura of integrity would have snared even the most cynical. Caught up in the memory, he could believe it still.

The heaviness in his loins pulled him out of his reverie. *Fool!* She would not pull the wool over his eyes again. John's revelations still reverberated in his head. If he lived to be a hundred, he would never shed that hateful voice.

Get out! You may have tricked Father into splitting my inheritance, but that's the end of it, John had growled the moment the solicitor was gone. His fingers had beat a furious tattoo on his copy of the will. *If you don't leave today, I will throw the Thompsons off their farm. They are worthless peasants, incapable of producing enough to cover their rent. And Cotter deserves a lesson in humility. It is time he learns who really owns that land.*

James had blanched, but he'd known protest would only make matters worse. He should have realized that helping the Thompsons and educating Cotter would cause trouble. But he had not expected his father to die.

Yet John's next words had driven even the tenants from his mind.

Don't consider taking Mary with you—not that she would agree to go. She is mine. His mouth had twisted into a smirk as he licked his lips, driving a stake through James's heart.

You lie! he had shouted, his temper shattering.

Never. But rest easy, dear brother. I didn't seduce her. She threw herself at me on her eighteenth birthday. Too bad you are so timid. If you had pushed her a little harder, you could have had the ride of your life. She has tricks you won't have run into elsewhere. I've never had a more eager wench, and that beauty mark on her bottom could stir lust in the coldest shaft.

He had laughed at James's white face. Laughed and laughed and laughed. It echoed still.

James clenched his teeth. The cruel words had haunted him for months, though he would never believe that Mary had instigated the affair. He knew John too well. The initial contact had either been seduction or force. After that, threats of exposure would have kept her in line. But it would explain why Northrup had married her.

This way lay madness. The past could not be changed. And he could not have known her as well as he thought. Her unwillingness to come to him for help belied the friendship he had thought they'd shared. She should have known he would protect her.

She had fallen silent and was looking at him in puzzlement.

"I will call on your husband tomorrow," he said to cover his inattention.

"You will find him in the churchyard. He died a year ago."

"What? He cannot have been more than fifty."

"Dear Lord." She backed her horse a pace, her stare making him squirm. "Did you actually believe I had married Frederick's father?"

"What was I to think when you introduced yourself as Lady Northrup?"

A sigh accompanied a rueful shake of her head. "I forgot you would not know about his death."

"You married Frederick?"

She nodded.

"Why? He was at least two years your junior." The question slipped out without thought, and he nearly kicked himself in disgust.

"My reasons are my own, my lord," she said coldly.

"Forgive me," he begged, unwilling to endure the shadows in her eyes. "That was intolerably rude. You say he passed away last year?"

"He fell into the quarry." She shrugged. "Justin is now the baron. I hope you and your friends will join us to welcome him home. Five years in India will have made him a stranger."

Turning away, she cantered in the direction of Northfield, leaving his mind a swirl of uncertainty. If five years abroad made Justin a stranger, what had a ten-year absence done to him? And why the devil had Mary wed a schoolboy?

But watching her disappear around a corner distracted his thoughts. Her horsemanship had improved immeasurably. As had everything else. The straight back flared into alluring hips that set his blood to boiling. He hadn't seen anyone that enticing in years.

Mary changed out of her habit without summoning her maid. She needed time to put the morning in perspective.

James.

He had changed considerably since she had last seen him, but she could not decide if that was an improvement.

The greatest difference was his demeanor. In memory, he was always smiling, his enthusiasm contagious, his heart as big as the word. He had been a gentle dreamer dedicated to healing the ills of the world. Despite the height that should have overwhelmed those nearby, he had never intimidated her. It distinguished him from John—whose arrogance and incipient brutality cowed nearly everyone—and made people forget that they were identical twins.

She shivered.

The dreamer was gone, vanquished as if he had never been. That was why she had thought for one instant that it was John she faced. In his years away, James had shed his gentle nature and now exuded a masculinity that took her breath away and left funny, prickly feelings crawling over her skin. She would have to stay clear of him, for he had become dangerous—perhaps even as dangerous as John.

There had never been a question about John's character. He had been arrogant from the moment he understood that he was Ridgeway's heir. His temperament had ranged from disdain to anger to an obsequious charm that made her skin crawl. He had expected instant service from his staff, instant gratification of any whim, and subservience from anyone he considered socially inferior. And he had never once lifted a finger for any of them. In fact, he had often gone out of his way to hurt people.

As children, the twins had been a study in contrasts. John was demanding; James, introspective. John dominated any gathering; James melted into the background. John took what he wanted; James gave what he could. John paid back any slight tenfold; James forgave even blatant insults. Despite attending different schools, their years away had intensified those contrasts. John returned harder; James, softer. John was devoted to wine, women, and gaming; James was fascinated by agricultural advances, inventions, and social reform.

Until now. James had hardened, becoming more purposeful. Anger had twisted his mouth into the same expression John had always worn. Yet she could still sense his moods. Something had been bothering him today. Estate problems? A grueling journey? He had to have just arrived, or she would have heard news of him in town.

The years had broadened his character and sharpened his impact. He was no longer a man who could fade away. His presence demanded attention. And that could be dangerous, reviving pain and shocking the populace.

She smoothed her hair before heading for the study.

Someone had murdered John. Most people believed that the culprit had been a chance-met vagrant, despite ample evidence to the contrary. She was not blind, but she now prayed the killer had followed John from elsewhere. If the man was local, what would he do when he encountered John's replica?

Chapter Three

James sipped brandy as he faced Isaac Church across a broad desk. He had known the squire all his life, for Isaac was only one year his senior. They had played together as children, attended the same schools, even contemplated a joint investment. But their friendship had not survived James's departure.

Hurt and disillusioned over John's claims and reeling from John's threats, he had severed every tie with home. His only contact during his years abroad had been with his London man of business, who had promised to keep his location private. Even after returning, he had not visited his former friends. They were part of the past—a past he had not wished to revive.

Thus he had avoided everyone he knew, settling in Lincolnshire, where he kept a low profile. And he had eschewed London society. Why tempt fate?

It had seemed reasonable at the time, for he had never expected to see Shropshire again. But now that he was back, his abrupt departure and its attendant rumors stood between him and the local residents. Isaac had greeted him civilly, but with the same lack of warmth he would have accorded a pushy tradesman or a petty miscreant. If it had been another man, James would have ignored it, but he needed to regain at least some of their former ease, for Isaac was the magistrate in charge of investigating John's murder.

"I heard there was some confusion about why I left home," he said, forcing the issue into the open.

Isaac took snuff and sneezed three times before answering. "Since you had announced no plans to leave, that should not surprise you. The most popular tale describes how you killed your father."

"By causing his fit?"

He nodded. "Though some claimed there was no fit. According to that theory, the family lied to cover the blow that struck him down."

"My God!" He shakily set his glass on the desk.

"The fight supposedly occurred during an argument over crimes you had committed."

"Lies, though we did have a heated discussion over one incident. I was innocent of the charge."

He nodded gravely. "No need to be coy. We all know about Meg Price. And I never believed you guilty of it. Another rumor swore that you fled to avoid marriage, either via compromise or because you debauched a well-born maid."

Mary? She was the only girl he had flirted with before leaving. But she was not that well-born, so he didn't ask. There was no truth to the speculation anyway.

"The arguments raged for months," continued Isaac. "Your father's servants kept passions high—in part to retaliate against John for turning them off. They swore you were innocent of every charge, reminding folks that your argument had preceded your father's attack by a full day, and that John had argued with him in the interim, but few accepted the claims."

No one could have done so, he realized. Not after John acceded to the title. Tenants, craftsmen, merchants. All owed their livelihoods to Ridgeway. John would have ruined anyone who blamed him. So they would have ignored the servants' claims, attributing them to fury over the lost positions.

"A few more theories were posed, but none was believable. The marriage tale died rapidly, for no one could produce a viable candidate. The doctor set the murder story to rest. Ridgeway met with those who blamed him for driving you off, and they decided he was innocent."

That sounded ominous. But claims that he'd killed his father accounted for his cool reception at the Court.

"Why *did* you leave?"

He shrugged. "John ordered me to. He was unhappy about Father's will and threatened to relieve his frustrations on the tenants unless I obeyed."

"No wonder you cut all connections." He relaxed with the

words, noticeably warming. "But you could have stayed in touch."

"No." Word would have leaked out if he had written, drawing John's wrath onto Isaac.

"I suppose not," he agreed, meeting his eyes. "But he is no longer here. Will you stay?"

"I doubt it. My home is now in Lincolnshire. But enough of the past. What can you tell me about John's death?"

Isaac sighed. "Very little. He was killed Christmas Day. But no one admits seeing or hearing anything."

"Cause of death?"

"Murder."

James glared. "I'm not stupid, Isaac. That much information accompanied news of my accession—as you well know. How did he die?"

He sighed. "Multiple stab wounds. His arms and legs were bound, so someone may have been questioning him."

Or torturing him. James shuddered. Torture indicated violent hatred, but John had been capable of inciting it.

"It wasn't a pretty sight," continued Isaac. "But I cannot think of a more deserving victim."

"No one deserves that," he countered, barely hiding his anger. "I don't care how grievous his faults were, I want his killer found."

"I've tried, but this is not a simple case. Little evidence was left near the body. No one has come forward with any information, and nothing new has turned up in six months. Where would you suggest I start? The list of potential suspects includes most of England."

"Surely you know something!"

"The killer was tall and strong."

"I thought no one admits to seeing anything."

"True. But the incident started with a brief fight. Even if the killer ambushed him, it would take great size and strength to have overpowered John that quickly. Yet I have no witnesses, and no one knows which of his dubious activities might have killed him. No strangers were sighted in the area."

"If no one saw a stranger, then the killer was local. So which of his *dubious activities* did he practice here?" Only great effort kept his voice cordial. He hated discussing his family's skeletons with others.

"You cannot assume the killer is local. The weather that day was the foulest we had all winter—blinding snow complicated by high winds. An army could have marched through Ridgefield unseen. As for his activities, he was rarely here. If one of his associates turned on him, it was undoubtedly an outsider."

"Are you aware that John's servants believe I killed him?" he asked wearily.

"Which explains why you are anxious to find the real killer. But you needn't bother. Only the Ridgeway staff believes it."

"Do you think I want the killer found just to divert suspicion from me?" he demanded, glaring daggers at his former friend.

Isaac paled.

"I want the killer found because I cannot condone taking a life. Any life. John may have caused problems, but he was still my brother."

"Very well." Sighing, he topped off their glasses and pulled out a sheaf of papers.

"Why do people believe I killed him? I've not been near Shropshire in years."

"Human nature. When someone is murdered, folks naturally suspect the one who benefits the most. And you must admit that there was no love lost between you. His death handed you the earldom and a tidy fortune."

"A title I don't need, half a dozen properties on the verge of ruin, and a mountain of debts that includes three mortgages. You should know me better than that."

"Debts? The Ridgeway fortune is legendary."

He shook his head. "It was never as large as rumor suggested." But Isaac's skepticism bared another of John's petty revenges. He ran frustrated fingers through his hair. "Damnation! I should have expected him to remain quiet about how Father left things."

"Which was?"

"John got the title and estates. I got most of the money."

"No wonder he tossed you out."

James cut off the retort that sprang to his lips. "That is ancient history. I want his killer found, Isaac. Start at the beginning and tell me about your investigation."

"He wasn't found until late Boxing Day, so the killer had ample time to make his escape. The wind had shifted so much snow that we don't even know which way he went."

"Where was he killed?"

"Near the lane across Brewster's Ridge. We found his body behind that rocky outcropping halfway to the top."

Something nibbled the edges of James's mind, but Isaac's next words drove the thought into hiding.

"The obvious conclusion was that he had been set upon by a highwayman."

"That seems unlikely."

"In retrospect, but it was a viable theory at the time, and investigating it gave me the opportunity to check the whereabouts of every large, strong man in the area. I learned nothing pertinent. Every potential local suspect is accounted for. If it wasn't a chance-met stranger, then his killer followed him here."

"Was he robbed?"

"No." He shifted uncomfortably. "His purse was intact, he was wearing an emerald ring, and his horse wandered back to the Ridgeway stables. But his assailant might have been interrupted before he could complete the job."

James frowned. He was a magistrate in Lincolnshire, so he knew the procedure. One could not ignore any theory, but he suspected that Isaac had followed a blatantly erroneous trail. A fight, binding, multiple wounds, lack of robbery. Why had he entertained thoughts of a highwayman for more than half a minute? "You know he was killed by a personal enemy, so who wanted him dead?"

"No one local," he insisted. "John had just returned after a six-month absence. That is a long time to hold a grudge. But since no one saw the culprit, I have no way to trace him."

"Are you sure John did not meet anyone after arriving home? He could incite fury faster than any man I know."

Isaac nodded. "No one called at Ridgeway, and John did not leave the estate until he went out to meet his killer. The servants would hardly lie about that."

"What do you think happened?"

"I think the culprit is from London, but I have no way of tracing him. No one is willing to hire a runner."

He would, but this wasn't the time to push. He was not yet convinced the killer was an outsider. "Are there no hints of local involvement?" he demanded, watching Isaac's eyes as the man again shifted. "Not a single rumor?"

"Well . . ." He sighed. "A new story started about six weeks ago—which makes it highly suspect—but it might contain a grain of truth."

James waited in increasing impatience while Isaac ordered his thoughts. Nursing a killing fury for six months was usually difficult, but not when John was involved. Every day he found new evidence of vindictiveness. John had saved all his childhood grudges, brooding over them year after year. How many had he avenged once he gained the title? Every victim would be a potential killer.

But he must watch his step.

Isaac's unwillingness to look close to home was going to be a problem. Was it laziness? If the killer lived elsewhere, the responsibility for finding him was out of Isaac's hands. Or was Isaac protecting someone? The squire might know the culprit's identity. The evidence for an outsider was sparse. In fact, it was less than sparse. A group could have overpowered John even faster than a large, powerful assailant.

"I suspect the tale started with Turnby."

"Father's head groom?"

Isaac nodded. "John turned him off with the others. He works at Carworth Lodge now, which is less prestigious than Ridgeway—whatever your father's weaknesses, he kept a fine stable. But Turnby has a history of exaggeration and outright falsity. He never forgave John, so I cannot trust him. He was the most vocal of John's detractors ten years ago."

James sighed. "We can determine veracity later. What does he say?"

"He blames the murder on an affair gone sour, though he did not name the lady. Personally, I have trouble believing it."

"John did have numerous affairs."

"True, but he rarely kept them secret. I have spoken with some of his former inamoratas. Few of them remember him fondly, describing him as selfish and arrogant. But he has been involved with no one here in at least three years—which merely makes the story more scandalous. The gossip-mongers are avidly trying to identify the lady in question. Their list of candidates grows daily, as does the list of proposed killers—a furious father, an incensed brother, a cuckolded husband, the lady herself—but I've found no evidence to support any of it."

"So you believe there is nothing to it?"

He nodded, sighing. "Turnby hated John. He also hates you. I think he started the rumors that you killed John, just as he exaggerated those accusing you of killing your father."

Turnby hated him? That was news. Turnby had been one of the few servants whose support he had counted on throughout childhood—which would have drawn John's malice, he realized on a new wave of guilt. Turnby must have discovered that supporting James brought painful consequences. Who could blame the man for publicly condemning him? He might even believe it by now.

"Could Turnby have killed John himself?"

"I doubt it. He isn't strong enough—he must be all of sixty—and he has always retaliated by using lurid accusations. He may have killed a few reputations, but I've never known him to raise a hand to anyone."

"Then why bring this tale up at all?"

"That is the problem with Turnby. Many of his tales contain elements of truth. Only a fierce hatred could survive for months. Debauching the wrong woman might do it. Or John may have betrayed a partner in some business venture. Or cheated a competitor."

And he did not know that Turnby had started the tale, James reminded himself sharply. That was Isaac's assumption, and he was already questioning Isaac's impressions. He had never known Turnby to lie, though the man had a knack for learning truths others wanted to deny. "So where does your investigation stand?"

"Nowhere. I have no evidence and no suspects. Your brother made enemies. Many enemies. Rumors abound—that he fleeced people through cheating and fraudulent investments; that he worked hand in glove with smugglers; that he abused servants and tenants; that he injured girls in some of the less reputable brothels in Birmingham and London. His supposed crimes are countless, but most take place elsewhere, so I have no way of confirming the truth. No one here admits to being a victim. Even those who swear they've witnessed misdeeds will not provide names. Most folks consider his killer a hero, for no one deserved death more than John Underwood, earl though he was."

Dear God. If even half the charges were true, John's vices were worse than he had thought. Gaining the earldom must have removed the last restraints on his behavior.

Goose bumps trailed down his arms. Here was yet another reason for the locals to distrust him. Most people expected identical twins to have identical characters. Facing his own past had been intimidating enough. Now he had to face his brother's and try to repair the damage. How low had John sunk?

An affair. Mary had been one of John's inamoratas—and not one whose identity was generally known. James would have sworn she was not the jealous sort, but then he had not known her as well as he had thought. When had the liaison ended? If it had been before her marriage, John might have threatened to expose her.

But that did not fit the facts. Her husband had died long before John.

"Did John have any friends?" he asked suddenly. A friend might know who had the strongest grievances, and might reveal the information to John's brother. People often spoke more freely to those who were not officially investigating crimes.

"Very few. His closest was Lord Northrup, but he died more than a year ago."

"How?"

"Stumbled over a cliff after imbibing a little too freely at the Lusty Maiden," Isaac said dryly, naming the local inn. "I suspect his wife was not the only one relieved by his death."

James raised his brows.

"Northrup was unwelcome in area drawing rooms. He shared most of John's vices but none of his charm. Lady Northrup had the entire responsibility of raising his siblings and seeing after the estate. At least her mourning is now complete so she can reenter local society. And her next husband will treat her better."

"Is she planning to remarry?" The question was not as idle as he made it sound. If she had despised her husband, she might already have a replacement in mind. If John had known, he might have tried to blackmail her. That was a lot of *ifs*, but it fit her reaction on meeting him in the forest. In retrospect, her eyes had contained more fear than shock. Whatever her feelings for John ten years ago, at the time of his death she had hated him.

"No, but she is a beautiful woman who will hardly remain alone for long. I am considering offering for her. Constance has been gone for two years now, and I still need an heir."

"Is she capable of producing one? No one has mentioned any children, and I understand she was wed for several years."

"Seven, but Northrup was rarely at home, so that means little." He sighed. "As to John's death, are you sure you want to pursue it?"

He nodded.

"Then perhaps you can help me. You look more like John than ever. People's reaction on seeing you might show how they felt about him. Stay alert. Perhaps you can find something that will point us in a more productive direction."

James took his leave.

He had not expected to find himself in danger, but now he had to consider the possibility. John's death had not resulted from a sudden fit of passion. He had been deliberately murdered. If it had been done in reprisal or because of a quarrel, the killer would have no reason to bother him. But that was not guaranteed.

What if the killer had suffered continuous mistreatment until he broke under the pressure? Faced with an exact replica of his nemesis, would such a man strike again? By poking into John's life, he might become a target. Thus he must remain alert at all times. It was not a comfortable idea, but justice demanded action.

An affair gone sour. He could disprove one theory immediately. Isaac would never consider offering for Mary if he knew about her affair with John, so it must not be common knowledge. How far might she go to protect her secret now that she was seeking a husband?

If she had arranged John's death, then threatening to expose her affair should trigger an attack on him. And not just because of Isaac. She had much to lose if society learned of it. A tarnished reputation was doubly serious for a girl who had not been born to the aristocracy. Marrying up had left her vulnerable. The truth would destroy her social standing and keep her from attracting a new husband.

If it is the truth, whispered a voice in his head.

But if the tale was false, she had an even better motive for murder. John's claims could have ruined her.

Stupid! This was getting him nowhere. No evidence connected Mary to John's death. He was as bad as Isaac, chasing after phantoms—and with even less cause. Imagining her guilt was a way to dissipate the lust that had gripped him from the moment she had ridden around the corner.

He did not want her to be guilty, he realized with a sigh. But he could not ignore the possibility until he had disproved it. The uncertainty was already eating holes in his stomach.

Mary set aside her mending as Justin crossed the drawing room. He had grown four inches since she had last seen him. His shoulders were broader and his face shockingly tanned. But every remnant of childhood was gone, leaving him too much like Frederick despite their difference in coloring. The length of his hair, the pallid blue eyes, the square chin, the oversized hands—all the same.

She shivered.

There were differences, of course. His nose was longer, his face narrower. His light brown hair had been bleached nearly blond by the tropical sun. He was muscular instead of paunchy, and smelled of horses and sandalwood rather than stale wine.

But the most obvious difference was demeanor. Justin exuded a confidence Frederick had never managed. He knew what he was doing and why, with neither the dithering nor the arrogance Frederick had employed. Justin would never need a mentor to point the way. Then there was expression. Frederick's face had always been furtive, as if it concealed vast stores of secrets. Justin's face was open.

Or seemed to be. Some men hid secrets behind charm. Others were cordial in public but brutal in private. So she must tread warily. He was Frederick's brother, which already gave him one black mark. And after years in the military, he would be accustomed to rough company and gruesome sights.

He also controlled her future. If he chose, he could turn her off or demand she remain here as a virtual slave. Even the jointure her father had negotiated as part of the marriage contract was worthless if the estate had no funds. All her hopes rested on him. A reasonable man would find a way to buy that cottage she wanted so badly.

"You look wonderful, Mary," he said, bowing over her hand.

"As do you. India obviously agreed with you."

"I wouldn't go that far, but I survived with my health intact. How are the girls?"

"Charming, as you will see for yourself. They are in town just now but should be back shortly."

They discussed his trip and his relief at having escaped India's sultry heat. But he skirted all topics of import. Was he trying to gauge her reaction to his return, or did he believe she was of no account? He would have to accept at least a temporary alliance, though. Even the steward did not know everything about the barony and the estate. But that could wait.

"I have scheduled a dinner party tomorrow, in honor of your return," she finally said. "The Earl of Ridgeway and two of his friends are visiting the Court, and the Holcolmes are entertaining an unmarried cousin. Perhaps one of them will find Amelia interesting. She is rapidly approaching the shelf."

He frowned. "I had not considered that. How is it that she is twenty and still unwed? Is there a problem?"

"Only money. She has no dowry and no means of staging a come-out. You know your father left little beyond the estate."

"So Frederick always claimed."

"It's true, as the banker will confirm when you meet with him."

He snorted. "Frederick lied to everyone, may he roast in hell.

He had several accounts in London and investments unknown to the local banker. Remember Uncle Horace?"

"His guardian?" And Justin's, she recalled. "The man never cared a whit for how the estate was run."

"Lazy."

"I know that well enough. He forced Frederick into wedding me so he could wash his hands of the lot of you."

"But that was not all. He transferred most of the cash into Frederick's own hands so he would not be bothered by requests for more funds. He told Frederick to prove his worth or sink trying."

"What?" She slumped against the back of her chair in shock. The estate had been flirting with the River Tick for years.

"He proved it, all right, despite losing that initial amount and then some. I don't know how he recouped, though I suspect at least some of his dealings were disreputable."

She didn't doubt it if John had been involved. But she also knew that Frederick had stripped every shilling he could from Northfield.

Justin shook his head. "Uncle Horace didn't care. He withdrew onto his estate, refusing any further contact. He died a couple of years ago."

"No one told us."

"Nor me, though the solicitor swore that Frederick knew. But that is typical. Frederick could easily have afforded Seasons for both girls, but I suspect he did not want any of you in London. It would have forced him to take responsibility for their future and might have interfered with his activities. Even in the few days I was there, I heard more than enough about his affairs to disgust me."

"Such as?" she prompted him.

"Nothing that need concern you now. Suffice it to say that he was neither honorable nor respectable. Nor is Ridgeway. I must request that John and his friends stay away from Northfield. Far away."

Her last letter had been the announcement of Frederick's death, which he would have received six months ago. So he would not know. "James is now the earl."

"When did that happen?"

"Christmas Day. John was murdered, though the identity of his killer remains unknown."

Justin's mouth hung open in surprise.

"His horse returned to Ridgeway without him. The staff believed he had passed out from drink and fallen off—it would not have been the first time—but they didn't find his body until the next evening. It took them another month to locate James." She shrugged.

"There are no suspects?"

"None that I know of. But I'm tired of talking about it—the topic dominates every conversation, and has for months. James's recent arrival at Ridgeway makes the gossip even worse."

"Of course. But I am not comfortable about inviting James, either. Twins are too alike."

"He was never like John," she reminded him, then chided herself for jumping to his defense.

"Not usually, but his temper was just as explosive. He lamed my pony when I cut him off one day by jumping a hedge without first checking the lane for other riders."

"How old were you?"

"Eight. He swore at me, delivered a diatribe about irresponsible children, then struck Rudy across both knees with a whip."

"That sounds more like John than James."

"It was James. I recognized the horse." John had always ridden black horses, while James preferred bays. "And I heard some unsavory rumors about him in India."

She raised her brows.

"He ran an export business there for a while—rather questionable in itself, for it was outside the jurisdiction of the East India Company, whose officials were less than pleased. But that was not all. At least one tale claimed he fathered a child on his mistress that he later killed rather than acknowledge."

"Surely that would bring prosecution." Her hand shook. She would have expected such behavior from John, but never of James. Yet they were identical twins. And James had grown much harsher in his years away.

"Not that I heard of." He stared at her white face. "He left about the time I arrived and was never part of the English colony, so I cannot vouch for the accuracy of the tale. The East India representatives hated those they considered poachers, reveling in any bit of scandal. But they could do nothing about him because he had the backing of several powerful rajahs and never traded with Europeans."

"We will proceed cautiously, then. But I do not wish to exclude him on the basis of unproven rumors and a single incident fifteen years old." She poured more tea. When he reluctantly nodded, she set herself to be chatty. "Lady Carworth was quite ill last winter. They feared that she would die, but the warmer weather allowed her to recover."

"Is she still the harridan I remember?"

"I would not go so far as to call her a harridan. She has been quite good to us this spring, escorting the girls whenever mourning prevented me from doing so. Perhaps your memories are tinged by youthful escapades?"

He grinned. "Perhaps. She was less than ecstatic about that foray I made into her orchard. And I managed to steal strawberries out of her hothouse one year."

"I know. I was the one to whom she complained. Her gardener had spent weeks forcing berries out of season so she could astound her house guests, and you ruined her surprise." She had been newly wed to Frederick at the time. The girls had welcomed her attentions, but Justin had resisted accepting the authority of a virtual stranger. "Her current tormentor is Philip Redfield."

"Sir Richard's son? I hadn't realized he was old enough to run about on his own."

"He is nearly eleven." She laughed at the shock on Justin's face. "You've been gone a long time. People grow, even when you aren't watching them."

He nodded.

"But the adults have hardly changed. Mrs. Bridwell is as self-righteous as ever, and Vicar Bridwell still puts us to sleep during his Sunday sermons. Young Barnes is gaining a reputation for his ale. Oh, and Tom Ruddy lost his daughter last year. I don't recall if I mentioned it in my last letter."

"No. Does he still run the linen draper's shop?"

She nodded. "Alice caught that influenza that swept the shire, but now that I think on it, she died just after I wrote you about Frederick."

"He took a tumble into the quarry?"

"Too much wine. He was on his way to Ridgeway after several hours in the Lusty Maiden."

"That's a dangerous area," he agreed. "Old Harry Smith died there ten years ago, as I recall."

"Right. And the Wilsons' oldest boy a year before that."

They shook their heads.

"Speaking of old Harry, his granddaughter Jenny married Ned Payne just before Christmas. They are already expecting."

He sighed. "I remember her as a hoydenish ten-year-old— but that was before I bought colors. Have you anything planned besides this dinner?"

"No. Why?"

"I know little about Northfield's operation, for I never expected to run it. I will need to spend most of my time with Branson—he is still steward, isn't he?"

"No. I dismissed him for theft eight years ago."

"*You* did?" His shock boded ill for working together.

"Sit down, Justin." He had surged to his feet. "I did not discuss estate business with you because it was not your concern, and in the shock surrounding Frederick's death, it slipped my mind in that last letter. Frederick had no interest in estate matters, leaving its supervision in my hands. I will only hit the high spots now. Once you recover from your journey, we can go over the books in detail."

"That sounds ominous."

"Not really. The estate has always hovered on the verge of destitution, but it is not carrying any debt. You might recall that Frederick left for London within days of our marriage."

He nodded.

"It did not take me long to realize that Branson was embezzling funds. Since Frederick wanted nothing to do with estate problems, I took the evidence to Mr. Collingsworth."

"The banker who oversaw father's local accounts—I doubt he ever knew of those Uncle Horace turned over to Frederick."

"He cannot have, but he *did* have authority over the estate until Frederick came of age. He had Branson arrested and transported. Little of the money was ever recovered, but the estate immediately showed higher profits. In order to prevent a recurrence, I started keeping the books myself, with Collingsworth's approval."

"So why is the estate on the verge of destitution?"

"Frederick came of age. Until then, I had run the estate myself, using Collingsworth's authority to make needed changes. But once Frederick gained control, he refused to approve spending for repairs or improvements, taking all profits for his own use. I've authorized the most urgent expenditures since he died, but the years have taken a toll on productivity. There isn't much to work with."

He still looked uncertain about trusting her judgment, but at least he did not seem angry about it. "Who is the new steward?"

"Fernbeck. He is a good man."

"Have him meet us in the library tomorrow morning."

Amelia and Caroline raced into the room, interrupting further talk. Mary cringed, but Justin showed no surprise at Caroline's garbled greeting. A few soft words brought her under control.

She relaxed. Justin's affection for his sisters was obvious, especially when contrasted to the polite manners he had accorded her. Which resolved one fear. Frederick had barely tolerated the girls.

Leaving them to catch up on the news, she went upstairs to see that Justin's rooms were ready. Tomorrow's meeting should go well. Everything was in order.

So why was the tension spreading across her shoulders? She had nothing to fear.

Chapter Four

James frowned as he turned toward Ridgeway. Today had been his first visit to Ridgefield since his return. Aside from his call on Isaac, he had passed the week checking the estate records and taking the first steps toward erasing ten years of neglect and mismanagement, starting with the stables.

His father had established a breeding and training program so good that Ridgeway horses had been prized far beyond Shropshire. James had shared his passion for the stables, which accounted for most of their rapport. It was one area in which the heir had been an admitted disappointment. John had been a good rider, but he had relieved his frustrations on anything handy, so animals invariably learned to fear him.

Thus John's desecration of the stables must have been deliberate. The damage far surpassed simple neglect. Had John struck back at his father and brother by destroying an interest he had not shared, or had it been an attempt to imprint his own stamp on Ridgeway by eliminating anything he did not like?

It didn't matter. The damage was done, and though he had no plans to live here, he had to repair enough stabling to handle his cattle during visits. Mistreating animals was unacceptable.

Estate business had not consumed all his time, of course. He had passed several pleasant hours with his friends. And despite the vast amount of work needed to restore Ridgeway, he had not neglected John's murder. His secretary would hire the most tenacious Bow Street runner to investigate John's activities. If the murder had roots in London or along the south coast, the runner would find them. In the meantime, he would look here. Isaac might prefer an outside killer, but he suspected the culprit would be found near the crime.

But the search would not be easy. The servants were no help. John had trained them to be deaf, blind, and dumb. Until they trusted him, they would reveal nothing. He had thought town gossip might help, for murder must still be a popular topic. But his visit had raised far more questions than it had answered.

The first man he had encountered had nearly expired of shock, as had the second. By the time he met the third, word had spread, but people still recoiled when meeting him face to face. They answered his questions with monosyllables, feigning ignorance on even innocuous topics. And though it was often mixed with uncertainty and curiosity, fear lurked in every eye.

So Mary's reaction had been normal, removing his only evidence against her. The realization lightened his heart far more than it should have—to say nothing of heating his privates. He shook his head in disgust. Lusting after a widow of questionable virtue usually led to a pleasant interlude, but not this time. Mary had once been a friend. Honor forbade him to bed her.

He snorted.

Who was he trying to gull? Bedding her was the most delectable idea he'd had in years. She had invaded his dreams every night since he had encountered her in the woods. But a liaison was out of the question. He would remain celibate for life rather than share a woman with John.

Shifting in the saddle, he forced his mind back to business. He had to find John's killer. And Mary might still be guilty. Her situation made her an ideal target for blackmail, so he must confront her.

And clear her of suspicion, whispered his mind.

Of course, he replied in irritation. And once he cleared her, he would solicit her cooperation. She had known John better than anyone, so she could reduce his list of suspects. Even if she had come to hate John, her sense of justice would force her to help.

He certainly needed her assistance. At the moment, his suspects were legion. The Ridgeway servants had feared John. His father's servants had hated him. Today's trip to town proved that everyone feared, hated, or distrusted him. As did the tenants.

So his list included hundreds of people from every social class. Hatred might not lead to murder, but fear was a powerful emotion. Even a weak man could strike back out of fear.

What had John done here? Isaac had hinted at various crimes in other places—and he knew of several problems in London—but the local situation was far worse than he had imagined. Arrogance would annoy people. Flagrant debauchery might disgust them. But every person he had met since his arrival acted like a victim of deliberate brutality. Could John have actually hurt so many?

Damn the guilt! He should not have let his twin drive him away. Surely he could have tempered John's conduct had he been here. At least he could have protected people from spite.

But admitting that John acted out of spite reminded him of why he had left. In the week between their father's death and the reading of the will, John's natural arrogance had hardened into a selfishness that had reveled in his new powers. Never one to follow orders, the new John had bristled at even the hint of a suggestion. His senseless commands invited protest that he gleefully punished—but often indirectly.

John enjoyed inflicting pain, especially long-lasting emotional pain. And he was a master at it—hurting James by mistreating the tenants; avenging a woman's rejection by ruining her husband's business; punishing a tenant who protested a rent increase by arranging the disappearance of his son. Rumors had suggested press gangs, but James feared the lad had been sold into slavery.

Those were just three cases he knew about, all occurring in that single week. How many others remained secret? How many new incidents had happened in the years since?

Yet John's spite did little to banish his own guilt. There must have been some way to keep his twin under control. Leaving had given John free rein to raise havoc among the Ridgeway dependents.

Sighing, he cantered across the park. Grass and shrubs ran rampant. Oaks were missing, weeds choked the drive, and the stone bridge remained damaged three years after a flood. Most of the problems related to money.

His fault, he acknowledged through a new wave of guilt. The

truth was written in the ledgers he had studied in recent days. The damage hadn't all been spite. John had plunged into rebuilding the fortune James had inherited, cutting staff expenses, squeezing every possible penny from the tenants, and throwing that income into any investment that promised substantial returns. Most had lost. And the estate James loved now lay in shambles.

He could hear John laughing.

If only their father had lived long enough to revise his will as he had vowed to do during their final confrontation.

His last visit had started innocently enough. He had returned from a house party at Holkham Hall, bursting with Coke's latest ideas for agricultural reform. John had been in London, but he had not considered that significant. After two weeks of discussions, and with support from the vicar and several neighbors, his father had agreed to make some changes—acquiring a second breeding stallion to expand the stables; combining two tenant farms to give Walsh enough land to make a decent living; giving the dispossessed Lane a stake he could use to emigrate to America; implementing a better crop rotation plan to improve productivity. The earl had also agreed to install James as an overseer to the steward until the man mastered the latest agricultural methods.

He sighed.

Not until John's return did he learn that his brother tolerated no interference in his affairs. As heir, he demanded a voice in every decision concerning Ridgeway. His fury had prompted the earl to abandon all the planned changes.

But retaining the status quo had not satisfied John. He had sought retribution, aiming his vindictiveness at anyone who might have benefited. Guilt had dogged James for years, for he had left before John's fury was spent, so he could only imagine the lengths to which his brother had gone. How many innocents had suffered because he had tried to help them?

It was that guilt that had delayed his trip to Ridgeway. He hadn't been ready to face the damage—or the victims. Without his interference, they would not have suffered, for John's actions had been devised to hurt James more than the hapless tenants and tradesmen who were his actual targets. John had long known that James felt other people's pain more deeply than his own, especially when that pain arose from injustice.

He had cursed himself daily for his blindness. Why had he never understood that John had been determined to sever his twin's connection to Ridgeway and would go to any lengths to achieve that goal? He should have stayed in London that year or built a new life for himself somewhere else.

But enlightenment had come much later. When their father had canceled the reforms, James had held his tongue, not even pointing out that the changes would benefit John in the long run. The earl had been glad to avoid a worse confrontation, dropping any mention of the subject. So when he had demanded a meeting two days later, James had thought nothing of it.

He had expected an apology for capitulating to John's tantrum. Or perhaps an offer to put the breeding operation under his control, since John had no interest in it. But the earl had been anything but amiable, lashing out before James even got through the doorway.

How dare you ravish the Price girl? After everything I've done for you, how can you repay me with this!

The shock had snapped his own temper. Accepting responsibility for John's pranks was one thing, but he refused to admit to such calumny. And so he'd offered his alibi and accused John.

Liar, his father had shouted. *I've given you chances to reform before, but this time you've gone too far. Denying your guilt is bad enough, but trying to pass the blame onto your innocent brother is unforgivable. I've often regretted your misfortune at being second, but I should have listened to those who recognized the malicious resentment you have harbored all these years. It is time to rectify the mistakes of the past by removing any opportunity for further trouble. You will leave Ridgeway forever. No more allowance; no more sweeping your crimes under the rug. I am writing you out of my will. You are no longer my son.*

But the earl had died before his solicitor arrived. And the will had left James a fortune with the explanation, *for my younger son, who missed a birthright through a quirk of fate.*

John had been furious. Never once had he suspected that James would inherit more than the usual second son's portion. And he had fired the solicitor on the spot when he learned that the accounts had been changed to James's name on the day the old earl died. Bradshaw had known John well enough to expect trouble. John would never have issued orders to turn over a shilling.

He frowned. *No orders.* John had been gone for six months before his death. The servants had done nothing during that time, for John had left no orders. Thus his departure must have been sudden. Why? Had he received bad news from town? Or had he been fleeing vengeance? Perhaps he had chosen the wrong victim for one of his crimes. It gave him something to investigate.

So which of the locals might have kept his anger hot for six months? He could not believe that a sudden argument had led to such a brutal crime. Killing, maybe, but not torture.

Don't lose sight of any possibilities. You don't know what started that feud—or when. It was important to identify the killer's grievance, but it might have started two or three visits ago, or even more. John's trips to Ridgeway had been sporadic. He had appeared without warning, inflicted instant chaos, then left within days.

He had no real suspects. And he needed help from someone who lived in the area. This visit to town proved that he had little chance of succeeding on his own. Fearing he was another John, people would tell him even less than they had told Isaac.

Which brought him back to Mary. It was odd how his thoughts always circled back to her. She knew everyone, so could direct him to people who might be willing to talk. She would know what rumors were current, who had started them, and might even know who was guilty.

But even with help, finding the killer would take time. There seemed to be a conspiracy of silence on the subject. He was going to be here far longer than the fortnight he had expected.

James set his plans in motion at the Northrup party that evening. But it wasn't easy.

"You look lovely," he told Mary, slipping up behind her the

moment she abandoned the receiving line. And she *was* lovely. Her blonde hair was caught up in an arrangement of waves and curls that made his fingers itch to touch it. It would cascade to her hips once he removed the pins. The image of all that hair spread in a halo over his pillow nearly blinded him.

He cursed.

Her only adornment was a locket on a thin gold chain that he recognized as having been her mother's. Its simplicity drew further attention to her charms.

She looked at him doubtfully. "Thank you, my lord, but I cannot hold a candle to Amelia. I doubt you recall her, since you've been away so long."

And somehow he found himself talking to Amelia Northrup, with Mary nowhere in sight. The elder Northrup girl was small, delicate, and so serene that she would have disappeared into the walls if she had been plainer. After exchanging a few innocuous comments, she asked about London, so he handed her off to Harry, claiming that he knew little of the city.

It took a quarter hour to corner Mary again, because every guest wanted a word with him. They were better at hiding their fears than the servants and merchants had been, but the same questions blazed in their eyes.

"I need to talk with you for a moment," he murmured into Mary's ear. "Is there someplace we could go that is private?"

"Gracious! Surely you were taught better manners!" she scoffed, making no attempt to sound genial. "No hostess can leave the drawing room this close to dinner. Why don't you relax and enjoy the evening?"

Before he could dredge up an apology, he found himself conversing with Caroline Northrup, a vivacious beauty who should have attracted his eyes earlier. But he had murder on his mind, and a ten-year-old affair was eating holes in his gut. He was so angry at the practiced way she had again slipped out of his clutches that it took him a moment to realize that Caroline's vivacity bordered on hysteria.

She was trying to control it, clenching her hands whenever she spoke, but fear lurked in her eyes; her gaze darted about the room, studiously avoiding him; her words bumped into one another, becoming so garbled he could barely follow her conversation; and her coloring brightened and faded, sputtering like a badly trimmed wick.

Either she was terrified of him, or the excitement of the evening was too much for her. So he introduced her to Edwin. If anyone could calm her down, Edwin could.

He grimaced. In the two minutes since their last exchange, Mary had worked her way to the far side of the room. He followed.

"Thank goodness Lord Northrup finally returned," said a horse-faced woman as he passed. "He will keep Lady Northrup in line. And about time." Creases of disapproval were permanently etched into her face, but the words hinted that Mary was not a pillar of the community.

Pressing on, he passed Miss Hardaway, who had been the most vicious village gossip since before his birth.

"Mourning. Hmph!" she snorted at her companion. "She did not care a whit for Northrup—not that any of us did. No one would have thought twice if she had refused to mourn him, but she pounced on the chance to escape scrutiny for a year." Another snort split the air. "But she was mistaken if she thought it would put her conduct beyond censure. We all know she visited Captain Stone twice a week for more than a month."

"But he was recovering from injuries," protested her friend.

"Not by then. He returned to the Peninsula when he left here."

James bit back a retort. It sounded like John was far from Mary's only paramour—not that her morals were his concern. But he had to wonder why Isaac was courting her if everyone knew about her liaisons. It didn't jibe with the man who had once been his friend.

Enough! They had business to discuss once he cleared her of complicity in John's death—he could not picture his response if she was guilty.

But she would be innocent. The fact that everyone in the room knew about her fall from grace eliminated any motive. If John had no leverage, she had no grievance. So he could solicit her help to find the killer.

Get this over with so you can relax.

But he could not reach her. Every time he paused to respond

to a greeting, she slipped farther away. Her unwillingness to
face him exasperated him beyond bearing. But not until dinner
did he realize her true purpose. He was seated between Amelia
and Caroline, with Harry and Edwin on their other sides.

Matchmaker! Damn!

His own purpose had blinded him to hers. How could he
have missed the signs? He would have to step as carefully as he
had done in London. Marriage had to wait until he had finished
with the past. But even if he were ready to wed, he would never
choose the Northrup girls. They might be fine young ladies, but
they seemed little more than children. So he set himself to be
scrupulously polite but aloof. It was an act he had perfected.

He couldn't really blame Mary, he decided over the second
course. He had haunted the Marriage Mart for two months,
using his spurious search for a wife as an excuse to avoid
Ridgeway. She had probably seen his name in the society
columns. And he *would* have to marry soon. A title carried
many responsibilities, one of which was to produce an heir.

But he would not look in London when the time came. He
wanted a wife who could also be a friend, one that saw beyond
his wealth and title. The girls making their bows had been gig-
gly and empty-headed, unable to converse intelligently on any
topic beyond fashion and gossip. Many of them hung on his
arm despite overt wariness over his kinship to John. And they
were so young, so ignorant, so incredibly naïve.

Perhaps his travels had aged him unduly, but every one of the
chits made him feel as old as Methuselah. Never mind that he
was only three-and-thirty. It was a problem that would only
worsen with time, so he had to wind up this business soon.

The ladies retired, leaving the gentlemen to their port. Conversation grew predictably bawdy as guests relieved themselves one by one in the chamber pot, but James remained
silent, assessing each man as he recalled what he knew of him.

Isaac, former friend and local magistrate. Had he investigated any of John's questionable activities? John would have
retaliated, which might have forced Isaac into an escalating battle. Or John may have persecuted Isaac solely because he had
been James's friend.

Sir Richard Redfield, whose son was the neighborhood

scamp. He had seen parents go to incredible lengths to protect their children. Had John threatened the boy in reprisal for a prank?

Sir Maxwell Granger, a staid, unimaginative baronet, whose estate was older even than Ridgeway. Sir Maxwell was excessively proud of its history, and frequently compared it to others—always in his own favor. Had he made disparaging remarks about Ridgeway that John had taken as personal insults? Ridgeway's deterioration made it likely. But how would that lead to murder?

Lord Holcolme and his cousin Edward. He knew little of either, but Edward was about his own age, so he would have known John in London, and perhaps also at Oxford.

Colonel Davis, still hale, though he must be seventy. His son had been stationed in India when James first arrived, though they had only spoken twice. Now the man was serving on the Peninsula. But he could imagine no conflict between the colonel and John—unless the rumors were true that John was involved in smuggling. Many smugglers aided French spies, infuriating every military man in the country.

The new vicar, who was oddly outspoken for a man of the cloth.

The doctor, two solicitors, and half a dozen young people he could not place—friends of Northrup, he supposed. They would have been children on his last visit.

His eyes finally rested on his host. Northrup had also been in India, though they had not met there. Did that hold any significance? Northrup was the one man who was truly innocent of murder, yet he was the most hostile man in the room. His eyes hardened whenever he glanced at James. Only the presence of others kept his teeth unbared. Was Northrup another who was reacting to his looks? But that made little sense. Northrup had been abroad for years. Even virulent hatred should have dissipated. Did his remain, or was it new?

Perhaps he had only recently learned of some serious offense. He might look askance on John's affair with Mary. Or was there a worse crime that had struck directly at Northrup's family?

*   *   *

"I really must talk with you privately," James murmured to Mary once the gentlemen reached the drawing room. She was settling the older guests at card tables. Most of the younger ones had repaired to the music room for informal dancing.

Irritation flashed across her face. "If you are offering for one of my sisters, talk to Northrup."

"I am not interested in either of your sisters, and Northrup cannot help me. He's been gone nearly as long as I have. Surely you can spare me five minutes. No one will miss you. They are engrossed in cards."

"Persistent, aren't you?" She sighed, but led the way to a small sitting room.

He shut the door firmly behind them. "Do you have to treat me like a pariah?" He regretted the question the moment the words burst out.

"Am I neglecting my guests so you can complain because I'm not falling at your feet in adoration?"

"No. I am trying to find my brother's killer," he said bluntly. "But it isn't easy. He accumulated enemies the way Shelford collects driving records." Shelford was a noted Corinthian who spent much of his life racing.

"Why come to me? Squire Church is conducting the investigation."

"I know. I already spoke with him, but he is satisfied to let the matter go."

"Without evidence, what would you suggest he do?"

He shrugged. "Maybe he is right, and the killer came from elsewhere. I have men checking that possibility. But I don't believe he ever seriously considered the local connection. Thus he hasn't asked the right questions. Every person in the district must have a theory about who killed John. Since you knew him better than anyone, I want to hear yours."

She frowned. "Where did you get that idea? He was Frederick's friend, not mine."

"Don't lie to me," he interrupted, anxious to get this phase of the conversation finished. "I don't care what either of you did. John was despicable, but that does not give anyone the right to kill him. Even you."

"Me?" she spat. "Did the Indian sun addle your wits? What earthly reason would I have to take a life?"

"I want justice, Mary." He walked close enough to loom over her. "And I don't care what secrets I have to expose to get it. I've known about your affair for years. I doubt you entered it by choice, but even if it continued until John's death, I wouldn't blame you. Your husband was rarely at home." He had not intended to say that much, but the words poured out, leaving gaping wounds behind. Damn John! And damn Mary. He cared, all right. No matter how much he deplored the idea, he cared.

"What affair?" she demanded, her face so white he feared she might swoon. She hadn't reacted that strongly to his accusation of murder. Did she think no one knew?

"Don't play the innocent with me, Mary. John told me about it ten years ago."

"My name is Lady Northrup," she snarled, retreating from his intimidating stance until she had put a table between them. She fingered a pair of scissors as if she considered stabbing him. "You are as despicable as your brother, and far more stupid. I can't believe you can be that credulous."

"*Credulous?*" His voice dripped ice.

"Are you blind, my lord?" She slammed the scissors back onto the table and glared at him. "Can you actually believe a word he said? You, of all people, should know how he twisted facts. He was no gentleman. Winning and exercising his power were more important to him than truth or honor. How many falsehoods did he spread about you?"

"But—"

"But nothing. I never believed that you killed your father, though John told everyone that you had fled rather than admit to striking him down. In fact, most of the rumors surrounding your departure originated with him."

Dear God! "I left because John threatened to evict the Thompsons and abuse Cotter and the other tenants if I stayed."

"That sounds like him. John was contemptible. He routinely cheated tradesmen. He reveled in making the tenants struggle to meet their rents—which he raised whenever higher corn prices made their lot bearable. He brutalized more than one of his servants. Whoever killed him deserves a reward for outstanding service to the community."

"Are you claiming that you never had an affair with him?" he demanded, struggling to understand her words. Had that white face been fury rather than fear?

"I'm telling you that your brother would say anything to carry an argument." She twisted her face into a sneer. "But you are like everyone else. Believing him justifies having designs on me yourself. Well, forget it. I deplore affairs and could never consider one with a man who can only remind me of the neighborhood scourge."

"No one gets that angry over injustices to others." He ignored her other charges as well as his own fury whenever he encountered injustice. "What did he do to incite such hatred? Did he ravish you?"

"Of course not! I would have killed him myself if he'd tried. I've seen the results too often."

"Why would a rape victim come to you? Everyone believed you to be his mistress," he scoffed, again failing to censor his tongue.

"Not everyone—especially before my marriage; the vicarage welcomed those in trouble." She sighed, turning away. "Calm down and think, my lord. John had no need to steal my virtue. He could inflict far more pain by stealing my reputation."

Which he had done. James clenched his fists, recalling the snide remarks that had filled the drawing room before dinner. Country memories were long, meaning that malicious rumors would remain forever. What had she suffered? And why?

Stupid! The why was easy—to hurt him. By befriending Mary, he had drawn John's wrath onto her head. So he must somehow rescue her reputation.

He should have questioned John's veracity long ago. Instinct had tried to warn him at the time, but he hadn't—and wasn't listening now, he realized grimly. She had been describing John's tactics, most of which he'd missed.

"And he drew my husband into repeated trouble," she continued, pacing the room. "John was a profligate wastrel—not that it mattered to a man of his means. But Frederick could not afford such a life. The ones who suffered the most were his sisters."

"Is that why you are throwing them at my head?" he demanded. "Am I supposed to pick one and launch the other to make up for John's sins?"

"Not at all. I would never approve a match based on guilt. Both parties would be miserable. Nor would I consider a match at all now that I see how unreasonable you have become. Perhaps I discounted the rumors too quickly. I had remembered you as a man who treated people fairly. Unfortunately, maturity has robbed you of your virtues while repairing none of your naïve blindness."

"That is hardly a fair assessment, my lady. And not typical of someone who used to weigh all the evidence before jumping to conclusions."

The address was an attempt to regain lost ground. He had badly mishandled this meeting. His biggest error had been believing John. Thus he had hurled unconscionable charges at her face. He would not have treated the lowliest tenant like that, so why had he done it to Mary? Her title might derive through marriage, but even the vicar's daughter he had once befriended deserved more respect than he had shown.

She was innocent, both of murder and of liaisons with John. His heart leaped for joy, swelling until he feared it might burst. *Slow down,* he admonished himself, fighting to steady his breathing. This wasn't the moment to pursue his desire. His accusations had put her back up—as her vow proved. His second mistake had been his failure to anticipate her reaction. Thus he had inadvertently alienated her. She would likely refuse to see him again.

He must remember this lesson in the future, he noted in an aside. He could not accuse anyone without shackling his hands. They were already tied too well by his kinship with John.

So he had two problems. He still needed her help. And now that he had removed John from the picture, he wanted her in his bed. But she would require wooing—especially after this fiasco.

Yet even wooing wouldn't work if she refused to see him. So he must convince her to join his investigation. It would provide frequent contact. By the time they discovered John's killer, they would have reestablished their friendship—and more.

"We have drifted far from the subject," he said, injecting as much respect as possible into his voice. "Please accept my apologies for allowing my emotions to control my tongue. John's insinuations had been eating at me, for I had not expected that from you. But that is no excuse for my unmannerly display."

She stared stonily at him.

"Please, Mary. Even if you cannot forgive my lapse, I do need help. And you are the best one to provide it. I have to find John's killer. Who had the worst grievances against him?"

She shrugged. "Take your pick. The only one who did not hate him was Frederick."

"But hatred does not usually lead to murder. That would take a mixture of fury and fear. Did he do anything worse than usual in the last year or two?"

"Who knows?" She wandered over to the window and gazed into the darkness for several minutes. He had nearly decided she would say no more when she turned back to face him. "Mourning prevented me from hearing gossip. In fact, I did not even know John had come to Ridgeway at Christmas until after his body was found. And I know of nothing that might keep someone's anger hot for months. But even if I did, I would not tell you. John was evil."

"Perhaps. But he was also my brother. I cannot condone murder."

"Nor I as a rule, but every rule has an exception. Instead of wasting your time looking for his killer, why don't you repair some of the damage he caused?"

He raised his brows in a silent question, hoping to learn more. He had already taken steps to address the problems revealed in the estate records, but he doubted they represented all of John's crimes.

"Your tenants pay twice the rent they should, and John authorized no repairs. Not even to Lane's barn, which has all but collapsed. The mill has stood empty since Tate died, forcing people to travel many miles to grind their grain. And you should talk to Barnes at the Lusty Maiden. John held a house party at Ridgeway last year. The guests gathered at the inn one night for a boisterous party that burned down one wing. John refused to pay for the damages, so Barnes could not rebuild. The next day, the same group trampled most of Wilson's crops, breaking fences and killing livestock for sport. I forgave Wilson's rents last year to keep him out of debtor's prison, but he is still suffering. I lacked the resources to do more."

"*You* did?" But his surprise waned when he remembered that her husband had died shortly afterward. He didn't know he had said the words aloud until she answered.

"Frederick's death made no difference. I have run Northfield for years. Even before John corrupted him, Frederick preferred that I do so." She glanced at the mantel clock. "I must return to my guests. Forget John's killer. No one will thank you for persecuting a man who did us all a favor. Redress his crimes, then turn your attention to the future."

She was gone before he could respond.

James paced the sitting room for several minutes. He could sympathize with her thinking, but he could not drop the subject until he understood what had happened, and why. Guilt would not allow it.

Yes, John's behavior had been despicable. But it was worse than it might have been without his twin's provocation. Left to his own devices, John would have lived out his life in London, wallowing in dissipation and debauchery—very like Devereaux was doing. The estate would have drifted into disrepair, but the tenants and staff would have survived.

But John had not been given that option. James had inherited the money that should have supported that London life. Disappointment and fury had erupted in a tantrum aimed at anything James loved.

Yet John's anger had run deeper than pique over the fortune, he admitted, sinking into a chair. The will had merely been the last straw on a mountain of grievances, not all of them minor. There was the time twelve-year-old John had spooked Cotter's team, spilling a load of grain into the river and ruining it. James had chided him for carelessly harming a tenant, not only proving that he alone genuinely cared for their dependents—and betraying the vulnerability John had later exploited—but inadvertently revealing the deed to their father, who had arrived in time to overhear the details. John's punishment had been severe.

There had been the incident in the stable when they were sixteen. John's rough handling had sent a stallion into a frenzy. It might have sustained fatal injuries, but James had calmed the horse, earning his father's gratitude and demonstrating the contrast between the brothers. Again John had been punished.

But that had not been the worst insult. By the time they were three-and-twenty, their father had been fretting over John's wildness, even while excusing most of the London gossip as wild oats. James had suggested placing John's inheritance in a trust so that youthful profligacy would not damage the estate in the event that John got the title before he settled down. The earl had dismissed the idea, but someone had overheard the conversation and sent word to John. That was what had sent him hurtling back to Ridgeway, where he found that James had convinced the earl to adopt agricultural reform. Meg Price had been ravished the next day. So, in a way, he *had* been responsible.

He shuddered.

Only now did he admit that a trust would never have worked. John had not been sowing wild oats. He had not been misguided or immature. Time had not made him more responsible. Even their father's mollycoddling and eagerness to overlook John's failings had not ruined his character.

John's problem had been far more basic. He had needed to be the best, the most powerful, the most successful. Facing a mirror image of himself every day of his life had eaten at him. James's existence had proved that John was not unique. There was another man who shared his looks, his talents, his breeding. A man who had earned respect and genuine affection—two things John had never experienced.

He shuddered.

John had been more depraved than he had ever suspected. His problems had arisen from his own character; his actions had been taken by his own choice.

James ran frustrated fingers through his hair. But even that could not excuse murder. And so he had to find the killer. Justice was more important than the victim's character. A man who could kill once would find it easier to kill a second time, and for less cause. He had called enough tragedy down on his dependents. He could not be responsible for more.

He returned to the drawing room and joined a whist table.

"Lady Northrup hosts delightful parties," said Lady Carworth while dealing the first hand.

"For one of her reputation," said Mrs. Bridwell with a snort.

"Martha—" began Lady Carworth.

"You know very well she is no better than she should be," interrupted Mrs. Bridwell. "I have heard revolting tales of her escapades. Estimates make her familiar with half the men in this shire."

"I doubt it," protested Sir Richard stoutly. "I've seen no evidence to support those tales, and I know for a fact that many of them are false."

"Ha!" Mrs. Bridwell pursed her lips as she arranged her cards.

"Be honest, ma'am," he urged her. "Every one of the stories you so gleefully cite predates your arrival in Ridgefield. There has not been a single new tale in eight years."

"That doesn't make them false."

"Where did you hear them?" asked James.

"Here and there."

"Discounting anything my brother might have said, for he delighted in prevarication, who else claims knowledge of misbehavior? I know of no tales before I left."

"There were a few," claimed Lady Carworth. "Though only in town. I doubt they would have reached Ridgeway. I believe the first surfaced in 1800."

"She would have been barely sixteen then," he protested.

"Old enough," insisted Mrs. Bridwell. "And why else would her husband all but abandon her?" Her triumphant smile made him long to wring her neck.

"Spade lead," said Sir Richard, determinedly turning the topic. "I find it distasteful to disparage one's hostess in her own drawing room."

James followed suit, but his mind was not on the game. If the stories had stared in 1800, then he was not responsible, for he had paid her little heed until two years later. So why had John turned on her? He had to be behind them. She had sworn that he was responsible for stealing her reputation. Which meant John had been making her life miserable for more years than he cared to contemplate.

Mrs. Bridwell continued to mutter imprecations under her breath. Mary was her favorite target, though her barbs skewered nearly everyone in the room. Since her eyes turned to him so often, her performance had to be for his benefit. Surprisingly, not one criticism touched on John.

Her attitude hardly became the wife of a vicar, raising new questions. The parish was under the earl's control. Already he suspected that the vicar was grossly inept. So why had John kept him on? The Bridwells were hardly assets—

Which answered the question, he admitted, hiding his glee as he trumped Mrs. Bridwell's ace. They were another plague John had inflicted on the district. But their loyalty to John's desires so long after his death was odd—and gave him yet another thread to investigate.

Mrs. Bridwell uttered more self-righteous criticism.

James grimaced. Didn't she understand that her husband's future rested in his hands?

Chapter Five

"The evening was quite a success," said Amelia once the last guest had departed. Justin had accompanied an old friend home, so the girls joined Mary in her sitting room. "Mrs. Bridwell grumbled, of course, but that was only to be expected."

"You enjoyed yourself, then?" asked Mary.

Amelia nodded, settling onto a couch with a sigh of relief. She had danced for hours.

Caroline was too excited to sit and continued to twirl about the room. "Wonderful night. I danced nd dncd n dncd——"

"Slow down, Caro," urged Mary. "You charmed everyone, but you are letting the excitement carry you away."

"I know." She inhaled deeply, then perched on a chair. "And I made some mistakes. Lord Ridgeway couldn't wait to get away from me."

"What happened?"

Caroline clenched her hands. "He is big and intimidating—and he scowls. I do not like gentlemen who tower over me."

"Did he say anything to disturb you?" asked Amelia.

"N-no. But I could not slow my tongue."

"It is all right, Caro. One needn't charm everyone," Mary reminded her. "Did anyone else give you trouble?"

"Not really. I stumbled a bit with Sir Edwin because I was still upset from Lord Ridgeway, but he did not seem to mind. He is a fascinating gentleman."

"And steady," observed Amelia.

Caro smiled. "He spent quite half the evening with me, talking and dancing."

"Was he in London this past Season?" asked Mary.

"Yes, but he did not enjoy it—except for the time he spent at the British Museum with their expert on Roman remains. Sir Edwin's estate might contain traces of an ancient settlement, so he is anxious to return and resume his hunt. He also needs to deal with his young brother, who was sent down from Eton for locking a dozen geese in his tutor's rooms." She giggled.

"Being sent down is no laughing matter," Amelia reminded her. "He should not have disclosed such ignominy, especially to someone he barely knows."

"Why?" Caroline appeared puzzled. "No harm was done. Prescott will return to school next term, and that tutor is dull, stupid, and bad-tempered—or so Sir Edwin recalls from his own school days."

"I expect he is, but that does not justify breaking the rules," put in Mary.

Caro scowled. "Perhaps, but I cannot condemn the boy. His prank was harmless—not at all like those Frederick favored. Remember the time he locked you in the dairy, Amelia? And that ghost caper, when he dressed up like Mad Cousin William, terrorizing a maid so badly that she broke a leg trying to escape?"

"And Frederick laughed." Amelia's eyes had hardened.

"Sir Edwin would never risk hurting anyone. Nor would Prescott."

Mary frowned at her vehemence. She had not expected Caroline to form a *tendre* for the scholarly baronet. Sir Edwin was quiet and calm, far more like Amelia than the excitable Caroline. But they had passed much of the evening together.

"Nor would Mr. Crenshaw," admitted Amelia. "I should not have criticized you, for we carried on a similar conversation. Mr. Crenshaw earned a reputation for playing pranks during his school days, though none were spiteful."

Mary nearly gasped at the warmth glowing in Amelia's eyes.

"But your assessment is correct," Amelia continued. "Not all pranks are alike. Frederick's were always cruel."

"Mr. Crenshaw's weren't?" asked Mary skeptically.

"Not those he mentioned. Even the one that got him sent down for a term left the headmaster laughing. I found him fascinating."

"Perhaps, but tread warily," warned Mary. "A gentleman would never tell tales that might call his character into question, so you do not know that all his pranks were harmless. And he is friendly with Lord Ridgeway, who has yet to prove he is not like his brother."

"Despite reducing the rents for all his tenants?" Caroline's voice had intensified. "And he will collect no rents at all this year."

"I have heard nothing of that."

"Lady Carworth mentioned it. He only made the announcement today."

"I am delighted for Ridgeway's tenants, but that does not negate my concerns," insisted Mary, suppressing the warmth creeping into her heart. Why had James said nothing when she'd mentioned Ridgeway's appalling rents? "Sir Richard has met Mr. Crenshaw several times in London and reports that the man is widely known as a rake. He might be welcomed into society's drawing rooms, but I would not take his words to heart."

"He considers me nicer than the young ladies gracing London this Season," Amelia said stubbornly.

"That is precisely what I mean." Mary sighed. "Amelia, a rake flirts with every female he meets, paying her pretty compliments that puff her vanity. It is as natural as breathing. I doubt he plans to seduce you, for your breeding would force him into marriage, but he will certainly try to lure you into indiscretions. Even an innocent-seeming kiss would ruin you if Mrs. Bridwell or Miss Hardaway heard of it."

"He wasn't flirting," insisted Amelia. "I can tell the difference between sincerity and flattery."

"With the gentlemen you have known all your life, but you have little experience with London beaux. Do you recall what happened with Charlotte McCafferty?"

She reluctantly nodded.

"I don't," said Caroline.

"It was five years ago, so you may not have heard about it."

"Charlotte was empty-headed and silly," said Amelia. "So when a London gentleman looked her way, she looked back, meeting him secretly and allowing him too many liberties. But he was merely amusing himself during a duty visit to his grandparents. Naturally, she heard nothing from him once he left. Anyone with sense had understood his purpose from the beginning."

"Be careful about casting aspersions," warned Mary. "Especially when your information comes from Mrs. Bridwell." She stared until the girl nodded. "While it is true that Charlotte lacked education beyond the finer points of manners and fashion, she was quite astute about people. Many of those who loudly condemned Lord Willis after he left had doted on him during his visit. In truth, he was a charming rogue who could talk water into flowing uphill. Charlotte believed every word he said—not because she was stupid or credulous, but because he made every word sound like gospel. And she had no experience with a manner quite common among London beaux."

"But—"

Mary ignored Amelia's interruption. "I am not accusing Mr. Crenshaw of being another Lord Willis. All I ask is that you be careful. I would hate to see your heart bruised because he chose you as his country diversion."

"What happened to Charlotte?" asked Caroline.

"No one is sure. She left not long after he did, supposedly to live with an ailing aunt. Few believed the tale, but nothing has been heard of her since."

"Why warn me and not Caroline?" demanded Amelia, ignoring their exchange. "Do you believe I am more likely to make a fool of myself?"

Mary blanched. "That was unfair, Amelia. You must both beware. I only mentioned Mr. Crenshaw because we know he is a rake, but Sir Edwin could be just as dangerous. We know nothing about him beyond his odd friendship with Ridgeway."

"Odd?" echoed Caroline.

"They would seem to have nothing in common—which proves how little we know about any of them. Perhaps their interest is genuine, but we must be wary. They have spent their lives in sophisticated circles. Sir Edwin has postponed an undertaking he is anxious to start in order to visit the earl. Sir Richard swears that Mr. Crenshaw usually visits Brighton this time of year—again, proving that he gave up his own pleasure to come here. And we know little about Ridgeway. How did he pass his years abroad besides dabbling in trade while in India? All I ask is that you guard your hearts until you know them better. Connection to Ridgeway is hardly a recommendation."

"Sir Edwin asked if he could call tomorrow," said Caroline.

"So did Mr. Crenshaw."

"Very well. They will be welcome. But you must promise that you will never make an unchaperoned assignation with either of them."

Caroline and Amelia readily agreed, then left for their own rooms. But Mary stayed, her forehead creased in thought. She had hoped the girls could interest at least one of the gentlemen, but now that they had, she feared it had been a mistake to invite any of them. Perhaps she should have taken Justin's warnings to heart.

James was no longer the man she remembered—if he had ever been. Why had he accepted John's lies without checking the facts for himself? She had thought him smarter than that and far less reckless. Nor would the old James have accused her so rudely, interrupting a gathering in her own home to do so. It made those tales of an Indian mistress and child seem more believable.

She huddled deeper into her chair.

His accusations had revived the pain of John's worst lies. People were so credulous—and James most of all, she concluded sadly. John was the last man she would have allowed to touch her. Intimacy with anyone was repugnant, but John's very presence had made her skin crawl since the day she had witnessed him bludgeoning a kitten. She had been six.

But James had always seemed different—kind, generous, and willing to help anyone in need, without the condescension his father employed on those few occasions when he had played benevolent lord of the manor.

James had genuinely cared. He had paid to fix the church roof, found new buyers for the potter's wares, rescued two of Payne's sheep that had been swept away during a spring flood—and Payne had not even been a Ridgeway tenant.

So his accusations hurt, even more so because she had not expected such vitriol from him. He was not the self-righteous

Mrs. Bridwell or the disdainful Lady Carworth. He had once been her friend.

But that had been many years ago, and now she had to wonder if he had ever been a friend. Her admonitions to the girls had breached the ramparts surrounding her own memories. Had she ever truly known James, or had she exaggerated every trait that set him apart from John?

They had seen little of James for several years before his last visit, for he'd spent most of his school breaks with friends, then moved to rooms in London. Only a month had elapsed between his return home and his father's death.

How naïve she had been in those days. James had grown to full manhood during his stay in London. The craggy face that intimidated when twisted into John's habitual frown could soften breathtakingly when influenced by James's crooked smiles. He had cropped his hair to a Grecian cap of dark curls according to the fashion of the day. And his laugher had been like a fresh breeze blowing through the neighborhood. Was it any wonder that his flirtations had turned her head?

What an idiot she had been. First with George, then with James.

Sighing, she wandered to the window and gazed up at the stars. She hadn't thought of George in years.

The son of another vicar, he had been visiting a school friend before assuming a post as curate to a Leiscestershire rector. She had been flattered when he chose to court her—and a little wary. Curates had minuscule incomes and could rarely support wives. But he had a small inheritance that would supplement his earnings until he found his own living.

They had discussed marriage more than once. But he had never spoken to her father. Then he'd left without a word, bidding his hosts farewell a full month early.

She had been devastated. Then furious. If he had suffered a reverse of fortune or a change of heart, the least he could have done was to explain it to her. It had to be one or the other. No message had summoned him away. No disagreements had occurred. Ten years later, she was still baffled.

And hurt. His defection had injured more than her feelings. Everyone in town had expected a betrothal. When he left so abruptly, the gossip-mongers assumed she had driven him off. She might have weathered the storm if she'd admitted turning him down, but lying had never occurred to her. So they'd concluded that her virtue had been compromised, letting their imaginations run wild over her supposed transgressions.

Her tarnished reputation had never fully recovered. The sly looks and snide remarks had made appearing in public a chore. Yet locking herself in her room where she could grieve in private had not been an option. Too many parish duties fell to her.

Thus James's flirtation had been welcome. It had quieted the gossip and added sparkle to her days.

Perhaps he had been trying to help her. That had been the effect of his attentions at first. Or perhaps he had been amusing himself. But he had not considered the inevitable consequences. When he left—which he had done within the month, slipping away without a word, just like George—his desertion had added fuel to the rumors, subjecting her to vicious attacks that still echoed in area memories. Everyone assumed that they had been conducting an affair, so his departure had cast further calumny on her reputation. Even worse, the suspicions that he had brought about his father's death also hurt her, for they were inextricably linked in the public mind.

But her tarnished reputation was not the worst consequence of his attentions. Any girl in her position would form a *tendre* for a handsome London gentleman who took pains to make her laugh and ease her burdens. She had never admitted her infatuation—had actually denied it more than once—but that did nothing to lessen her pain. Thank heavens Charlotte McCafferty had provided another example she could use with the girls, making it unnecessary to bare her own soul.

What a fool she had been. Who, in her right mind, would believe that an earl's son could entertain serious thoughts about a vicar's daughter? It would have been odd enough if her father had been a well-born younger son, but she was three generations removed from the closest aristocratic tie—and even that was to a little-known baron. Yet she had embraced his interest, using it to heal her bruised heart. And her feelings had rapidly strengthened beyond anything she had felt for George.

Idiot!

She had not even accepted the truth when he left. At first she had excused him, assuming that he needed time to sort through the rumors and eliminate the fiction. When he didn't return, she forgave him. He was only three-and-twenty and was unready for a serious relationship, so he must have forgotten that she was of marriageable age.

But as the gossip swirled and grew more lurid, forgiveness had faded. He had used her, then abandoned her. Her rationalizations had been no more than a way to keep despair at bay. Having experienced the same treatment from two vastly different gentlemen, she could only conclude that she was unworthy, just as the gossips declared.

Abandoning the window, she headed for her bedroom. As much as she wanted to forget the past, she must deal with James. John had told him that they had conducted an affair. Since James believed him, he must also have believed the other rumors—which put a new slant on his youthful attentions. Perhaps he had not been rescuing her from the gossip after George's defection. Had he expected her to fall into his bed, abandoning the idea only because he declined to share with his brother?

She shuddered.

If that were true, then he was more like John than she had ever suspected. Which boded ill for everyone. Would he resume John's long campaign against her? Only time would tell.

But a more immediate enemy was herself. Her attraction remained. He had done more than adopt a more impressive demeanor in his years away. He had also changed his style of dress, abandoning his former experiment with dandyism for something more elegant. A brilliant sapphire had sparkled from the folds of his cravat tonight, drawing attention to his blue evening coat and to the silver embroidery on his white waistcoat. The fit of his gray pantaloons had been the perfect compromise between fashion and movement.

Then there was that deep, velvety voice. His compliment on her appearance had thrilled her. Trading words had been exhilarating, tumbling chills down her back, and not from cold or fear. Even her fury had contained no fear.

But she must fear him. He shared too much of John's blood.

Despite his show of openness and kindness, he had hidden basic parts of his character. She did not know him.

Which brought her full circle to his friends. Mr. Crenshaw was an earl's younger son, giving him a higher social standing then Amelia. So could he seriously be interested? Considering his reputation, she had to doubt his intentions.

Sir Edwin was easier to believe. Wedding Caroline would be a step up for him, and he was probably attracted by her vivacity. But he did not yet know the full extent of her problem. And his friendship with Ridgeway raised questions. What did the men have in common?

Yet without evidence against them, she could not forbid them the house. She needed to investigate their circumstances. In the meantime, she must make sure that both girls were closely chaperoned whenever the gentlemen were nearby.

Perhaps Justin could spend time with each of Ridgeway's friends. Men behaved differently with each other than with women. And their morning meeting had gone a long way toward convincing her that Justin was nothing like Frederick. She could trust his judgment.

"Tell me about Miss Amelia," demanded Harry as the carriage bounced away from Northfield.

James shifted so his legs would not become entangled with his friends'. "You know more than I do. I hardly spoke with her this evening, and I didn't notice children on my last visit."

"Then what do you know about Northrup?"

"Again, very little—he is ten years my junior and was away at school when I left home. I understand he just returned from several years of military service in India."

He hid a frown. If Frederick had been John's closest friend, then what were his sisters like? They had seemed conventional, but public facades rarely revealed true character. And even their facades had been odd. Amelia was too quiet, while Caroline had been crazed. But he had paid them little heed, being too caught up in confronting Mary and listening for any gossip about John.

"The older brother was not a steady character," Edwin noted. "In fact, several people compared him to John. But he was rarely here, so he exerted little influence on the girls. Miss Caroline says they were raised by Lady Northrup."

"Is that supposed to be a recommendation?" asked James sharply. However much he wanted her, he could not overlook her unladylike conduct. "She wed Frederick, who was two years her junior; she has been running the estate by herself; and though they are undoubtedly exaggerated, more than one rumor questions her morals."

"All false," snapped Harry. "Amelia easily refuted the one about an affair with Sir Richard, for he was in London when it supposedly took place—as I know from personal observation. Not a shred of evidence has ever supported the tales. They would have died years ago if judgmental harridans like that prune-faced Mrs. Bridwell didn't keep them alive."

"You sound like you are smitten," observed James.

"Perhaps. Amelia is the sweetest girl I've ever met. But despite that delicate appearance, she is neither helpless nor gullible. I intend to see more of her."

"Be careful about raising expectations you cannot meet," warned James. "Whatever my suspicions about her family, I do not want her hurt."

"I will keep an eye on him," offered Edwin. "It will be no hardship. Caroline is a delightful young lady."

Harry choked. "Surely you jest. One cannot understand one word in ten that she says. What would you want with a pea-brained widgeon?"

"Excitable, certainly. But never pea-brained. You probably rattled her," said Edwin. "All that sparkling charm. But once she slows down so her tongue stops tripping over itself, she is quite knowing."

"Are you saying she thinks faster than she talks?" asked James, frowning.

"It would seem so. Whether that is usual with her, I cannot say. But she was clearly wrought-up tonight. I promised to call on her tomorrow."

James turned his thoughts inward as his friends compared impressions of the Northrup sisters. He did not like this development at all. Mary was clearly plotting to marry off her sisters and would grab the first gentlemen to show interest. She might even stoop to compromising them.

But they were determined—moonstruck, both of them. All he could do was accompany them whenever they called at Northfield and make sure that neither of the girls tried to draw her escort off alone. Which would complement his own plans nicely, he realized in satisfaction. He had not yet convinced Mary to look for John's killer.

A burst of heat at the prospect of seeing Mary again made him grimace. What was wrong with him? No matter how delectable she was, he could not afford to lose control. If she suspected his motives, she would never agree to help.

Down, he ordered his raging body, but it ignored him.

Again he shifted his position.

Their confrontation had not gone as he had expected—starting with her vehement denial of an affair with John. He had believed her—and not because his heart had leaped with joy at her words. She had to have heard the rumors. They were too ubiquitous for her to remain ignorant. So the white face could only have been from fury that a former friend had turned on her. Or perhaps pain?

But he thrust that thought aside. Pain would indicate stronger feelings than friendship—unless she was upset because he had accepted that she was dishonorable, while she had dismissed more dastardly tales against him.

Yet she was far from the sweet innocent he remembered. Now that he was removed from proximity to that delectable body, he could think more clearly. She had succored John's victims before her marriage. What had her father been thinking?

He remembered Vicar Layton as a devoted parent and dedicated servant of the parish. Neither role was served by discussing sexual encounters with an innocent, especially involuntary ones—which cast new suspicions on her virtue. She might not have met with John, but he had heard tales of a suitor crying off.

He stiffened. *Consider all the facts.* Was Mary a better actress than he had thought? John had not merely claimed an affair. He had offered evidence—a mark visible only to a lover.

He would never have mentioned something that might be easily disproved. So he must have seen her naked.

Pain clenched his stomach.

He twisted facts. Mary's voice reverberated in his head. There must be another explanation for John's knowledge. If only he could think of it.

His expression was growing grimmer, but this was not an appropriate place for serious thought. When they arrived at Ridgeway, the light would expose his face. Glancing across at his friends, he forced his mind back to the conversation.

"Lady Northrup is the only mother Amelia remembers," Harry was saying. "Her own died when Caroline was born, and their father never remarried. Their governess was an ancient crone who disdained anything frivolous. Fortunately, Mary replaced her with a younger woman and took the girls under her own wing."

"Caroline mentioned that. They were shocked when Frederick married within a month of their father's death—and to a vicar's daughter of little breeding—but they soon learned to love Mary. Without her, Caroline fears she would have been judged insane. It was Mary who realized that her problem was excess energy, and who taught her to control herself."

"And they rejoiced that Frederick rarely returned home. He was a brutal man when crossed."

"How?" asked James, though it was hardly surprising in one of John's friends.

"He broke Amelia's arm knocking her across the room one day. She had interrupted him to ask a favor despite his orders that he not be disturbed. The servant who let her in was summarily dismissed."

Which sounded exactly like something John would have done, he had to admit.

The carriage pulled up before Ridgeway.

Chapter Six

Mary rode along the rim of the abandoned quarry, keeping her horse as far from the edge as possible—which wasn't very far. Trees crowned the crumbling cliff that rose on her right. Piles of rock had accumulated at its base. Wind and rain had gouged out the quarry walls until the road was only twelve feet wide in spots.

People had talked for years about moving the road to the other side of the hill, but so far nothing had happened. She hoped James would consider it. The decision would ultimately be his since the proposed right-of-way would cross his land. In the meantime, she shuddered every time she passed this spot. Frederick had tumbled to his death here.

Not that she missed him.

As she rounded the sharpest corner, a hawk exploded out of the pit, clutching a squirrel in its talons. Acorn shied, swinging dangerously close to the edge and kicking loose a rock that bounced twice before landing twenty feet below.

The Ridgeway gentlemen had called at Northfield the morning after her dinner. Justin had been out with the steward, so she had been the girls' sole chaperon. But the job had been surprisingly easy.

Mr. Crenshaw had entertained them with humorous tales of the London Season, drawing giggles from the usually sedate Amelia.

A very proper couple had been thrown into hysterics while walking in Hyde Park one day. Two boys and a dog had raced past in a game of tag, knocking them into the Serpentine and ruining their clothes. Though Mary rarely laughed at anyone's misfortune, his narrative had been so witty that she hadn't been able to help herself. And the tale of the climbing-boy-turned-burglar was even funnier. The lad had been released by his master, who deemed him too old to work. The master had been right. When oaths awakened Lady Benchley, she had discovered his head dangling in her fireplace, his shoulders firmly stuck in the chimney. Nothing could dislodge him. They had finally sent a smaller boy down to tie a rope around his ankles so they could haul him out the top.

Mary sighed. She could see why Amelia found Mr. Crenshaw so fascinating.

Sir Edwin was not a sparkling entertainer, but his conversation was just as interesting. He had described why he believed the remains of a Roman villa were buried on his estate, painting such vivid word pictures of the Roman invasion that she could see the legions marching across Britain. Caroline had hung on every word, and she had stayed in control for the entire visit with hardly a clenched fist to help.

Neither of the gentlemen had said or done anything to justify her suspicions. The only surprise had been the way James had studied every move and analyzed every word. Had he feared his friends would reveal some secret? Or were her earlier suspicions correct? If he were like John, then his friends would be like Frederick. Hiding their faults could be a ploy to inflict pain by winning their regard before crushing their spirits.

She didn't want to believe it, but ignoring the possibility could be dangerous. Somehow, she must discover his ultimate intentions. Their conversation during that morning call had merely raised new questions.

They had retired to a corner of the drawing room. He had still been harping on John's recent visits, demanding a detailed list of who his brother had met.

"How should I know?" she'd finally burst out, though she managed to keep her voice pitched low so the others would not hear. "I avoided him as much as possible, for I despised the man."

"But he was your husband's closest friend. You must have seen him often."

She glared at him. "Yes, he was Frederick's friend and led

him into trouble more often than not. But even when Frederick was home, John never visited here."

"Why? Was your husband afraid you preferred him?"

She wanted to strike him, but a lady could not do so. And drawing attention to them would raise questions she did not want to answer. Her relationship with her husband was no one's business.

James still believed she had succumbed to John's wiles, despite his soothing words at their last meeting. Frederick would never have jumped to such an unwarranted conclusion. If he had considered the question at all, he would have feared that she might slip a knife into John's back if he visited Northfield. She had warned him against John too often for him to mistake her feelings.

"Frederick was understandably concerned for his sisters' reputations," she finally claimed, though she doubted he had cared one way or the other. "Allowing John near them would have courted disaster."

"Yet he left them in your charge."

Red haze pulsed before her eyes. "Do you practice being offensive or does it come naturally? I rue the day I ever considered you superior to your brother."

"How dare you?" he snapped.

"At least I base my judgments on the evidence of my own eyes instead of proving my gullibility by accepting the unsubstantiated claims of chronic liars." She immediately regretted the outburst, but it was too late to recall the words.

"Chronic liars?" He seemed on the verge of losing his temper.

She forced control on her voice, but something prodded her to continue. For years, she and every other person in the district had avoided talking about John. Though he was gone, the fear remained. Why else had she softened her condemnation when James had cornered her the first time? But it was time to lay the past to rest. If James wanted the unvarnished truth, she must provide it.

"John never spoke an honest word in his life, even when telling the truth would have been easier. But he was your family, so of course you believed him. Just as you accept every sensationalized tale Mrs. Bridwell spouts. After all, she is a vicar's wife, so why would she lie?"

"I am aware that John frequently exaggerated," he protested. "And I know very well that Mrs. Bridwell is overly judgmental, but those are not my only sources."

"What you don't accept is that John was an unconscionable bully who would employ any tactic to achieve his goals. And the goal was often to inflict as much pain as possible. Not only was he a liar who frequently fabricated stories out of whole cloth, but he intimidated everyone he met. No one dared counter him. If he'd said the sky was green, people would have rushed to spread the word lest he destroy them for daring to oppose him. If a lie is repeated often enough, people accept it as truth. Even if they doubt the details, the core remains viable— where there is smoke, there must be fire," she quoted bitterly.

He let out a long sigh. "I am not as gullible as you imply, and I know that John preyed on most of you. But that is not what I wish to discuss just now. In addition to your husband, who did John usually see when he was here?"

"I've no idea."

His eyes bore into hers, raising odd prickles on the back of her neck—quite different from those John and Frederick had incited. *Not now,* she chided herself, stifling the warmth even as his voice softened into that soothing velvet that stroked across her skin, caressing her, enticing her.

"Surely gossip included talk of who John saw when he was in the area."

"You still don't understand, do you?" To hide her emotional confusion, she glared at him. "Anyone with an ounce of intelligence ignored him—they didn't see him, didn't hear him, didn't discuss him. They certainly uttered no word against him, for attracting his attention guaranteed reprisals. Even when he was away in London, no one spoke of him. When commiserating with his victims over their bad fortune, a look or nod toward Ridgeway might hint that John was responsible. But that was the most anyone dared."

"You heard nothing else?"

"If people whispered in private, I would never know. His lies have always isolated me, and not just because of my reputed escapades. You are not the only one who erroneously believed we were close."

"Let's try this another way, then. Who were Northrup's friends?"

"I don't know."

"Why?"

"He never discussed his disreputable acquaintances, and he had no others. In fact, he had never discussed anything. The only difference his presence had made was casting a pall of tension over the household, fraying tempers and inciting fear."

"But you must be able to guess. You were married to the man for seven years."

"So what?"

"Who did he see during his last trip home besides John?"

"Give it up, my lord. I know nothing."

"You mean you will reveal nothing."

"Don't put words in my mouth." Her temper snapped. "I know nothing. Even when Frederick visited Northfield, he split his time between Ridgeway and the Lusty Maiden. He knew no one and liked it that way. He could have passed the steward or a tenant on the street and not recognized him. I've no idea who John knew, so I can't help you. I know even less about his last visit home because I was in mourning. If you need to find out who he saw, ask your servants."

"I already did, but they are a close-mouthed lot. They claim he saw no one, but I suspect they are hiding something."

"Perhaps they are telling the truth."

"Then what triggered his death?"

That parting question had teased her ever since. If John had spoken to no one, then who had killed him? And why? No one had liked him, but she had heard of no new tragedies that could be laid at his door. So why was he dead?

The obvious answer was that an argument had exploded out of control—which explained why James was determined to discover who John had seen that last day.

She sighed.

Drat the man. He was forcing her to become involved. Despite her vow to leave well enough alone, she would have to ask questions.

It was his voice, she decided as she thankfully left the quarry behind. It had deepened since he had left, taking on a honeyed quality she could not resist. Even when he was absent, it echoed at the most inconvenient times, seducing her with promises of things that didn't exist.

She must expunge it. Already, under its influence, she had revealed more discontent and more details about her barren life than she had exposed to another living soul.

The clatter of hooves diverted her thoughts. And just as well. Her agitation had pressed Acorn into a canter. They were rapidly approaching the forest.

She was reining in when a phaeton emerged from the trees, its team moving at a ground-devouring trot. But the ends of the ribbons bounced along the road. The driver had collapsed across the side, every bump edging him closer to falling out. At the rate he was going, he would do so just about the time he passed the yawning pit of the quarry.

She spurred Acorn forward even before she recognized the man. James.

"Easy, fellows," she called, cutting in front of the team in an attempt to slow them. They were not yet spooked, but without a steady hand on the ribbons, they were picking up speed as the road sloped downhill.

"Halt! Stop! Whoa!"

The commands had no effect. The team swerved around her, sliding James closer to disaster. His head and right arm dangled inches from the rear wheel, which posed a more immediate threat than the quarry.

Curses reverberated in her head. The horses were not trained to voice commands. Her best chance of halting them would be to rein in the wheeler, though she wasn't sure she could manage it. Yet she had to try. Turning, she gave chase.

The team responded by breaking into a canter, bouncing the phaeton harder and accelerating James's slide. Would the carriage overturn? Phaetons were notoriously unstable and this one was becoming unbalanced.

She fought down terror. The offside ribbon was fluttering out of reach between the horses. But the nearside one had come unhooked from the backstrap and now floated along the wheeler's right side, so it should be possible to grab it. Yet she didn't have much time. She would be squeezed between the team and the quarry in another minute, giving her little room to maneuver. And the only way to catch the ribbon was to lean far off her horse.

Panic licked her veins as she glanced back at James. He was jolting up and down, precariously balanced across the side rail. And the quarry was looming closer.

She had not seen Frederick's broken body, but her imagination conjured increasingly horrible images. James must not die. He was important to her—which was the most horrifying thought yet. She would not feel this crazed about another man. He was upsetting her world, changing her perceptions. And he didn't even realize it.

Thank God for that. If he again turned his attentions to her, he would destroy her. Somehow, she must deflect these growing feelings. She had no intention of wedding again, and no desire to conduct an affair. Even friendship would not work. It could only cause new pain when they separated—which they inevitably would. Whether he stayed at Ridgeway or not, she would soon be moving on to her dream cottage.

Keep your mind on business.

She shook away the images. Whatever her fears for the future, she must stop this phaeton.

Shifting both reins into her right hand, she inched closer to the wheeler. He was in full stampede, with white-ringed eyes and foam-flecked bit. Sweat caked his hide. Gripping the leaping head with her knees—and thanking the fates that she had chosen a saddle equipped for jumping today—she leaned down and tried to catch the fluttering ribbon.

"Easy, easy, easy," she chanted, but the wheeler paid no attention. They swept onto the narrow ledge ringing the quarry, the ribbon still tantalizingly out of reach. It flicked across the back of her hand, teased her fingers, then plunged nearly to the road before floating up to shoulder height.

She drew closer to the horse's head. He snorted, shifting toward the cliff and again swerving the phaeton sharply. James's arm brushed the wheel.

"Slow down."

She tried using her crop to catch the loop where the ribbon split into two reins. No luck. Acorn tensed as the road narrowed. They were approaching the sharp corner.

In desperation, she lunged farther, her knees barely clinging to the saddle, her hand banging against the wheeler's shoulder, increasing his panic. The ribbon slapped her fingers once . . . twice . . .

She had it. Acorn was fretting over the unexpected weight shift, so she spared a moment to pull herself back into the saddle—a more difficult task than she had expected.

"Easy does it," she crooned, pulling back as sharply as she dared.

The wheeler tossed his head, fighting the pressure, but he broke stride, throwing his teammate into confusion.

"We're going to stop now, fellows." She managed to keep her voice even. Another break slowed them to a trot. But they didn't halt until they had reached the narrowest point in the road.

She stayed atop Acorn, gasping for breath. Reaction was setting in. Her legs were so weak that standing would be impossible. All three horses were trembling.

Now what?

A quick glance showed that James still hung half out of the phaeton. His right glove was shredded, revealing a bloody hand. But she could not attend him just yet.

She stroked Acorn's neck. Her voice might calm the team, but it would take time. They were rolling their eyes and twitching. The wheeler stamped one foot in agitation.

"Easy, there," she crooned softly, adding words of praise and even a song or two. Forcing gentleness into her tone calmed her own nerves. Gradually, their ears began flicking in her direction. Less white showed around their eyes. Tails swished more naturally.

It took several minutes before she dared dismount. Several more minutes of stroking the horses' heads and necks finally settled them enough that she could attend James.

He remained unconscious, but he did not smell of wine. Had he suffered a seizure? New fears made her hands shake.

She was trying to push him back onto the seat when something landed on her boot.

Blood. And not from his hand.

"Dear Lord," she murmured as another drop fell. A good-sized patch had already soaked into the road.

His head had grazed the wheel, but the resulting scrape was not responsible for the blood. A deep cut lacerated a large knot just behind his left temple. Swallowing nausea, she pushed his hair aside. It was a fresh injury, but positioned where it could not have been inflicted by the wheel or railing. Yet there was no trace of blood on his coat, so he had not incurred it before beginning his drive.

She had to stop the bleeding before the smell spooked the horses. They were still nervous. Ripping the bottom flounce from her petticoat, she fashioned a bandage that pressed a thick pad into the wound. Now all she had to do was move him back onto the seat.

Easier said than done. He was a big man, broad-shouldered and well over six feet tall—intimidating even in unconsciousness. Pushing did no good. The side rail was so far above the ground that she could get little leverage. If only he would wake up, he could help, but nothing roused even a flicker of awareness. Giving up, she tied Acorn to the back, retrieved the off-side ribbon, then climbed into the phaeton.

A rock was wedged under his boot.

Shivers stood her hair on end despite the heat of the day. The rock was roughly four inches across, with jagged edges. And one of those edges was smudged with blood that had trapped a dark hair.

Someone had tried to kill him.

She glanced at the forest a quarter mile away, suddenly feeling far too vulnerable. The quarry yawned its sinister mouth only a few feet beyond James's head. The phaeton sat at the base of a cliff, open to attack from above. She had to get him away before his enemy could strike again.

Tugging moved him only an inch before his coat caught on the rail. Pulling harder had no effect and left her panting from exertion.

The attacker had arranged a very clever accident. The rock

might have killed James outright, but its main purpose had been to knock him across the right side of the phaeton, where he would eventually fall. Even if he did not immediately roll into the quarry, a helpful push would have ensured his death. The landing would erase any sign of the initial attack.

Just like Frederick.

Dear God. Frederick had been riding along this same road in the same direction, headed for Ridgeway after an evening in the Lusty Maiden's taproom. Everyone had assumed that he'd passed out from drink and fallen. Now she had to wonder.

Later! This is no time to panic. James has no connection to Frederick.

Invisible eyes bored into her back. Was the killer still watching?

James needed help. She could not drive with him draped over the side, but she dared not leave him alone while she fetched assistance. Fear and desperation gave her a new burst of energy. Tugging finally tore a button loose and pulled him onto the seat, but tears were streaming down her face by the time she was finished. His sprawl filled the space. He remained unconscious, with new blood trickling down his cheek.

She frowned as she retied the bandage. His breathing was fast and shallow—not a good sign. At the very least, he had a concussion, but his injuries might be worse than that. He needed a bed and care.

Perching precariously on the edge of the seat, she set the horses to a walk, fighting the urge to spring the team. Jarring could only make things worse.

Was the culprit still watching? A fast horse could have circled the hill to get ahead of her. She had no idea how much time had elapsed since she had first spotted James. Would the man waylay her at the park gates or the stone bridge? Who was he? And why had he attacked?

The trip to Ridgeway seemed endless, though the Court was barely two miles from the quarry. Her fear increased with every step. As did her uncertainty.

James had claimed only yesterday that the servants were hiding information. John had hired every member of the staff, so she could not trust them, despite knowing that they had not liked him. She had no reason to believe they liked James, either. A disgruntled servant might have planned this attack. Or an angry tenant. Or any number of other people. Had one of his changes threatened someone? Was there a man who hated all Underwoods?

But that made no sense. James had not been near Ridgeway in years.

Think logically!

The only real threat James posed was to John's killer. So either his investigation was making progress, or the culprit had decided to prevent it from doing so. Thus she had to help him search for justice. If the culprit was willing to strike at anyone who threatened to expose him, then they were all in danger. They had to catch him before anyone else died.

But the man was smart. Knowing that a second murder would force Squire Church to reopen his inquiry, he had chosen to stage an accident, taking Frederick's as his pattern. Everyone knew the quarry road was dangerous. Every few years the pit claimed a new victim. Who would question another fall?

It fit all too well. But she still had no idea who was behind it. And an unconscious James could not protect himself against a second attack.

She could not remain in a bachelor establishment to nurse him, so the only protection she could provide was to keep the nature of his accident a secret. The killer must believe that no one suspected the truth. As long as James remained in bed, he was vulnerable.

"What happened?" demanded Harry, bursting outside in response to a footman's summons. Edwin followed more slowly.

She shrugged. "It looks like he fell. I found him out by the quarry. Can you carry him inside?"

"Of course," said Edwin.

They made lifting him look easy. Harry sent a footman to fetch the doctor.

"He will need constant watching. Head injuries can be quite unpredictable," she suggested as she held open the door to James's room—which was not the master suite, she noted in passing. Did he dislike the idea of occupying a bed John had slept in? But this was not the time to think of such things. Especially when the sight of his dark head against the white pillow sent heat sizzling through her veins. She had to leave before she offered to nurse him.

James had been right about the staff. They were sullen and antagonistic. Would they turn on him? But she had hardly formed the question when Edwin proved that his thoughts matched hers.

"We will watch him," he promised, exchanging a thoughtful look with Harry. "We can take turns. The servants are not overly friendly."

They were hiding something, but she did not question them. Perhaps they were helping him investigate John's death. Or they might know of some other threat on his life. It didn't matter. They would protect him until he recovered, and that was the important thing. Taking leave of them, she headed for home, the rock wrapped in his handkerchief and tucked inside her reticule.

By the time she reached Northfield, reaction was shaking her in long waves. New fears tormented her. Had the killer watched her stop the phaeton? Had he seen her bandage James's head or pick up the rock? Did he know that she recognized an attempt at murder?

She played out the scene in her mind again and again, but she had no answers. He must have remained. If James had not tumbled into the quarry on his own, the killer had to be ready to help him. So he had seen her. Which accounted for her edginess. It had been eyes peering out from the forest that had made her so nervous, not the yawning quarry.

How obvious had she been when she'd found the rock? She frowned. Had she glanced at the cliffs? Someone who had not seen the phaeton emerge from the woods might believe the rock had fallen. If she was lucky, he would expect her to accept the incident as an accident, but she could not count on that. A rock from above would not have struck the side of his head.

Thus she had yet another reason to help James find the killer. If the man had attacked because James had learned something, then he would have to eliminate her as well. So she had to protect herself. And the only sure way was to identify him.

Perhaps she should approach the problem from a different direction. She could hardly ask questions about John without drawing attention. But James had found no evidence of an argument or even a meeting on the day John had died, so his death probably had its seeds in his last trip home with Frederick. By investigating Frederick's final days, she might learn something useful. John and Frederick had always acted together. She had turned a blind eye to most of their escapades, knowing that she had no power to stop them. But perhaps she could use a desire to make amends as her excuse for peering beneath this particular rock.

That last trip home had been unusually eventful—the inn fire, the damage to Wilson's farm, a week-long orgy at Ridgeway, and finally Frederick's accident. What else might they have done?

She could eliminate one possibility immediately. As soon as she brought her nerves under control, she would pay a call on the Wilsons. She had thought that her intervention had defused his fury, but she may have been wrong. Had he struck out at John for instigating that ride? Was he afraid James would learn about it? If he had been away from the farm this afternoon, she must suspect him.

Evil had stalked the district for too many years, but it had not died with its principal perpetrator. It had taken new root in the man who had killed John. Until he was exposed, none of them were safe.

John's killer slouched in the corner of the taproom, nursing a pint of ale while he listened to the voices rising from a nearby table.

"Doctor was called to the Court today. Seems 'is lordship 'ad a little accident."

" 'Tweren't no accident," muttered his companion. "He had a fit. Foaming, he was."

"Says who?"

"Dunning."

"You'll never want for moonshine if you listen to 'im. 'Is wits is addled."

"I heard the earl got into a fight."

"With who?"

"Don't know. Some says the groom, others claim 'twas a tenant."

"I heard he was poisoned," put in a man from the next table. "The cook didn't like his complaints."

"It were an accident," insisted the first speaker. " 'E were climbing around by the quarry and slipped. But the doctor says he'll recover."

Everyone grumbled.

He ceased listening. None of the rumors hinted at the truth. So Lady Northrup had seen nothing incriminating.

Again he cursed the interfering widow, as he had been doing since he'd arrived at the edge of the forest to see her standing beside the earl's phaeton. He should have made the horses bolt—would have if he had expected anyone else to be on the road. The team must have stopped when the rider approached.

A perfect plan ruined.

But justice would win in the end, he swore, downing his draft of ale. God would provide another opportunity, and he would make sure that the next encounter was conclusive.

Only then would he find peace.

Chapter Seven

Mary was helping the housekeeper inventory the linens. Now that Justin had authorized the expenditure, they had to decide how many pieces needed replacing.

"Hopeless," she agreed, adding yet another sheet to the rag pile.

Footsteps raced along the hall.

"Cm-sb-kil-rg!" Caro babbled as she stumbled into the linen room.

"Calm down," urged Mary, grasping her arms to look into her face. Caro was more agitated than ever before. Every muscle was quivering.

"Cm-Cm-Cm-sty-boy-bpt!"

This wasn't working. "Can you show me the problem?"

Caro tore free and raced out. Mary followed, though it wasn't easy. Caro always moved like the wind when she was excited, but she had never been this bad, even as a child.

Once they emerged from the house, Mary had little doubt where they were heading. Shouts arose from the stable, and several footmen were running in that direction. Various disasters flitted through her mind, from mad horses to fire, but they faded when she rounded a corner.

Men crowded close together, forming a ring.

A fight.

"I'll take care of it, Caro," she promised, sending the girl back to the house. "Thank you for fetching me."

Caro was trembling with reaction, but she managed to nod.

Too bad Justin and the steward were out, she thought grimly as she pushed through a cluster of gardeners. Where was

Brown? The head groom was supposed to maintain order in the stables.

He was watching and cheering, she realized when she reached the inside of the ring. One of the stable boys was attacking James with a pitchfork, goaded on by everyone assembled. Though no more than fourteen, the lad was tall and muscular.

"Stop this!" she ordered, glaring at Brown.

The female voice distracted everyone, allowing James to catch the pitchfork and tackle his opponent.

"M-my lady," stammered Brown.

"I am appalled that anyone on my staff would treat a visitor so rudely," she said scathingly, staring at each servant in turn. "Brown, you will remain here. The rest of you will return to your duties if you wish to stay in Northfield's employ. Lord Northrup will speak with each of you when he returns."

Having the fight replaced by a furious mistress sobered most of them. She took note of which ones were still muttering as they shuffled away.

"What happened, my lord?" she demanded, turning to James. His wound had broken open, staining his bandage with fresh blood.

"I rode over by way of the shortcut, then made the mistake of dismounting in the stable yard. This lad jumped me."

"Brown?"

"I arrived just afore you, my lady."

She doubted it. He had been too enthusiastic in his cheering. But that was for Justin to address. "Yet you made no attempt to break up an attack by one of your staff on a lord of the realm who was paying a call on your employer."

He shifted his feet. "Nobody likes Ridgeway."

"Unacceptable, Brown. It is not your place to judge any visitor to this estate. You might remind your staff that we will not tolerate anyone doing so again. Nor will we tolerate avenging grievances against the old earl by attacking the new one."

"Yes'm."

The boy was squirming to escape James's grasp. "What's his name?"

"Will."

"Why did you attack Lord Ridgeway, Will?"

"M'sister," he mumbled, freeing an arm to strike James anew. Brown jumped in to pin him down.

"Who is your sister?" demanded James.

"Betty. You smashed her jaw so she can't eat good."

"No."

"What is he talking about?" she asked Brown.

He shrugged. "He's one of Farmer's lads," he said, naming one of Sir Richard's tenants. "Whole family's a bit simple—though the boys make good enough stable hands—but the girl can't do nothin' for herself."

"When was Betty hurt?" James asked, gentling his voice.

"Couple of years ago."

"Did she claim I did it?"

"I doubt she'd recognize her own father," muttered Brown.

"*One o' the twins,*" Will quoted.

"John, then. I've not been here in years."

Will glared suspiciously.

"It's true, Will," Mary said. "This is James, the new earl. The man who was here two years ago was his twin brother John. I know, because he traveled from London with my husband, Lord Northrup."

Will's sullen face flushed.

Mary turned to Brown. "I will leave him in your charge for now. You will make him understand that the twins are two different men and that neither is responsible for the deeds of the other. Northrup will discuss the situation when he returns."

Brown jerked Will toward the stable. She was confident that the boy would assault no one again.

"My profound apologies, my lord," she said, leading the way to the house. She knew why he had called alone, though she had not expected him for another day or two. He would have questions about the accident, and this incident would not make answering them any easier.

"It wasn't your fault." He gingerly fingered his bandage. His coat sleeve had a new hole where Will had caught him with a tine. "It would seem that John was even less popular than I thought. Why would he attack the Farmer girl?"

"I am only guessing, but he probably ordered her out of his

way. When she responded slower than he liked, he struck her down. Do you wish to speak with Northrup about this?"

"No. I doubt an officer needs help disciplining his staff. But I have several questions for you."

"I will answer what I can, but first, you need to clean up."

Summoning Justin's valet, she sent him upstairs. After apprising Trimble of the scuffle, she left him to deal with the errant footmen, then paced the study while she reviewed recent events.

James's arrival was disrupting the neighborhood. She had been right to fear his appearance. It was opening old wounds, reviving old grievances—and doing it with a suddenness that bypassed the usual curbs on behavior. Two attacks, by two different people, put a new twist on the incident at the quarry.

"Lord Ridgeway, my lady," announced Trimble from the doorway.

A fresh bandage wrapped his forehead. Pickins had brushed his blue jacket and mended the tear, but mud still streaked the dove gray pantaloons, and blood stained his shirt. She bit back a groan when she spotted the scratch on his top boots. Gentlemen hated it when anything damaged their boots.

"Sit down, my lord." She motioned to the chair in front of the desk. He looked pale, but she was determined to keep the meeting businesslike. Her serenity would disappear if she did not maintain her distance.

"No more apologies," he begged, forestalling further comment.

"Very well." She handed him a glass of wine before seating herself behind the desk.

"Harry claims you brought me home yesterday."

She nodded. "What was the diagnosis? I am surprised to see you up so soon."

He grunted. "Concussion, but I hate being confined to bed."

"Yet if you were not still weak from blood loss, Will would have been less successful." Or if his clothes had been less fashionable. Even though his were looser than some—Mr. Crenshaw's, for example—they constrained his movements. His last lunge to tackle Will had torn the shoulder seam of his coat.

"Hmph." He sipped wine. "According to Harry, you found

me unconscious near the quarry, loaded me into my phaeton, then drove me home."

She said nothing.

"Arrant nonsense. You could not possibly lift me."

"I never claimed to have done so. You were in your phaeton when I found you."

"Still arrant nonsense."

"Are you calling me a liar? I did find you near the quarry, and I did drive you home."

"Perhaps, but that is far from the whole story. What really happened?"

"Do you not recall?" Even before the incident in the stable yard, she had questioned her original conclusions.

He paced the room, tossing back the wine and helping himself to more. "I had spent the morning in town. People no longer recoil in shock at my appearance, but they remain aloof, even those who used to be friendly."

"That should come as no surprise, my lord. You have been absent a long time. People no longer remember you clearly and have to wonder if you resemble your brother in more than looks."

"It is more than that," he insisted. "I've done enough since returning to ease most fears."

"You have rolled back the rents and postponed turning off any servants, but that could be a prelude to harsher measures—something John often did. You cannot regain trust in a fortnight that took ten years of deliberate cruelty to destroy. And you cannot expect people to willingly abandon years of prudence to discuss the unmentionable subject of your brother."

"Always, we come back to John," he murmured.

"You cannot ignore him," she agreed. "And whatever your reasons, the fact that you are searching for his killer counts against you."

"Are you suggesting that I stop?"

She frowned. "At first, I thought it a futile attempt and an unnecessary one, but I am no longer certain. I had not looked beyond the fact that John's death benefited many deserving people. But what of the killer? Can I feel secure knowing that one of my neighbors is capable of brutally dispatching an enemy?"

"A valid concern. Where does he draw the line between friend and foe?"

"And what constitutes justice?" she finished for him, then felt her cheeks warm at her temerity. Shivers rose at this apparent bit of mind-reading.

"Exactly, but we have moved far afield. Tell me about this accident. If I was still in my phaeton, why do I have a knot on my head?"

"What do you remember?" she asked again.

"I had been asking questions about last Christmas—strangers who might have passed through, holiday visitors, John's actions. But no one admitted anything new."

"Of course not."

He sighed and resumed his seat. "I was mulling the responses as I drove back to Ridgeway, trying to decide if I had any hope of surmounting people's suspicions. But I remember nothing after I entered the forest."

"You met no one on the road?"

"I passed the doctor and a farmer, but we did not speak."

"So much for one theory," she muttered, but he heard.

"What theory?"

"I had hoped that an argument had exploded into violence." He raised his brows.

"A rock knocked you senseless," she admitted, shrugging. "I found you and drove you home."

"A rock?" He straightened, his eyes darkening in fury. "There was no argument, not even an exchange of greetings, so just how did a rock hit me as I drove through the forest?"

"Someone threw it."

"Hence the argument theory. But that won't wash."

"I was afraid of that. Which is why I began thinking about John's killer. Did you note any reaction beyond professed ignorance from those in town?"

"No. I have been keeping my questions casual, hoping that the different approach might uncover something new."

"So who was disturbed?" she murmured, half to herself.

"No one—or everyone. The response was uniformly unhelpful."

"Not surprising. You may lack Isaac's official standing, but they must assume you are seeking revenge."

"But I'm not."

"Of course you are, though you dress it up in words like *justice*. What is law but a way to retaliate against wrongdoers without incurring the stigma of dirtying your own hands?"

"Don't hit me with philosophy when my head is pounding," he begged, pressing his temples as if to suppress the pain. "So you think I should forget the killer and return home?"

"No, but many people will. Few openly rejoiced at John's death, but most did in their hearts."

"I agree that he was not a good man—"

Her snort cut off his words.

"All right. He was evil. I wish I had recognized it sooner—and I apologize for believing his tales. But I cannot condone murder."

"I would not ask you to."

"Good. That is doubly true now that the killer has attacked me."

"Slow down. We don't know that it was he."

"But you just said that my probing incited the attack. He must protect himself from exposure."

She shivered. "Even discounting an argument, I can think of three possibilities. And there may be more."

"I can assure you that I've made no enemies on my travels."

"That is not one of my theories."

He groaned. "Then what are they?"

"The first is the most obvious, that the killer—or someone who is trying to protect the killer—decided that your death was the only way to prevent disclosure. The second is that the killer or his protector was warning you to drop the investigation and leave. The third is that Will is not the only simple-minded soul who might attack because you look like John.

"Which do you believe?" His face had paled further.

"My first impression was an attempt on your life, but reflection makes me think it was merely a warning." Or so she hoped. Gossip contained no hint of her involvement, instead offering half a dozen explanations for the earl's sudden indisposition, which made it likely that the attacker had not remained long enough to see her.

His gaze sharpened. "You are hiding something. A rock to the head would hardly guarantee death, so why suspect murder? Start at the beginning and tell me exactly what happened. Why did you mislead Harry?"

The harsh voice grated on her ears, but she could hardly blame him. He had always been intelligent—and far too good at reading her thoughts. "I did not exactly mislead him. I reported that you had fallen. Since you were unconscious, he assumed you must have fallen to the ground. I saw no need to correct him."

"Why?"

"At the time, I believed someone had tried to kill you, but I had no idea who or why. If it were connected to John's death, the culprit might have been anyone, including one of your servants. You were helpless. The only protection I could offer was to make no accusations that would threaten the culprit."

He stared to say something, but she overrode his words. "After I left Ridgeway, I realized that I'd overreacted. The attack was most likely a warning."

"Fustian!" he snorted. "Quit tiptoeing around the truth. I want facts, starting with how you know someone threw a rock at me. You cannot have seen him, or you would know his identity."

She sighed, then pulled open her reticule. He leaned across the desk to accept the rock she pulled out. The blood had blackened, but enough smudged the handkerchief to make clear what it was.

"Rather a large weapon if the purpose was merely a warning," he observed.

"And thrown with enough force to knock you half out of your phaeton. The horses picked up speed when they hit that downhill stretch leading to the quarry. Every bump pushed you farther over the side."

He abruptly sat down, as if his knees had collapsed. "That sharp corner where the road narrows would have tossed me out entirely—or overturned the phaeton, which amounts to the same thing."

She nodded. "And if someone wanted you dead, they need only roll you a time or two to send you into the pit."

"Thus hiding the blow on my head."

"The likely conclusion would have been accident." She sighed. "But enough of this speculation. The idea is ridiculous. The attack had to have occurred in the forest, for you were already unconscious when you emerged from the trees. He made no attempt to panic the horses, so he cannot have expected them to continue all the way to the quarry."

"Perhaps." He sounded skeptical.

"A few questions would hardly pressure the killer into striking again. Surely he would wait until you actually learned something."

"Unless he has more to fear than John's death."

"Or unless you made an enemy of your own without realizing it. Did you meet anyone from here in London or elsewhere. Sir Richard is often in the city."

"No."

"Had you decided to let any of the servants go before announcing that reprieve?"

"The butler and housekeeper. Both stole freely, but I need to identify John's killer before making changes."

"You should also investigate why they stole."

He glared. "You knew about that?"

"Most people did. Forbes and Mrs. Washburn despised John, for they witnessed much of his venality. The food and supplies they pilfered went to tenants in danger of starvation and servants turned off without a reference."

"I had no idea."

"Nor did John, for he visited rarely and never checked the household accounts. Walden dealt only with estate records—he was truly John's servant, carrying out every command to the letter."

"So that is the real reason you misled Harry. You suspected Forbes of killing John, then turning on me."

"Don't put words in my mouth. Forbes would be more inclined to circumvent your orders than to kill you. And if he had been in the woods, I doubt he could have reached the house before me. He doesn't ride. The gig he uses could not have covered the long route around the hill in time. And he is getting on in years, so could never have run that fast."

"How did you stop the horses?" he asked abruptly.

"Caught the ribbon controlling the wheeler. Your team is well-trained."

"That cannot have been easy. How fast were they traveling?"

"Panicked," she admitted with a shiver. "Which was mostly my own fault. They objected to being chased."

"Were the ribbons still in my hand?"

She shook her head.

"Look at me, Mary."

Compliance sent fire along every nerve. He was radiating that intense masculinity that alternately fascinated and terrified her. She had to hide her reaction, or he would take advantage of her.

"How did you do it?"

"I had to." She managed a negligent shrug.

He shook his head. "Few people could have. You have my eternal gratitude for saving my life. But one point puzzles me."

Only one? She must be under better control than she thought.

He ran his fingers through his hair. "Why did you suspect murder the moment you found me?"

"It wasn't quite that soon. I had no time to consider how you had fallen into that predicament until after I stopped the team. That was when I found the rock."

"But why suspect murder rather than a prank?"

"My husband died there."

"By accident, you claimed."

"Yes. He had been drinking heavily, and probably fell from his horse—he was a poor rider even when sober—then stumbled off the road in a daze. If you had died, the conclusion would have been the same, though some might have wondered how a sober man could slip on a sunny afternoon. But the incidents were too similar. If someone wanted to kill you, Frederick's accident gave him a perfect plan. No one takes the long route to Ridgeway from town, so an attacker would expect you to pass that point. Everyone knows how dangerous that road is, but you might have forgotten during your absence. By the way, we all hope you will consider moving it to the other side of the hill," she added.

He nodded, but absently. "Are you sure your husband's death was an accident?"

"Of course." But she could feel her face paling. "Who would want to kill Frederick?"

"Who knows? He and John ran many joint ventures. I find it suspicious that they are both dead."

She shook her head. "His only connection is that someone used his fall as a model."

"But he died, so why do you insist that my attacker was issuing a warning?"

She gave up sitting quietly behind the desk. She hadn't expected his insistence. Thinking was easier if she paced the room. "There are too many questions and even more contradictions," she said at last. "No one has a reason to kill you, at least not until your investigation shows some progress." She looked at him.

"I've learned nothing except that John lied more often than I had believed."

Nodding, she resumed her rambles. "Unless this was another attack like Will's—which means any resemblance to Frederick's accident is coincidental—I have to believe it was meant as a warning. Yes, it could have resulted in death, but that was far from likely when the rock was thrown."

James fingered the bandage again. "I still think Northrup's death is suspicious. Are you sure that no evidence points that way?"

"Not that I know of—and I have been asking questions about his last days, hoping to learn something that might explain John's murder."

"Any luck?"

She shook her head.

"How about tenants and servants? Obviously, your staff hated John."

She grimaced at the reminder, resuming her seat. "True, and I did wonder if Wilson might have taken revenge for the damage to his farm, but he was cutting hay all afternoon yesterday, in company with half a dozen others, including Justin. As to Frederick, he was mostly an object of ridicule. He was a wastrel, and could be quite unpleasant when in his cups, but he generally ignored underlings."

"Yet one of them might have sought his death—just as Will sought mine."

"Why bother? He was rarely here. I ran the estate without his interference—which everyone knew."

"I still think he was murdered."

"I don't, though I will concede that it was possible. If someone *had* been determined to attack him, finding him would have been easy. Everyone in the taproom knew he was headed for Ridgeway that night."

"If you turn up any evidence, will you tell the squire? After all, your husband was nearly as unscrupulous as my brother."

Damn him. Very little escaped his notice. She had wondered at the time if Frederick had had help falling over that cliff—his death had culminated a week of almost unimaginable savagery—but she had never seriously considered the idea because widowhood had been so welcome.

She forced another shrug. "We already agreed that killers make dangerous neighbors. Deliberately taking a life cannot be justified by citing the victim's faults."

He nodded. "Enough about your husband's death. We've strayed far from the subject. What did John do that might have incited murder?"

"If I knew that, I would have told Squire Church. John's public actions harmed broad groups—tenants, artisans, servants, and so on. Anything aimed at an individual remained private— on both sides. Revealing details always brought reprisals. And he was rarely here, especially in recent years. His visits never lasted more than a fortnight. At Christmas, he arrived only a day before his death."

"How about earlier visits?"

"Usually he and Frederick traveled together. I heard he left the day after Frederick's death. That trip was eight months after the previous one."

"You seem quite familiar with his travels."

"Not really. As I said, he and Frederick usually arrived together. If John ever paid Ridgeway a brief visit alone, I would not have noticed. But your servants would know."

"They are uncooperative. Some even blame me for his death."

"Credit you, most likely."

She could have named a dozen people besides the exonerated Wilson who had hated John, but the words would not form. None of them needed James's suspicions. All still suffered— women coerced into John's bed, men whose livelihoods had been jeopardized, the potboy at the Lusty Maiden who had run the chandler's shop until John put him out of business. But none of them had recent grievances, so she discounted them as potential killers.

James finally gave up and left, though he couldn't shake the notion that she was hiding something—perhaps several things. But it would be difficult to learn what. She had remained cool and aloof—again he berated himself for his clumsy accusations. Was that the cause of her reticence, or was she protecting someone?

Beauty mark. He gritted his teeth. No matter how logically he debunked John's claims, the suspicion lingered. Was the person she was protecting herself?

Mary was not a typical lady. She had charged into the stable yard and taken control of an explosive situation without a second thought. Judging from everyone's reactions, it was not the first time she had restored order to a group of rowdy men. He had seen many women on his travels who were capable of brutality. War forced everyone into new roles.

John had been waging a war against the inhabitants of Shropshire. Had gentle Mary finally snapped? She had the imagination for plotting John's death. She'd come up with possibilities he had not considered. And her reluctance to concede that Frederick's death might have been murder supported his suspicion. She had protested too vehemently. Had she killed both of them?

He shuddered, doubling over with pain. If that proved true, could he turn her in?

But this whole line of thought was ridiculous. John had lied about having an affair with her. Yesterday's attack had been provoked by his investigation—which itself vindicated Mary, he realized. She had not thrown that rock, and he doubted any of the area's residents would lift a finger to protect her.

Imagining the effort Mary must have made to stop his phaeton left him dizzy. His last memory had been of approaching the center of the forest.

He held up his right hand, finally understanding the pattern of abrasions that covered its outside edge, which proved how close to death he had actually come. Regardless of the quarry, falling would have landed him under the phaeton's wheel.

Mary could have been killed trying to rescue him.

He ruthlessly suppressed the thought. Dwelling on the past was pointless. She was right that asking questions alone would not have pushed the killer into striking, so he must have heard something important in town. But what?

He passed from Northfield land to Ridgeway's as he reviewed every scrap of gossip. Miss Hardaway's grand-niece was in an interesting condition for the fourth time. Mr. Morton was betrothed again; his first two wives had died, probably from his chronic brutality.

He grimaced. Morton had a long history of cruelty and vengeance, but John had done nothing to Morton or his wives—or nothing he knew of.

Colonel Davis's son had been promoted to colonel after the battle of Badajoz, adding to the old man's pride. Isaac had almost single-handedly led his cricket team to victory over a team from Shrewsbury. Barnes had narrowly defeated Ruddy at quoits, ending the merchant's long reign as Ridgefield champion. Several young boys had tossed rocks through the windows in Lady Carworth's hothouse, drawing the wrath of parents forced to pay for repairs.

None of the tales had any connection to last Christmas. And he had heard nothing about John.

Chapter Eight

Having three London gentlemen and an unwed baron in the neighborhood caused an upsurge in entertaining, particularly among families with marriageable daughters. The Northrup dinner might have been the first, but other hostesses were soon vying to see who could produce the most memorable event.

Lady Granger, wife of Sir Maxwell, was no exception. A ruined castle overlooked the lake on their estate. It had originally belonged to Sir Gryfyd Wellwyn, who had received both the land and a knighthood from Edward I in exchange for renouncing his allegiance to all Welsh princes. The castle had passed into Granger hands during Elizabeth's reign, then burned during modernization. Rather than rebuild at a site many believed had been cursed by the last Wellwyn, the Grangers had erected a manor across the valley.

Time had continued the destruction begun by the fire, knocking down walls one by one. But the south tower remained sturdy enough to provide access to a stretch of battlements that offered a spectacular view of the valley, the manor, and the distant mountains.

The second attraction was the lake. Sir Maxwell had a dozen boats available for rowing. Fanciful gardens covered the island, which was crowned by a faux Grecian temple. A maze of romantic pathways on island and shore earned his estate accolades for being the most pleasing to visitors—as well as the oldest in the district. Thus no one was surprised to receive invitations to a picnic.

"Sir Maxwell needs a suitor for Lucy," Amelia warned

Justin, who was riding beside the carriage as they approached the picnic site.

"Lucy?"

"His youngest daughter; I doubt you remember her," explained Mary. "Unfortunately, she is quite the antidote, and her manners are sadly lacking. Sir Maxwell is desperate to see her off his hands, though to his credit, he turned down an offer from Mr. Morton. But I would not be surprised if he arranged a compromise with someone more eligible. Be careful, and avoid accompanying her to the island or the ruins. Miss Brentwood accidentally became shut in the dungeon with Mr. Gardner some years ago. It might have given Lucy ideas."

Justin nodded.

Amelia and Caroline chattered about the picnic. Each was looking forward to spending more time with her beau. Mary ignored them, too intent on her own problems.

She had done little more to investigate Frederick's last days, for James's questions had raised disturbing ideas.

If Frederick had been murdered, then asking about his activities would be tantamount to teasing a bull. A killer would believe she was suspicious. He would feel threatened and attack.

Just as he'd done to James.

The image of that runaway phaeton flashed before her eyes. No matter how much she scoffed at his suggestion, she could not afford to ignore the possibility. Even if someone balked at killing her, her reputation was more vulnerable than most.

So she must keep her questions discreet. And that meant talking only to those people who would remain silent about her interest. Friends or not, she couldn't trust the Northfield servants when it came to gossip. All servants freely discussed their masters, both within the house and with those from other houses. So the only new person she had questioned had been her personal maid.

Flora was a gem. Because she had grown up on one of Ridgeway's tenant farms, she remained friendly with the other servants despite her elevated position. Yet she was loyal only to Mary, who had taken her into service after John had ravished her at age fifteen, and who had kept the incident a secret. Despite knowing John, half the population would have condemned Flora.

Flora swore that no one had discussed Frederick's accident. No rumors suggested he had been killed. Despite all the anger he had provoked during that visit, nothing hinted that an argument or prank had gotten out of hand. He had been so obviously intoxicated that his death had surprised no one.

And Flora could add nothing about Frederick's activities during that last visit. The entire group had stayed at Ridgeway. Even after the other guests departed, Frederick had remained at Ridgeway, riding into town to visit the taproom, then heading back to the Court. So she had no way of learning who he might have seen.

She considered asking Squire Church what he had discovered about Frederick's last days, but she doubted he knew anything. He had not investigated beyond interviewing those in the taproom that night. Besides, he had declined to give her any details at the time, citing female sensibilities. He had not even allowed her to view the body.

She sighed. Justin must ask for all the particulars. If Frederick had suffered a head wound like James's, she would have to seriously consider the question of murder. If not, there was no point in digging into the matter, for without a confession, they would prove nothing.

The carriage rolled to a halt. She had hardly greeted Lady Granger when Squire Church commandeered her arm.

"My dear Lady Northrup, you look remarkably fine today. Lord Northrup's return has agreed with you. What a relief it must be to have the estate burdens removed from your pretty shoulders."

"Not at all, sir," she protested absently, her mind immersed in questions about Frederick's death. Even if the squire had not asked as part of his official investigation, he might know what Frederick and John had done during their last days together. Was there any significance in the fact that their friends had left the morning of Frederick's accident?

And there might be a way to prove James's theory, she realized suddenly. If Frederick had fallen, then rolled or slid into the pit, he must have had help. The road sloped away from the edge at that point.

But would asking the squire do any good? He considered her an unorthodox hoyden who lacked any sense of propriety. It was a wonder that he condescended to speak with her.

His smile was distinctly superior. "So gallant. I will escort you to see the ruins."

She started to object, but he continued without pause. "Northrup can chaperon his sisters. His return finally gives you the freedom to enjoy yourself."

"I have always enjoyed myself," she countered, irritated by his patronizing tone. Perhaps stretching the truth would get the information she wanted. "When Justin returned, he asked me a question I could not answer. You examined the road where Frederick fell. Did he roll into the quarry, or did he walk off the edge?"

"It doesn't matter, my dear. You are well rid of that wastrel. And so is Northrup. Reviving such ancient history serves no purpose. It is time to put the past behind you."

"His question piqued my curiosity. I want to know," she insisted, making a mental note to inform Justin of his interest. "I would rather not remember him as a being too foxed to see where he was stepping."

He shrugged. "I couldn't say. And it really does not matter. Darkness would have obscured his view even had he been sober. Shall we climb to the battlements?"

"Not today. I promised to help Lady Granger organize the children's games." It was another lie, but she would learn nothing useful. And he was unusually tense today. *Enjoy yourself.* Would he be the latest to offer her carte blanche? He had rejected the rumors in the past, but his proprietary glances were making her nervous.

His face darkened, but he turned toward the lake—by way of the woods. His insistent flirting intensified her unease as he complimented her gown, her dinner party, and the pretty manners displayed by the girls she had raised.

What had gotten into the man? His wife had been her closest friend, and he had advised her on estate matters when she had first assumed control, using her willingness to solicit help to excuse her intrusion into men's business. She had been grateful and had long considered him a friend, but he was not acting like a friend today.

"I have long admired you, my dear," he said at last. "Had my father not contracted me to Constance, I would have offered for you years ago."

She recoiled, berating herself for her blindness. Constance had died two years earlier, without providing him an heir. Her own bereavement just as he was emerging from mourning must have given him ideas.

She muttered imprecations under her breath. If only she had realized his thinking sooner, she could have turned his eyes elsewhere. She had no intention of wedding again. Ever.

She opened her mouth, but he gave her no chance to protest.

"Now we can both leave the past behind, taking what should have been ours ten years ago. You will make me the happiest of men by accepting my hand in marriage."

"I wish you had not brought this up, sir." She kept her tone very formal. "I have too many responsibilities to consider marriage."

"You take too much on yourself, Mary," he protested, interrupting. "Northrup will assume all those responsibilities—which is only right and proper. If Frederick had not forced you into taking over such unladylike chores, you would never have attracted the attention of malicious tongues. But you can finally resume a lady's proper pastimes and forget all those indignities."

"I am sorry, sir, but I am quite content with my life and have no plans to remarry now or in the future. While I am honored by your consideration, I cannot accept your offer."

"Fustian. If Northrup expects you to continue slaving for him, I will set the lad straight."

"You are misinformed," she said icily. "My activities are mine by choice. And pressing a failed suit because you dislike my answer belies your standing as a gentleman."

His eyes narrowed, but even her insult did not distract him. They argued for another five minutes before he would accept her refusal—for the moment; his parting words implied that she remained mired in unnecessary grief but would soon come to her senses.

As she left him, two things were clear. Their friendship would not survive this confrontation. And she could never trust his judgment again. He saw only what he expected to see. Since he had formed a *tendre,* he assumed she reciprocated. Because he believed ladies should live lives of frivolous leisure, he supposed her to yearn for an end to her estate duties.

Which led to new questions about Frederick's death. Within moments of finding the body, Isaac had concluded that the death had been an accident. Had he then overlooked evidence to the contrary?

Perhaps she was doing him an injustice, but she doubted it. So where did that leave her? The answer to that simple question should have disproved James's suspicions. Now other questions reared their ugly little heads. Frederick had known that road better than the drive leading to Northfield. If his senses had been so disturbed that he could walk off a cliff, how had he stayed in the saddle long enough to cover the three miles from the Lusty Maiden to the quarry? And if Isaac's impressions were worthless, could she believe anything he said about John's murder?

By the time she returned to the company, Amelia was walking with Mr. Crenshaw, and Caro was talking animatedly with Sir Edwin.

"The ruins gvgd view," she was saying as Mary approached.

Mary cringed, but Sir Edwin did not seem to mind. "The view must be lovely from the top," he agreed soothingly, stroking the hand that lay on his arm. "And the lake also looks inviting. Which would you prefer first? A boat ride would be wondrously relaxing."

His tone calmed her. Mary was amazed. He was the first one outside the family to truly accept Caro's problem.

"The lake," Caro decided, glancing at Mary for permission.

"Enjoy yourself," Mary said.

They had hardly moved out of sight when James brought her a glass of lemonade. "Edwin will take good care of her."

"I know." She sipped her drink, wondering how he had sensed her uncertainties. "Have you seen Justin?"

"He headed for the ruins a quarter hour past, in company with two gentlemen wearing yellow pantaloons. They were discussing dungeons."

"The Adams brothers." She bit back a sigh. If Justin had teamed up with them, he was unlikely to return before refreshments were served. But the squire would not be in the dungeons, so she could speak with Justin later.

Or could she? She must never try to anticipate Isaac's actions again.

What a mess. The last thing she needed was a suitor. Justin must discourage Isaac's courtship. And he must also press for every detail about Frederick's death. Even if Isaac's conclusions were faulty, he might have noticed something useful.

She was beginning to think James was right. So she must find Justin as soon as possible. Urgency and a sense of impending doom were tickling the back of her neck.

"Don't run off," James begged, again reading her mind. "I must remain occupied so Sir Maxwell does not foist his daughter on me."

Isaac was speaking with Sir Maxwell, she noted, so she could delay seeking Justin for the moment. "Very well. You may use me as your escape, though Lucy is not quite as bad as she seems. Company has a way of bringing out her worst behavior."

"Is that what you told Northrup? He is of an age to settle down."

She shuddered.

"So I thought," he said, chuckling. "But you cannot protect him by casting me to the wolves."

"I would never go that far." But he was right. She had been excusing Lucy's manners in hopes that someone would remove her from the area.

And him. That unwanted attraction tugged harder with each meeting. And he must know it, for he dressed to draw her eyes. Today's cravat jewel was a deep-hued emerald that perfectly matched his forest green coat, and raised green glints in his dark eyes. Shivers rolled down her arms, making her glad she had chosen an unfashionable long-sleeved gown to hide her unladylike tan.

"Have you learned anything since we last talked?" he asked, abruptly changing the subject as they wandered away from the crowd.

"Very little. No one discusses John, even six months after his death. No rumors have ever hinted that Frederick might have been helped into the quarry. But if you are right, I cannot ask questions without risking a reprisal. Killers do not want people poking into their affairs."

"I had not considered that." He frowned. "Perhaps you should stay out of this."

"No. But I will be careful. And I did learn one fact. Squire Church is unreliable."

"Are you sure?"

"It is something I should have realized sooner. He ignores anything that does not fit his perceptions. And he is so convinced that his perceptions are right that he rarely questions them."

"How do you know?"

"I've known him since birth, and his wife was a good friend. In Frederick's case, he confronted a drunken corpse at the bottom of the quarry—an obvious accident. I asked him if the road showed marks of rolling or sliding. He refused to answer."

James frowned. "You want to know if he was dragged to the edge."

"Exactly. If he was, then you are right, and he was probably murdered. If not, we have no evidence one way or the other. Now Isaac may just be sparing my female sensibilities, but I fear he never looked."

"He looked at everything in John's case."

"Perhaps. A simpleton could see that John was murdered. People do not stab themselves, particularly when their arms are bound. But he may have overlooked something. His initial assumption was that a highwayman did it. He did not start looking at other possibilities for several days."

"Despite the fact that every piece of evidence disproved that the culprit was a vagabond." He snorted. "I had wondered why he spent so much time chasing phantoms, though he passed it off by claiming the man might have followed John from London."

"Possible, but that seems unlikely now. I cannot accept your attack as another incident like Will's." The reminder drew her eyes to his temple, but he had shed his bandage and combed his hair over the cut.

"So we must start at the beginning. And that means going back at least a year. What do you know about your husband's death?"

"No more than I already told you. Frederick drank too much, then insisted on riding to Ridgeway. Isaac found the horse wandering alone and recognized it as Frederick's—it had a white face that was hard to miss. The patrons at the Lusty Maiden confirmed that Frederick was heading for Ridgeway, so he took three grooms and followed, finding him in the bottom of the quarry."

"Three grooms?"

"And a wagon. Frederick had grown rather stout. They took him back to the inn and cleaned him up, but I've no idea what injuries he suffered, for I never saw the body. Isaac refused to let me in—those female sensibilities again." Why hadn't she recognized that proprietary attitude then? But she had been in shock.

"The conjecture was that he either dismounted or fell from his horse?"

"Exactly. Since there was no sign that he had dismounted to cast up his accounts, Isaac decided he had passed out. He made no attempt to discover whether he had rolled into the quarry when he fell, or if he stumbled in when he later tried to reach Ridgeway on foot."

"Surely he checked the road, though."

"I doubt it, but you can ask. Justin will demand details of Frederick's injuries—Isaac will not be able to duck that question. An army officer won't be squeamish, and a brother has every right to know. Not that I expect the condition of the body to help much. That fall would have covered any trace of a blow."

"Or explained it." He bit his lip, lowering his voice so it

wouldn't carry. "I have been debating whether to tell Isaac about the attack on me. He might have some idea who was behind it, but talking about it would alert the culprit that I know what happened."

"Unless it was unplanned, he must already know. A killer would have watched to make sure you landed in the quarry. He could hardly expect me to remain quiet about how I found you."

"So I need to speak to Isaac. Perhaps I can draw parallels to Frederick's accident and find out more about it. And if Northrup also asks, it might force Isaac to rethink his ideas."

"You can try, but I doubt it."

They dropped the subject, talking instead about the beauties of the day and speculating on the surprise Lady Granger had promised to produce after eating. The change in focus relaxed her—until she realized that James had placed a hand on her back to guide her up the hill. Unwanted warmth flooded her, trapping butterflies in her stomach.

He knew exactly what he was doing, she fumed, stepping aside so his hand dropped. She could see the laughter lurking behind those quizzical eyes. Men were all alike. They didn't care who they hurt as long as they satisfied their urges.

She shivered.

If he persisted, she must decline to help him investigate. As long as their contact focused on business, she was safe. But allowing a resumption of their old friendship was dangerous. It should never have started the first time.

But perhaps she had been wrong. He made no move to touch her again. Instead he drew her laughter with an improbable story about a Neapolitan donkey and a mountain of switches.

James dropped his hand, allowing Mary to slide another step away. She was an enigma he found more fascinating every day, especially now that he had laid his final suspicions to rest.

As he had lain awake last night, tormented by that mention of a beauty mark, he had suddenly seen it for himself—a reddish brown splash on her right hip, shaped vaguely like England.

He'd nearly kicked himself for mistrusting his instincts. Yes, John had seen it. So had he, Isaac, and a couple of tenant lads. They had been playing in the forest when Mary's pony charged along the trail, tossing her into the ford and tearing her dress half off. She had been six.

He had ignored her half-nude body in his rush to save her from drowning. But John had never forgotten. Twelve years later he had used the memory to concoct a lie that hurt James, Mary, and probably her father.

Retribution for backing James's suggestions for the estate? He shook his head.

It didn't matter now. Mary was innocent. So why did she cringe from his touch even as she welcomed his company?

He had rested his hand on her back because he enjoyed flustering her. His growing desire was strong enough that he needed this sign that she returned his interest. But his pleasure died the moment he met her eyes.

Yes, she was flustered. Her attraction showed in the heat that had softened their color. But she was also terrified.

Fool! He should have seen it before—would have if his thoughts had not been tied up in John's lies. The slightest sign of affection, the briefest contact, sent her skittering away—physically if she could manage it, but always mentally. Frederick must have hurt her.

Every muscle tensed. Frustration fizzled along his nerves, combined with a protectiveness that surprised him. If anything, he wanted her more than ever. But he could not touch her again until she learned to trust him.

So he entertained her by describing the silliest sights he had seen on his travels. When she had relaxed once more, he recounted some of the world's wonders—the Austrian Alps, the pyramids of Egypt, India's pearl divers. . . .

But keeping his hands to himself wasn't easy. Her scent surrounded him. A gust of wind pressed her gown close, revealing every detail of those long, long legs. A tantalizing glimpse of shapely ankles pooled heat in his groin that made walking difficult.

He wanted to help her surmount her fears. He wanted to see those blue eyes glaze with passion, feel her skin against his own, hear her moans. . . .

But thinking about it would drive him insane—and reveal his desires to the world if he did not get his body under control. At least her refusal to look at him kept her from noticing his problem.

"A race," he said, pointing to three boats on the lake below as they emerged from the trees.

"It's Amelia and Caroline."

"And Miss Granger."

Mary grinned at his lack of enthusiasm.

"Who is rowing her?"

She shaded her eyes. "Colonel Davis's grandson."

"Why isn't he on the Peninsula with his father?"

"The two older boys are, but Vincent is the family black sheep."

He laughed. "What did he do?"

"Turned his back on generations of tradition by refusing to buy colors. Instead, he is studying for the church."

"Black indeed," he agreed on another laugh. Her eyes were glittering with pleasure in a way he had not seen in ten years.

"Absolutely. I doubt Vincent's father has gotten over the shock yet, though he made the decision five years ago. Vincent has spent long breaks with the colonel since his mother died."

The race was nearing the halfway point, with all three boats rounding the island. Harry was in the lead, with Edwin and Vincent only one length behind. Feminine shouts of encouragement echoed across the lake.

The crowd swelled along the shore as the boats raced back. The gentlemen had removed their close-cut coats, which would have hampered their rowing. Muscles rippled across their shoulders as they dug the oars deep into the water. One of the girls on the bank swooned at the sight of so much undress.

Harry was losing ground.

"Not enough time in Gentleman Jackson's boxing rings," murmured James.

Mary's expression revealed her conviction that Harry spent all his days in boudoirs.

"He is not *that* bad," he protested. "But he is more interested in marksmanship than boxing, so he gets little exercise in town."

"How did you know what I thought?"

"Reading your mind, Mary. It isn't the first time. Was I wrong?"

She shook her head, then blushed.

"Almost to the finish." He ignored her discomfort. "Come on, Edwin. Two good pulls should do it." Edwin and Vincent were still neck and neck, though Harry was now half a length back.

"He won!" Mary laughed as Edwin shot ahead.

Actually, Vincent had swerved off course. At the last moment, Lucy had leaned over the side to better see the finish line, throwing the boat off balance and pulling one oar out of the lake. It sprayed her with water as the boat twisted, losing momentum and letting both opponents cross ahead of them.

Lucy's shriek disturbed the dearly departed in the Ridgefield churchyard. "Clumsy oaf! You've ruined my gown!" She jumped to her feet, brushing frantically at the spots.

Vincent stammered an apology.

"Sit down, Lucy," ordered Sir Maxwell, pushing through the crowd. "It's only a little water. And it's your own fault for upsetting the boat. Sit down before you fall in."

"Water ruins silk!" wailed Lucy, ignoring him as she twisted to survey the damage. Tears coursed down her cheeks. "How could you be so horrid? I should never have gone rowing with you!"

"Why would anyone wear silk to a picnic?" asked Mary as they raced toward the lake. Everyone within hearing of that screech was doing the same thing. She stumbled, grabbing James's arm to steady herself.

"Undoubtedly it's a new gown," said James absently, ignoring Lucy's megrims. Mary's grasp on his arm tingled clear to his toes, yet he dared yet he dared not respond lest drawing attention to her continued grip raise new fear in her eyes.

"Stupid." Mary shook her head. "This is her most idiotic display yet. And her mother isn't much better," she added as Lady Granger's screams joined Lucy's.

"Somebody save my baby! She'll drown!"

Lucy was counting water spots, dancing up and down as her hysteria mounted.

Vincent was trying to calm her, but she remained deaf to his instructions, rocking the boat so badly that he had no chance of reaching her. "Sit down," he finally ordered in exasperation. They were only ten feet from shore, but he could not pull them closer without knocking Lucy into the water.

"Spiteful boy! You've ruined it," sobbed Lucy. "On purpose. My newest gown. How could you?"

Everyone on the shore was shouting for her to sit down. Harry and Edwin helped their passengers out, then returned to the lake.

"Grab her!" shrieked Lady Granger, realizing that the other boats would never arrive in time. "Don't let her fall."

"Sit down, Lucy!" shouted Sir Maxwell, his face red with fury. No one in attendance would dream of offering for the girl now.

Vincent inched forward, swaying to counterbalance her antics and steady the boat.

"Get out!" cried Lucy, abandoning the spots. "I hate you." She slapped him, rocking the boat sharply to the left.

"Sit down!" Sir Maxwell's bellow made the onlookers jump, but Lucy ignored him.

Vincent grabbed the gunwale as the boat swung hard to the right, then lunged forward in an attempt to tackle her.

"Stay away. Don't touch me," Lucy cried, jumping onto the seat. "You've caused enough trouble."

She retreated another step and fell into the lake.

Lady Granger swooned.

Harry arrived and pulled Lucy up by her hair. She choked a couple of times, then screamed.

"The water can't be more than waist deep," Mary called.

"Thanks." Harry shifted his grip to Lucy's arm. "Stand up."

She kicked her feet, screaming louder.

Edwin maneuvered close enough to grab the other arm. They dunked her.

"Stand up," growled Harry when she came up sputtering. "You are perfectly safe, but you are making a complete cake of yourself and risk becoming a laughingstock if you do not pull yourself together."

One of her feet hit the bottom and she gasped.

"Stand up."

The moment she got both feet under her, they dropped her arms.

"Now walk."

"Poor girl," murmured Mary.

Lucy slogged toward shore. Her gown clung to her unprepossessing figure. Weeds dragged at her legs. Hair dangled down her back. When she noted the size of her audience, her face flushed.

Someone coughed. Several of the younger guests giggled.

"That's cruel," snapped Mary.

"Even though her own silliness brought this on," agreed James. He glared at the laughers, silencing them. It was the first time John's reputation had worked in his favor.

Mary released his arm, backing away a step. He bit back a sigh, feeling how she distanced herself, though not as far as usual. One small step of progress. There was no need to rush, he decided, clasping his hands behind his back so they would remain under his control. The day was already a success.

"May I get you some refreshments?" he asked, turning from the lake. Most of the company followed.

A glance over his shoulder spotted servants wrapping Lucy in a rug. Her hysteria revived as they carried her to the house. But no one cared.

The rest of the afternoon passed peacefully enough. Lucy never did return. The surprise was a play performed by a traveling theater company against the backdrop of the ruins. But while it was quite charming, its drama paled beside Lucy's theatrics. Lady Granger had gotten her wish. Her picnic was the most memorable of the summer.

*   *   *

"I had no idea Frederick was so irresponsible," said Justin, joining Mary in the drawing room that evening.

"What do you mean?"

"Why did you let me leave the country instead of asking me to help with the estate. I should have known better—and would have if you had kept me informed."

"Sit down, Justin." She waited until he reluctantly dropped into a chair. "First of all, leaving the country was your decision. We did not even know of it until after you sailed."

"What? I only transferred because Frederick pointed out that I could advance faster in a fighting regiment. We discussed it for months before making a decision."

So Frederick had wanted Justin out of the country. Had he hoped to hide his wealth, or was he trying to conceal his dishonorable activities? Justin's first regiment had been stationed near London. "He did not inform us. But to address your other complaint, his faults were not your concern. Nor was the estate or the barony. Even if you had known exactly how things stood, he would not have welcomed interference in his affairs. Now suppose you explain what brought on this surge of guilt."

"I heard stories today," he admitted. "Frederick and I never got on, which was one of the reasons I bought colors. He wasn't a particularly nice person, but I was shocked to discover that he all but abandoned you. Carousing in town was bad enough, but he rarely stayed at Northfield even when he was in the area."

Their previous talk had dealt mostly with the present conditions and future needs of the estate, she realized. She had said little that would reflect badly on his brother. "It doesn't matter," she insisted.

"But it does. How could he have ignored his responsibilities?"

"He did not want them."

"But why would he waste his life when he could have enjoyed Northfield?"

"What did you hear that upset you so badly?" she asked. When he hesitated, she continued. "I doubt there is anything you can tell me about Frederick that I do not already know."

"He and John were friends."

She nodded.

"Ralph Adams claims that the pair often cheated at cards. There is hardly a lad in the area who did not lose to them, sometimes large amounts. And Mitchell swears they robbed men who had consumed too much wine."

"It fits his character." That explained how Frederick had supported himself in London. But fleecing people was dangerous. Had someone retaliated?

Justin repeated more gossip, but she already knew the rest. The only surprise was how much the neighbors knew about her private life and Frederick's—which confirmed her decision not to question the servants. They would never remain quiet about it.

Once Justin had expended his indignation, she elicited his promise to question Isaac about Frederick's death.

"Don't let him manipulate you," she warned. "I turned him down this afternoon, and despite his conviction otherwise, I have no intention of changing my mind."

"Determined, is he?"

"Pigheaded."

"I knew an officer like that. He refused to believe any intelligence that cast doubts on his battle plans. It killed him in the end. Too bad he took so many good lads with him."

She slept better that night than she had in weeks. Justin was nothing like his brother.

James poured wine before joining Edwin by the fire. Harry had decided to make an early night of it.

They sat in companionable silence for several minutes while he considered all the ways John could have acquired several barrels of fine French brandy. Edwin finally spoke.

"Caroline claims John seduced innocents. Lady Northrup banned him from Northfield."

"So I've heard. Does Caroline know anyone John seduced?"

He shook his head.

"Doesn't it bother you that you cannot understand so much of what she says?" James asked, changing directions. He had not bared John's worst crimes to his friends, not wanting to reveal the blackest marks on the family name.

"When she is calm, she speaks quite clearly. Only excitement bothers her, or fear. You probably upset her, but she will grow out of this trouble. It would be gone already if her brother hadn't provoked her so often."

Was Edwin's interest becoming serious? James frowned. Caroline Northrup was a beautiful girl, but she would never manage in society. What man wanted a wife who could barely function in company?

Yet he had to admit that Edwin did not enjoy London. He was happiest when grubbing about his estate, digging for antiquities. Before meeting Caroline, he had talked of visiting Shrewsbury, which occupied the site of the Roman town of Viroconium.

"To prove that her suspicions of you were unwarranted, I told her about that orphanage you set up in Naples," Edwin continued, swirling brandy so the candlelight sparkled through it.

"Where did you hear about that?" He deliberately unclenched his fists. He hadn't thought anyone knew about the place, and was vaguely embarrassed to be discussing it.

"Meeker mentioned it," he said, naming his valet. "Your valet recounted the tale at dinner one night to prove that the staff was wrong when they swore you were uncaring."

He turned the subject by asking Edwin about the Roman lighthouse near Dover.

It was too late to recall the tale, though revealing it served little purpose. No one could verify its truth. And it wasn't quite as altruistic as Edwin thought.

His stay in Naples had been delightful, in part because of his odd friendship with the working-class Portinis. Luigi Portini had been a man of many trades, one of which was a guide. His fascinating tales had kept James in the area longer than he had originally intended. Luigi had also been fearlessly loyal. When a band of brigands had attacked them, Luigi had tried to protect his employer, sustaining crippling injuries.

James had been appalled and unable to suppress his guilt. After all, if he had not asked to visit Mount Vesuvius, they would not have encountered the brigands. So he had hired Luigi's wife Maria as his cook and housekeeper, hoping that time would improve Luigi's condition. He had also hired caretakers for Luigi and their eight children. But Luigi never recovered. When Maria died shortly before he left Naples, he had set up a trust to provide for the Portini family.

Luigi had passed on six years later. The four older children were married or established in business, but he continued to provide for the rest and for two young cousins Luigi had taken under his wing.

Hardly an orphanage.

Chapter Nine

James trotted along a narrow lane, heading for the place where John had died. If he was going to start at the beginning, then he must look at the murder site.

It had snowed heavily on Christmas Day, though it had been tapering off by the time John had gone out. But his errand must have been urgent to drive him into even a waning storm.

The lane was hardly more than an overgrown track. He frowned. It provided access to remote grazing areas and a shortcut to an estate in the next shire, but it was rarely used. It would have been difficult to follow when covered with snow, so why had John been here?

His horse splashed across a stream and up a hill. A quarter hour later, he reached Brewster's Ridge.

What a fool Isaac had been—and still was.

During his years away, he had forgotten how desolate this area was. That was the memory that had tried to intrude that day in Isaac's office. Yes, there was ample cover, making the spot perfect for an ambush. The track was barely a yard wide and climbed steeply at this point, forcing horses to slow. Trees and rocks made it impossible to see past the next bend.

He shivered.

But though the ridge formed the boundary between estates, he could not recall who owned the next one. The families were not close, meaning that few people used this particular track. No highwayman would know this lane existed, let alone expect to find custom here.

An ambush meant that the killer had already been in position when John arrived, so he must have known in advance about John's errand.

But given the weather that day, waiting could not have been comfortable. The man would have needed shelter. Dismounting, James tied his horse to a tree and scrambled over the hillside.

It took him an hour to find it. Tumbled boulders formed a shallow cave. Charred wood remained from an old fire, though he had no way to prove who had built it. The opening faced south, and though trees obscured most of the view, he could see the ford in the distance.

Harry and Edwin were splashing through the stream. As he watched, they jumped a hedge and galloped out of sight across a meadow.

He would bet his last shilling that the killer had huddled here, dousing his fire when John reached the ford, then taking up a position to attack.

But how had he known John would ride this way?

He must question the staff again. Someone must have heard about John's plans and mentioned them to others, unless it was a servant who had killed him. But until he knew where John had been headed and how many people had known of the errand, he could eliminate no more names from his suspect list.

Those already gone had never been serious contenders anyway. This attack bore no marks of a highway robbery gone sour. The attempt Mary had quelled by the quarry made it unlikely that the murder was connected to John's affairs elsewhere. There had been considerable unrest among England's working classes for several months now, but it had not started until after John's death, and it was not aimed at the aristocracy—yet.

Memories of France flitted through his mind. When he had been in Paris ten years after the worst of the Terror, fear had still lurked in many eyes. Even lords who had thrown their money and support behind Napoleon's new regime did not feel entirely safe. He doubted much had changed in the ten years since. He hoped to God that England would never face such chaos.

But he digressed. Perhaps Mary could discover where John had been going.

The thought brought a smile to his face. Drawing her into

this investigation had been a masterful stroke, for it gave him an excuse to see her often without raising her hackles.

Mary was prickly about anything personal, but he had made progress at yesterday's picnic. And he would make further progress when he next called on her. Perhaps they could stroll through the gardens where the servants would not overhear. Or maybe they could ride. He would use the murder as an excuse to recall the people they had known and the concerns they had shared ten years ago.

Sooner or later, he needed to discuss those subjects anyway. John would have targeted those people for his most vicious crimes. Learning the details was his first step toward making restitution, and discussing how best to resolve the problems John had created would soften Mary's antagonism.

Lust again snaked through his groin. How long before he could find relief?

The man crouched in a fern brake, listening.

Leaves rustled from a passing breeze, then fell silent as if they, too, were listening. The stream flowed sluggishly, almost soundlessly, to his left.

Patience. He knew all about patience. Watching. Waiting. Always ready to take advantage of the perfect opportunity. The earl would ride this way soon. Had to. The ford offered the shortest route back to Ridgeway from Brewster's Ridge. That had to be where the earl was heading this day. He had been lucky to catch sight of him as he left the park.

Not luck, he reminded himself. God was on his side, providing this opportunity so he could find peace.

This time no one would interfere. Especially not Lady Northrup. He still had not decided if he must take care of her, too. Had she recognized the truth?

But he had more important matters to consider at the moment. He had planned every step of the accident. A rock would knock the earl into the water, senseless. He would stop the horse so he could lame it as if a stone had shifted, causing a stumble—he had already moved one. That would be his only moment of risk, for the water might awaken the earl while he dealt with the horse. But it was unlikely, he assured himself. The blow would do more than stun him.

Finally, he would make sure the earl was lying facedown. So tragic . . .

He swallowed his fury, forcing stillness onto his body. But he flinched when a fish jumped in the river.

Hoofbeats approached.

He hunkered lower, fingering the fist-sized rock in his right hand. Invective swirled through his head, pictures and memories reminding him why he was here. Some people did not deserve life.

Harsher invective swirled when he realized that the two approaching horses rode away from Ridgeway.

The earl's house guests laughed at some joke as they splashed across the ford. But they were not looking for the earl. Just two gentlemen out for a ride, he decided as they jumped a hedge and cantered across a meadow. Yet they posed a complication. He must be quick—quicker than he'd planned. They might return, and with little warning.

Silence. The sun inched higher, pressing a blanket of heat onto the earth. An animal scurried through the ferns. Silence.

He flexed his fingers as faint hoofbeats again approached, but a laugh stopped the anticipation. The earl's friends were returning—which got them out of the way, he realized, breathing a prayer of thanksgiving.

Silently shifting, he peered through a low shrub, then cursed. Ridgeway had joined his friends.

Another opportunity lost. Sighing in frustration, he dropped his head to the ground. How much longer until he could rest in peace? Job's trials were minor compared to his.

Horses splashed through the ford.

He did not move until they were gone, but as he crept away to his hidden mount, he was already planning. Next time . . .

"I saw one of your tenants today," said Harry as he and James walked back from the stables. Edwin had stayed behind to talk to his groom.

"Which one?"

"Jem Cotter."

"Problems?"

"Not that I know of, but you need to talk to him. He asked me several pointed questions, but what he really wants to know is if you plan to continue John's policies."

"Surely lowering the rents answered that question." James could still remember Walden's shock when he had ordered the reduction. The steward's mouth had worked silently for nearly a minute before he could get words out. And James's decision to collect no rents this year to make up for past injustices had nearly sent the man into a swoon.

"Not entirely. Cotter is wary. Perhaps John enjoyed raising false hope because dashing it caused so much pain."

My fault again. Or was it? If John had been seeking to hurt him, then he must have expected him to return to Ridgeway. How else would he learn what John had done?

Yet that was ridiculous. John had never been stupid. After tossing James out and threatening reprisals against innocents, he would never expect him back. Unless he had somehow intended to use the tenants' plight to blackmail him into permanently leaving the country . . .

He had avoided attracting John's attention when he returned to England, staying in London only long enough to arrange purchase of the Haven. But John could have found him if he'd wanted to—could have kept track of his travels, for that matter.

And probably had, he admitted, ignoring the pain in his stomach. Thus John would have known about the second fortune he'd earned in India, would have heard about the Haven's prosperity and the growing respect James received from his neighbors. Despite exploiting the tenants, and despite the regular infusions of unexplained cash, John had died deeply in debt. How that must have rankled.

Jealousy. Even admitting John's need for power had not opened his eyes to the entire truth. Why had he never understood? Despite his instinctive decision to never compete against John—even choosing to attend different schools—he had earned numerous accolades over the years. Only now did he realize that John's most vicious acts had always followed one of his own triumphs.

He could never again chastise anyone for naïve blindness. He had suffered from that affliction for three-and-thirty years.

His stomach turned over, forcing him to swallow hard. John had craved respect, but he had never understood it, instead settling for fear. To validate his worth, he had exercised his power on everyone he met, demanding obedience, punishing any transgression, and accepting the resulting terror as proof of his stature.

His eyes itched.

"I will talk to Cotter," he said aloud. "Jem was always the brightest tenant. Perhaps I can set his fears to rest."

And maybe learn something useful. Would Cotter know where John had been going that last day?

Cotter was repairing the latch on the barn door when James rode into the yard and dismounted. The look of terror in the man's eyes smote his heart. No matter how often he saw it, he still cringed. Perhaps he should wear a sack over his head or grow a beard—anything to differentiate him from John.

"My lord," said Cotter, doffing his cap.

"Jem." Tears tickled his eyes as he took in the barn and other buildings. All seemed on the verge of tumbling down. The thatch on the cottage was rotting. Fences were in disrepair. Dear God, how could anyone force his dependents to live in such squalor?

He turned back to Jem. "Somehow I will rectify my brother's abuses."

Cotter nodded, but said nothing.

"Give me a chance, Jem," he pleaded. Not that the tenants would have much choice, he conceded silently. They had nowhere else to go. He closed his eyes. When he reopened them, Cotter hadn't moved a muscle. "We'll discuss your farm later, but first I need to ask about Walden. I cannot keep him on, for he is associated too closely with John's spite. Did he willingly carry out John's orders, or did he do so under duress?"

"Why?"

"I must decide whether to write him a recommendation. Talk

to me, Jem. You are the smartest man on the estate and the only one I can trust to tell me the truth."

Something flared in Jem's eyes. He held his pose of studied deference a few seconds longer before fury engulfed him. Grabbing James's shoulders, he slammed him into the barn door.

Stars exploded through his head.

"Trust?" Jem bellowed. "How can you claim to trust me after threatening to throw me off my land unless I stopped ignoring John's orders?"

James made no effort to fight back, though this was too much like his last call at Northfield. Then the import of Jem's words punched him in the stomach.

"Oh, God!" Every drop of blood drained from his head as the full extent of John's evil penetrated. "When was this?"

"Eight years ago." But his voice was suddenly uncertain.

"Jem, I haven't set foot in Shropshire since my father's funeral. Eight years ago, I was in Naples—Italy."

"Then that means—"

"He was impersonating me, may he roast in hell for all eternity. Devil take it, I never believed he could go this far."

Jem was shaking as he brushed splinters from James's coat. "I shoulda known. I shoulda known. But you always looked so different. I never had no trouble tellin' you apart before."

"Yet the faces were identical." John had not always glowered. He had been capable of smiles and charm. That was how he had seduced so many women.

"You really stayed away?" Jem's voice cracked, driving new pain into James's heart.

"I thought it would help. John threatened reprisals against all of you if I returned. I should have realized that he had other reasons for wanting me gone."

"He always was a shifty one."

He nodded. "I did not return to England until five years ago. I've lived in Lincolnshire since then."

"Forgive me for striking you, my lord."

"Of course," he said, though they both knew the offense was grounds for transportation. "You had more than ample cause. How often did he impersonate me?"

"Often enough the first couple of years. You'd show up at the Court for a day or two—looking for something to pawn, like as not, striking any as tried to keep you out, then reminding them to stay quiet because John would do worse if he learned they'd let you in. Everyone knew that meant a beating besides being turned off—and sometimes transportation. After that, he stopped identifying himself by name. We never knew who was here. He'd do things one visit that he denied the next. Many's the man who won't believe it wasn't you, but it's glad I am to know you haven't changed so very much."

"Thank you, Jem." A weight lifted from his shoulders, lightening his heart. This explained the staff's continued suspicion. He would have to sit down with Forbes and Mrs. Washburn. If he could convince them of the truth, perhaps they could persuade the rest. If not, he would have no choice but to let the servants go and start over.

He frowned. It might be better if he paved the way by encouraging his valet and groom to talk about their travels. Proving he was out of the country would raise enough doubts that most would accept the rest.

"You asked about Walden." Jem paused in thought. "I can't say how he really feels. He carried out every order, right enough. Real scrupulous about it, but he never pressed beyond the exact order. If John told him to raise rents if the price of rye went up, he would do nothing if barley rose."

"Did he ever lend a hand like Forbes and Mrs. Washburn?"

"So you know about that?"

He nodded."

"There's some as woulda died without them."

Another nod.

"No, Walden never helped a soul—but more from weakness than evil. The earl woulda turned him off and seen he never got another position. Walden has no family he could turn to if that happened."

"I will write him a reference, then. But I cannot keep him here. I need men of conviction in my employ—and compassion. I can't know everything, so I want people to tell me their problems."

"You'll have to be patient. Most will hold off for a good long time out of fear."

Too true. James bit back a sigh before turning to new business. "How much of the neglect here can be repaired, and how much will require tearing down and building new?"

Jem laughed. "I am in better shape than it would appear. The insides are fine." He led James into the barn, which showed care. "I learned real quick to make the place look as bad as possible. That kept my rents lower than they might have been. John wasn't here much, and he never did more than ride past. Walden investigated only when John told him to."

"You always were a wily one. So your problems can be readily repaired?"

"Most. Thompson's same as me, but Lane is in bad shape— worse than anyone, I expect. He often complained, so he drew a lot of attention before he learned to keep his mouth shut."

Which would have taken time. James doubted the other tenants had taught him the lesson. Lane was too loose-lipped to have chanced him mentioning their ploys to Walden.

He let out a deep sigh, hoping his next question would not resurrect Jem's distrust. "I have to find out who killed John. Any idea where he was going that last day?"

"You'd best let it go," advised Jem. "If ever a man deserved death, it was you brother. If I knew who did it, I'd pin a medal on the lad."

"That may well be, but killing is wrong. You know that, Jem. And once a man kills, he is likely to do so again. The second time is easier. I have to know who, and I have to know why. Only then can we let it rest. Who had he harmed the most in the last year?"

"I won't name anyone," insisted Jem. "There is not a man in the parish that didn't have a grievance with him. Who's to say which one acted? Who's to say what broke the fellow's control? Mayhap it wasn't the worst offense."

"Mayhap. But someone attacked me last week, staging an accident that might have proved fatal. Perhaps it was related. Perhaps not. But don't expect me to ignore it."

Jem's face grew troubled. "I hadn't heard."

"It is not something I want passed on. But knowing that John impersonated me suggests that it was the same person who killed him. So who has a grievance?"

"Everyone."

"What's yours?"

"Besides the farm?"

James nodded.

"He raped my wife."

"Oh, God."

"It happened not long after you left. She was a servant up at the house—Molly."

"I remember her, I think. Brown curly hair, always laughing?"

"That's Molly. She was barely fifteen and hadn't had the position long. John first noticed her about the time the old earl died. He already had a bad reputation with the servants, so she tried to avoid him. But he cornered her in the linen room. I found her trying to drown herself in the lake."

"How badly was she hurt?"

"Bad enough. She refused to go back to the house—I would have fought her if she'd tried—but her parents would not allow her home. So I married her."

"Was there a child?" He had to ask, though the idea choked him.

"No." Jem let out a long breath. "I thanked God for sparing me that. I doubt I could have raised his child."

"Nor I. You are a good man, Jem. And a lucky one. I'm surprised he didn't penalize you for helping her."

"He may not have known. He left for town before we wed. I doubt he remembered her by the time he returned."

"Try to recall anything that happened either during his last visit or the one before. Even the small things. As you proved just now, a minor event can push a man over the edge if he has enough previous provocation." He nodded toward the barn door. "It's no longer simply a matter of justice. I will not live in fear of my life."

Jem looked uncertain, but he nodded.

James's heart was heavy as he rode back to the estate. Every new fact about John made his evil more apparent. How could he have turned out so different from his twin?

That's what scared him the most. He and John were identical, so the seeds of John's evil must also exist in him. Would they someday sprout?

A word with Mrs. Washburn confirmed that John had stalked the maids, especially the young, pretty ones. She had hired only older women, but that had not prevented all abuse. John had assaulted one of the women two years earlier, in partnership with Lord Northrup.

He shook his head, diverted from his own problems. John and Frederick had shared conquests. What must Mary have suffered married to such a man? Had Frederick forced her to entertain his friend?

Nausea rolled through his stomach. But a moment's reflection dismissed the possibility. Mary had not produced an heir. No matter how debauched Frederick had been, he would never have risked her bearing another man's son.

But this added evidence that Frederick's death had been deliberate. Isaac had dismissed the idea that John's murder was the result of an affair gone sour. But it might still be connected with a girl. And Frederick might have been involved.

He had to interview Turnby. The old groom must know something.

Chapter Ten

"Lord Ridgeway is asking questions about the murder," reported Miss Hardaway as she poured a second cup of tea.

"Hardly a surprise," replied Mary. "John was evil, but he *was* Ridgeway's brother. He wants to know what happened."

"He should leave well enough alone. If ever a man deserved death, it was the ninth earl."

"Agreed." Mary nibbled a biscuit, wondering if her hostess knew anything that would help James in his quest. But asking would tie her name to his and shut off any confidences. So she would change the subject. Disinterest usually drew more information from the gossip. And even if it didn't, every conversation in months had eventually returned to the murder. "I hear the Thompson girl is working at the Court now."

"Dangerous. How does she know this earl is not like the last one?" said Miss Hardaway with a snort. "She should have waited until we knew more about his lordship."

"James was always different from John."

"He tried to give that impression to establish his own identity, but blood always tells in the end—as Becky Thompson will learn all too soon, if she hasn't already. She is no better than she should be." Her glare implied that Mary knew exactly how that felt.

"A little flirting after Sunday services does not make her unchaste." Yet she was worried about the girl—and not because of James. She could not imagine him misusing servants as John had done. But what would a rake like Crenshaw do with a comely maid?

"Hmph! I don't trust any of those gentlemen. No sensible girl would seek employment in a bachelor household. And what has

Ridgeway been doing these last years? Nothing good, I'll warrant."

"Traveling. Northrup says he spent some time in India."

"*Traveling!*" A crumb landed on the floor that her pug promptly licked up. "Why would anyone want to visit such heathenish places?"

Mary sipped her tea, offering no answer.

"Evil," Miss Hardaway intoned. "He shares his twin's evil. The vicar heard that he had dealings with Napoleon."

"I cannot believe it."

"How else can you explain his presence in France long after the peace collapsed? He had Napoleon's protection." She nodded in triumph. "Ridgeway may still be working for that monster."

"But what could Napoleon want here?" asked Mary, trying to defuse her intensity. The tale sounded shocking, but she knew from long experience that the vicar reveled in malicious gossip and had no regard for accuracy.

"To murder us in our beds, most like." She shuddered. "But that's not all. Ridgeway knows some very suspicious people in London, according to Mr. Dunning."

"Perhaps, but I'd need more than Dunning's word before I believed it. Why he claimed only last week that his great-grandfather's ghost killed four of his cows."

"Well . . ." Miss Hardaway bit into a lemon biscuit, then slipped the rest to her pug. Every year the dog became noticeably fatter. "That was silly, of course. But even if he is wrong, the Thompson girl will be sorry for taking a position at the Court. No matter how well they behave in public, gentlemen are bound to drink more than is seemly and assault the servants. Sir Richard met that Mr. Crenshaw in town—and you cannot dispute his credit."

"No. Even Sir Edwin agrees that Mr. Crenshaw's reputation is less than decorous." The admission revived her fears for Amelia.

"You see? I hope Robby can protect Becky Thompson. He's been sweet on her for some time."

"Robby?"

"Robby Hayes. My footman's brother. He is generally quite

sensible—except for working at Ridgeway, of course. He only met John on that last day, but if the earl had not died, he might have turned the boy off. Or worse." She shuddered delicately.

"Really?" She tried to sound disbelieving. It was the first time anyone had mentioned that day to her. Most of the talk speculated on why John had been murdered.

"Robby was carrying a table along the hallway when the earl burst from the library and struck him down. Then he waved a piece of paper in his face and demanded to know who had delivered it. Robby didn't know, but the earl accused him of lying, then struck him again before he strode off, muttering."

"Muttering?" asked Mary, trying to keep her voice neutral. "How odd."

"Very. Robby's head hurt, and blood was dripping from a cut the earl's signet ring had made on his cheek, but he dared not move until the earl was gone. He thought about fleeing—the earl's eyes had been that furious—but Ridgeway never returned."

"I wonder why the paper angered him so."

"Robby thinks it was a demand that John meet someone, but he has no idea who or why. Whatever it was, the earl was not pleased."

"But if it was a demand to meet someone, why would he comply? He held the highest rank in the area. He could have ordered the other man to call at the Court."

"The meeting must have concerned something illegal," said Miss Hardaway, lowering her voice to a conspiratorial whisper. "I've heard tales that he was involved with smugglers away south. I tried to tell Squire Church about it, but he dismissed the whole notion, insisting that the killer was a highwayman who was interrupted before he could rob the corpse. No letter turned up at the house."

But how much time had elapsed before Isaac had looked? Again, jumping to conclusions had interfered with his job. Idiot! If someone had interrupted a robbery, it would not have taken a full day to find the body. And if passers-by had not noticed John, then the culprit would have finished removing the valuables as soon as they left.

James would want to hear about this, but asking further questions might pique the gossip's curiosity. And he would learn more by questioning Robby directly. "I take it Robby recovered?"

"Oh, yes. It was hardly more than a scratch. His fear was the worst of it."

"What does he think of the new earl?"

"He doesn't know what to think. None of them do. Ridgeway talks nice, but his poking about makes everyone nervous."

Time to change the subject. "Mrs. Ruddy seemed more morose than usual when I called at the shop this morning."

"Poor woman." Miss Hardaway shook her head as she refreshed their tea and slipped another biscuit to her dog. "It has been a year since their daughter died. The date brought it all back."

"Of course. It doesn't seem that long ago."

"For any of them. Influenza is a curse. Polly Sharpe still hasn't recovered her strength."

Didn't want to. But Mary kept the observation to herself. Miss Sharpe was another spinster. Since her failing memory couldn't compete with Miss Hardaway's nose for gossip, she drew attention to herself through ill health.

Miss Hardaway's eyes suddenly gleamed. She cocked her head to one side, a sure sign she had a new tale. "Mrs. Bridwell was quite upset with Lord Northrup yesterday."

This was the first Mary had heard of it, though that was hardly surprising. Justin had spent nearly every waking hour with Fernbeck since his return. He had shocked the tenants by personally helping with repairs and by working in the fields cutting hay. Was he trying to prove that he was different from Frederick, or did he really enjoy manual labor? She had not found an opportunity to ask, for he kept to his military habit of rising at dawn, so she saw him only at dinner. And he had not discussed estate matters with her since they had gone over the books together. "So what is Mrs. Bridwell upset about now?" she asked.

"He succumbed to heathenish influences in India. She admonished him quite sharply—just in front of the chandler's shop, it was. He denied everything, practically calling her a liar to her face, though he could hardly do otherwise after attending services last Sunday."

"I wonder what bothered her so."

Miss Hardaway sniffed. "I couldn't hear all of it, for I was talking to Lady Carworth at the time—" Her face twisted in frustration. "But she demanded that he speak with the vicar, then prattled on and on about Jezebels and Baals and false prophets. He responded with something about King David sleeping on hillsides while tending sheep, though I've no idea why."

"Ah!" Mary laughed. "She discovered that he sleeps with his windows open."

"He'll make himself ill."

"At the moment he is reveling in England's cool air, though I doubt he will continue the practice once summer ends. But he hated the heavy heat of Indian nights. The servants are appalled, but I see no harm in it for now."

"The devil walks at night and can enter through open windows."

"I don't believe the devil relies on carelessness. The previous earl did not sleep with open windows—or did his servants suppress that fact?"

"No." Miss Hardaway relaxed. "As usual, Mrs. Bridwell is finding fault. She has been positively bursting with excitement now that she has four new gentlemen to admonish. She chided Sir Edwin this very morning for his unnatural interest in barbarians."

"The Romans." Mary smiled.

"And she is appalled over Mr. Crenshaw's reputation."

The rest of the call passed pleasantly. Miss Hardaway vented her own pique at the vicar's wife. Mary let her talk as she mulled the new information about John.

A note that drew him to his death put another face on the incident. Perhaps the writer had been an unsavory business associate here to report a problem. John had not been a man to accept failure, which explained the fight and accounted for the murder once the partner had won. John would have retaliated for the ignominy of defeat. Or a conspirator might have decided that John made an uncomfortable ally. But how did that tie in with a local killer? And he had to be local, she admitted. James had also been attacked.

Taking leave of Miss Hardaway, she turned Acorn's head for home. But she had barely left Ridgefield when she met James.

"Quizzing the gossips?" he asked.

How had he known? But she merely nodded. "I heard something interesting about John. And a rumor about you."

He raised his brows and waited.

"The rumor claims that you were quite friendly with Napoleon and might still be working for him."

"Surely you cannot believe that." His voice cracked, the shock in his eyes proving his innocence. It was rapidly overwhelmed by fury.

"I don't know you," she pointed out, wondering what he might say.

"I'm the same man I was before," he protested.

She merely stared.

He inhaled twice to bring himself under control. "I met the Corsican monster at a reception shortly after he was declared Consul for Life. He made a point of personally greeting all the English who were in attendance—several dozen of us, for many flocked to Paris during the Peace of Amiens, you might recall. I found him charming on the surface, but calculating beneath. It was obvious that he was only biding his time until he felt ready to attack again."

"Bridwell also claims that you remained in France long after the peace collapsed."

"No. I was in Vienna by then. Once we heard about the decrees against Englishmen, I moved on to Naples. Austria has changed allegiance more than once since this affair started, and I didn't want to take any chances."

"So who would know you had met Napoleon?"

"John."

"Why would he care?"

"I no longer try to explain his actions. He must have delegated someone to follow me when I left Ridgeway."

"Of course!"

He raised his brows.

"When John fired the staff, he kept one man on—your father's valet."

"It makes sense. Rigby—his own valet—would have done anything for him, so delegating him to follow me is not surprising. Morrell was the obvious man to keep. Without a reference, he was unemployable. He could not afford to retire, for Father had left him only a modest legacy. And John hated him."

"Why?"

"More than once Morrell divulged the truth when John was blaming me for his own escapades. Father never questioned Morrell's word, even when it implicated John."

"Poor Morrell. No wonder he killed himself."

"What?" James blanched, his sudden fists jerking his horse off the path.

"He jumped from the tower a year later."

"Another sin on John's shoulders. I just discovered that he impersonated me, making me appear equally cruel."

"You didn't know that?" She pulled Acorn to a halt, her mouth hanging open in shock.

"How could I? I wasn't here."

Why had she spoken aloud? She shifted uncomfortably, wishing herself elsewhere.

"What are you hiding, now?" he demanded.

"Nothing. I was just amazed at your ignorance. He has impersonated you for as long as I can remember."

"Why did you never tell me?"

"I thought you knew. You must have known. Only the most credulous could have fallen for his act, for he wasn't all that good at it. I never had any trouble telling you apart."

But some had been fooled, she recalled. John had tricked the Adams brothers half a dozen times before she had revealed the truth. And her father, who was far from stupid, had been confused more than once. So it must have been something else that gave him away. His soul, perhaps? She had always sensed the character beneath the face, not even needing sight to tell the difference.

He sighed. "You are one of the few then. Most people accepted his word about his identity. And he deliberately sought to destroy me. Spreading lies—like the spy tale—wasn't enough to satisfy him." He explained his conversation with Cotter.

"Calumny was one of his specialties," she agreed, recalling the many stories John had spread about her. "But it means the servants will never trust you."

"Why should they matter more than tenants and neighbors?"

"They may know something vital. John was unexpectedly summoned to meet a man on the day of his death. He attacked one of the footmen, demanding to know when and how the note had arrived, but the boy knew nothing." She repeated Miss Hardaway's story.

"Who was it?"

"Robby. His brother works for Miss Hardaway. She believes John's killer followed him here to repay him for double-crossing him in some illegal scheme."

"It won't do. That attack on me was connected."

"I know, but arguing with Miss Hardaway would have revealed that. Yet it is unlikely that John was deeply involved with any local wrongdoers, for he was rarely here. Of course, he might have stumbled across another man's crime."

"How ironic if he died for something he didn't do. Did Miss Hardaway mention the summons to Isaac?"

She nodded. "But he dismissed the notion—this was during his search for the mythical highwayman. He never spoke of it again, but she did hear that no note was found."

"I will look into it." He sighed. "That explains what he was doing on that road, and why the killer expected him. But it makes it less likely the staff knows anything useful." He recounted his morning explorations and his hope that someone had overheard John making an assignation.

"So we haven't made any real progress."

"Yes, we have. Robby may know more. In particular, he may have understood some of John's mutterings. And the killer is definitely local—no outsider would know Brewster's Ridge. We just don't have a name yet."

She nodded.

"I tried to find out who was at the Lusty Maiden the night Northrup died, but no one remembers. The usual crowd includes merchants, servants, tenants, and members of the gentry, but until Northrup's body was found, nothing had seemed different from any other night. There were no arguments, no unpleasantness. I don't want to press or the questions will raise suspicions."

"I doubt anything will turn up. If there had been anything odd, rumors would have started long ago."

"I don't know. Memory can be a funny thing. Sometimes hindsight offers a new perspective on events. Remember Miss Crabbe? She could cite chapter and verse of every mistake made by every resident in Ridgefield for the previous fifty years."

"True. And wasn't she proud of it! I always held my breath when she came to call for fear I would do something awful. She would have made sure every person in town heard about it."

"But she was not above admitting that she'd been wrong. She had one story about old Barnes that made his face turn red every time he heard it, but after Tate's wife died, Tate admitted that the fault had actually been his. Miss Crabbe apologized very publicly to Barnes and even claimed she should have figured out the truth for herself. In reviewing her memories, she was able to point out the evidence that she had misinterpreted."

"I don't recall that."

"You wouldn't. I was only ten or eleven at the time, and she rarely mentioned it again. Too bad she is not still here. She could have solved this mystery in no time. What happened to her?"

She shook her head. "Dropsy—or so the doctor claimed. Her legs swelled to twice their usual size, making it impossible to walk. It was almost a relief when she passed on."

"How about Mr. Morwyn?" he asked, naming an elderly man he had called on regularly during his last visit home.

"He died about six months after you left."

"Did John annoy him?"

"No. He died quite peacefully in his sleep, leaving his man a large enough legacy that he could retire. Remember how he always wanted to have his own garden?"

He nodded. "I'm glad for him, and more than pleased that Morwyn lived peacefully to the end."

She frowned as their horses entered the forest. "Did you expect John to bother others besides your tenants and servants?"

"I had wondered. He seemed to single out those I cared about."

She shook her head. "I doubt he even knew who they were. Just as few people ever discussed his deeds, no one ever told him anything. Unless he had delegated someone to watch your every move, he would have had no idea where you went or who you saw."

"He knew about you."

She shivered at the implication, but thrust her sudden pleasure aside. Of course John had known of their friendship. He had kept a close eye on her activities for years. But she offered only a bland, "That was different."

"Good. I feared that I had directed John's attention to the old people. I am not sure I could live with the guilt if he had harassed them."

"Rest easy. He left them alone. John cared nothing for others, so he wouldn't have understood your concern. Visiting the vicarage explained your trips to town. He never knew the pleasure you brought to people like Miss Crabbe and Mr. Morwyn just by listening to their tales. And I know you helped several of them with money."

"It was no hardship. Miss Crabbe had me laughing every time I called."

She smiled, but reminiscing about more innocent times was dangerous, building warmth and rapport that could only hurt her in the end. "Are your friends staying long?" she asked, changing the subject.

"As long as I do. Why?"

"I do not wish to see my sisters hurt when they leave. Flirtation may make their stay more pleasant, but they need to understand the effect."

"I will speak to them, but I suspect they are both serious."

She frowned. "Can they be trusted?"

"I believe so, though you will have to make your own decision. You don't trust me, so how can you accept my assessment of others."

It was such an astute observation that she stiffened, startling her horse.

But you do trust him, whispered a voice. *He is different. He's always been different. You just admitted that recognizing character allowed you to tell them apart. If their characters had been the same, you would not have seen through John's impersonations.*

It's an act, she insisted, wheeling Acorn down a side path to ride alone. James let her go, further confusing her. Men were always kind and considerate when they wanted something. James wanted information, but she sensed an edginess about him that hinted at less acceptable desires.

And how did she know that she had always told them apart? she fumed, ducking a low-hanging branch. Perhaps she could only recognize them when an impersonation was intended to tease. A serious attempt might have fooled her.

You knew serious, countered the voice. *John wasn't teasing that day. Remember? James is real. Trust me. He's not like the others. How does his touch make you feel?*

He only wanted to seduce her, she insisted, ignoring the warmth welling in her heart.

Then why did he let you move away from him at the picnic? Even when you grabbed him, he did nothing.

She cursed the voice. But James's restraint only proved that he had patience. She couldn't believe him. She couldn't. All men lied. Experience had taught her too well.

But she did believe him, she admitted as she dismounted outside the Northfield stable. And that was dangerous. She wanted to touch him, which was even more dangerous, because she knew he would hurt her. Physically. Mentally. Emotionally.

And it was already too late. The pain hovered, ready to pounce.

James watched Mary gallop away. There was more here than even her usual distrust. And he would bet his entire fortune that John was involved.

He forced himself to sit quietly until she was out of sight. If he moved too soon, he would follow her. He wanted her—and not casually. So how patient must he be to win her?

He was still reeling over her revelations. John had impersonated him since childhood. It put a different face on his father's apparent capriciousness. He had believed in James's guilt, because the victims had believed him guilty. So it had not been laziness. Weakness, yes, for he had blindly clung to his fantasy of John's worthiness. But he had not struck out in uncaring ignorance.

A knot in his chest unraveled, revealing just how much pain his father's apparent disinterest had caused.

And deep down, his father must have questioned whether James had truly been guilty. Why else had he drawn up that will? Had he discovered the truth about Cotter's dog? James had sworn he'd been at Isaac's at the time, though no one had listened. Or perhaps Miss Crabbe had mentioned that he'd been in town during the incident involving Justin Northrup's pony.

The last of his guilt faded into oblivion. John had been bad from childhood. The excuses, the second chances, his efforts to remain in the background had all been useless. John had victimized him all his life, but he had been too blind to see it. Yes, John had chosen his friends as targets, but only to derive extra pleasure from his usual activities by twisting a knife in his brother's heart. The truth was simple. John had hated him—not for anything he had done, not for any flaw in his character, but merely because he existed.

Stupid! Why had he not seen it earlier?

Now that he knew Rigby had followed him abroad, he could see John's continued meddling. No one had ever explained his odd encounter with the Parisian footpad or that near-fatal accident in Austria. Had John believed the money would return to Ridgeway if James died?

If so, he must have realized the truth, for no more accidents had plagued him. Maybe John had paid a visit to his solicitor. Bradshaw had known that James was abroad, but his clerk might have produced a copy of the will he had revised before leaving.

Had Rigby been responsible for that contretemps in Naples? Or the problems in Bombay? It no longer mattered. He had done well in Bombay despite that original setback. And he no longer had to fear John. He could concentrate on wooing Mary.

She was fighting him—as this latest escape proved—but he'd taken another small step today. So how should he approach her tomorrow?

He turned toward the Court. Calling on Turnby in the morning would give him an excuse to see Mary in the afternoon. In the meantime, he had to interview Robby.

Chapter Eleven

James followed Turnby into the stable office. It had taken some fancy talking to get him this far, and he suspected that the groom had agreed only to avoid assaulting a lord where they might be seen.

He felt like he was batting away fog. No one would talk to him until they learned to trust him, but no one would trust him while he was looking for John's killer.

"You've got some nerve, Master James," growled Turnby the moment the door was shut.

The address left him feeling ten years old again. Turnby had chastised him in this same tone for riding his father's prized stallion without permission. Of course, the groom had later admitted pride in his horsemanship, for he had stayed on the animal and ultimately controlled him.

"What am I supposed to have done to you?" he demanded wearily. "I did not replace the staff."

"I know that." His face hardened. "And truth to tell, I'd not have worked for John anyway. He never understood horses and mistreated every animal he rode. But you often vowed to take me on when you set up your own stables, yet you didn't even give me the courtesy of an explanation when you left me behind. Or were you praising my skills all those years just to make the old earl think better of you?"

"What stables?"

"No more of your games," he pleaded wearily.

"What stables, Turnby? At least answer the question before you condemn me to hell."

Turnby glared, but finally settled back with a shrug. "You moved your horses out the day your brother turned us off—

right after the funeral, it was. I was still packing when you come back the next morning to take the best half of the breeding stock. Disgruntled, you was—as you know quite well. 'Twas all the earl left you, you said, slamming buckets around, breaking harness, and kicking poor Bones half to death."

James blanched. "You're wrong." What had John done to Bones? If he had realized the extent of John's hatred, he would have taken the dog with him.

But Turnby ignored the interruption, railing at him as if he were still a wayward child and not a lord of the realm. "After that, is it any wonder Bones turned on you? When he caught sight of you a few months later, I had to lock him up to keep him from attacking. Another beating would have killed him. By then, we all knew that you were working hand-in-glove with your brother. Was that your way of keeping access to the Court, or had you helped John even while pretending to care?"

"Enough!" His tone was rough, but he could stand no more. Tears stood in Turnby's eyes. "I let you rant because I need to know how many lies John told, but now it's your turn to listen. I took my own cattle from the stables the day of my father's funeral. By sunset I'd reached Shrewsbury. Two days later, I was in London. I did not see Ridgeway again until two weeks ago. I not only left Shropshire, I left England."

"Must you still lie, my lord?" asked Turnby wearily. "Forbes has become my closest friend. Despite your orders to keep your visits secret, I heard about every despicable act you committed."

"Forbes didn't know me," he said gently. "I just found out yesterday that John often impersonated me, beginning when we were boys. Playing identity games with the staff was his way of forcing them into absolute obedience. And why should they question it? All they knew about me was that I was John's twin. It is no stretch to accept that our characters matched as well as our looks."

Turnby frowned, but his skepticism was clear.

"Damn, I wish Bones were here," muttered James. "He would accept the truth." But Bones had already been six when he'd left.

"Good idea. He remembers you, all right," growled Turnby.

"You're about to get your comeuppance." Opening the door, he summoned a groom. In minutes an old hound hobbled into the office.

"Bones?" said James through the tickle in his throat. A broken leg had been badly set. One eye stared blindly at nothing. "I can't believe you're still alive, Bones," he choked as the dog snuffled his hand.

Bones laid his head on James's knee with a contented groan and sat down.

Dear Bones. James absently scratched around the dog's ears. He had led a rough life, starting when only a pup.

He'd been walking in the woods just after his seventeenth Christmas, working off his anger over John's latest escapade, when a whimper had caught his attention. Following the sound, he'd found a pup wedged between two rocks. Someone must have mistreated the animal, for he was nothing but a bag of bones.

But he'd felt a connection the moment his eyes met those deep, brown pools. Tucking the pup into his greatcoat, he had carried it home. By the time they'd arrived, Bones had a name and a permanent attachment to his rescuer. But it was Turnby who'd raised Bones. James had returned to school two days later.

"What happened to your leg, boy?" he crooned, sinking onto the floor so he could hug the dog. Bones crowded close, collapsing half in his lap as James stroked his coarse fur. "And your eye. Did John do that to you? Poor Bones."

"It really *was* John," gasped Turnby, eyes focused on Bones, who was weakly licking James's other hand.

"It really was. John threw me out once the will was read. I wish Father *had* left me the stable—John might have accepted that. Instead, I got most of his fortune."

"Tantrums. I shoulda known. Forgive me for doubting you, my lord."

"Stick to James. You've always been more of an uncle than an employee."

Turnby nodded.

"I need your help, Turnby."

"Anything."

"You had best hear me out before making any promises. I have to find John's killer." Bones lifted his head at Turnby's protest, settling back when Turnby stilled. "I cannot approve anything John did, but neither can I condone murder. A man who has resorted to extremes once might do so again, and with less cause."

"I doubt it."

"I know it. John made sure my name was associated with his crimes, and he worked hard to call as much hatred onto my head as onto his. Someone made an attempt on my life last week, which can only mean that John's killer is now stalking me. I've encountered too much passion since returning to dismiss the threat as trivial."

Turnby's face was troubled. "I wish I could help you, but I don't know who killed John, and I don't want to speculate. People have enough trouble."

"Squire Church mentioned an affair gone bad as a possible motive. He thinks the story started with you."

"No. But one of the servants at the Court might have said something. They saw plenty that they couldn't repeat on pain of a beating or worse. Or maybe the vicar knows something. He was privy to many secrets."

"Sooner or later, I must compile a list of John's crimes—and not just as a motive for murder. I have to make up for his cruelty, Turnby."

"You always were too soft-hearted for your own good. But there's no remedy for most of his deeds. Stick to turning around the big things, like you already started."

"I need to do more."

Bones sighed, burrowing into his chest.

"You can't," insisted Turnby, lowering his voice. "What can you do for the Prices? James ravished Meg, as you well know, for the truth of that came out the day before the funeral. Nine months later, she died birthing a stillborn son."

James shuddered.

"Can anything bring that girl back? Will raking up the tale and reviving all that grief help her parents any? And what about Lady Northrup? I heard John spinning lies to that beau of hers. The lad was so appalled over her supposed fall from grace that he left that very day without even bidding her farewell. And those same lies made the rounds of the drawing rooms within the week. What can you do to make up for years of suspicion? 'Twas long in the past, and she's moved on to make a reasonable life for herself."

"But—"

Turnby refused to listen. "Nearly everyone can cite at least one case just like those. And in every instance, talking about it would do more harm than good."

He sighed, but he could see Turnby's point. "You said Forbes was a friend. Would you encourage him to talk to me about recent events that might shed light on the murder? I won't stir up memories among the innocent, but I must find the killer before he dispatches me."

He nodded.

"But don't mention the attempt on my life just yet. I'd rather not give anyone else ideas."

"It might at that. If I'd thought of it, I might have killed John myself after what he did to Morrell."

"I heard he made him serve as his valet—he'd sent Rigby to keep an eye on me."

"Mistreated him badly, then refused to bury him in sacred ground despite the vicar being willing. I never believed Morrell jumped."

Whether he had jumped or not, his death was John's fault. Bless Vicar Layton for overlooking an apparent suicide. "Do you know where he is?"

"Out by the woods."

In the pet burial ground. His fingers smoothed Bones's neck. "I'll see that he is moved to the family plot as soon as I replace Bridwell. I don't want him praying over Morrell."

"Thank you. And I'll write a note to Forbes. Do you want to take Bones now?"

"He's used to you, Turnby. And you to him. Besides, he's safer here. I don't want someone to strike at me by killing my dog. But I'll be back."

Giving Bones a final scratch and a vow to return, he scrambled to his feet and headed for the Court.

*   *   *

Mary clipped a fading blossom from the apothecary rose, holding it close to inhale its powerful fragrance. The rose garden had been her special place since the earliest days of her marriage, its stone walls providing a secluded thinking spot that offered shelter from cold northern breezes and Frederick's hot words. The scent relaxed her, bringing peace to mind and body—which was why she made the fading blooms into potpourri for her bedroom and sitting room.

"Beautiful place."

She nearly dropped her basket. "What are you doing here?"

"Such a gracious hostess." The sarcasm belied the twinkle in James's eyes. "My friends and I came to call. Your butler offered to summon you, but I preferred to do it myself."

"Arrogant. What if I don't wish to be at home to visitors?"

"But you would never turn us away, despite your suspicions. You want to see your sisters settled. Yet they must be chaperoned—hence your presence and mine."

"Yours?"

"Two couples. Two chaperones. A gentleman must guard against compromise."

"I would never—"

"I know," he interrupted soothingly. "But I wasn't sure when this started. You were so obviously matchmaking."

Her cheeks warmed. He was right about her suspicions, she conceded as she turned toward the house. Mind-reading again? She didn't trust the girls to any man. Women had so little control over their lives.

"Stay a moment," he begged, laying a hand on her arm to stop her progress. "You needn't rush off just yet. Northrup is in the drawing room. Or are you afraid of me?"

"Of course not." She was, though. And after she had fled him yesterday, he must know it. She wasn't sure what he wanted, but it was more than help with his investigation. Was he looking for a new mistress? Caro had mentioned an orphanage in Naples that he supported—a strange charity for an English gentleman.

Unless it houses his by-blows, whispered that voice, recalling Justin's tales from India. But even the basest suspicions did not mitigate the growing attraction she could not seem to banish.

Backing away, she fingered the ruffled petals of a striped rosa mundi, then clipped several of its flowers, though it was not a rose she usually used for potpourri. Every time she saw him, the yearning grew. The only way to reduce the inevitable pain was to stay in crowds. Those terrifying urges were easier to ignore when others were present. And today the crowd was in the drawing room. What was Justin doing home in the afternoon?

James broke into her reverie. "I spoke with Turnby this morning. That makes three people who now accept that I have not changed."

"He believes you?" Turnby had loudly condemned both twins for years.

"Bones convinced him."

"Your dog. I had forgotten about him. How is he?"

"Old. But even identical twins smell different. He always hated John."

"With cause. So did Turnby know anything?"

"He claimed the offenses he knows about are too old to matter."

"That is true of many of us. I know of nothing less than three years old." She caressed the pink and white blooms of a York and Lancaster rose, wondering yet again how one bush could produce two different flowers. "Did Robby tell you more about the note John received?"

"No. He barely admitted the facts you had already discovered, and he insists no one knows how the note arrived. Am I to believe that someone entered undetected?"

"It is quite likely in a place the size of the Court. Even an adequate staff does not watch unused wings."

"And John kept a very reduced staff," he finished for her.

"It is also possible that a servant conspired with the killer. Are there any with particularly serious grievances, or who were singled out for especially severe punishments?"

"I don't know, but I can check. Turnby and Forbes are good friends. Forbes may cooperate now that Turnby accepts me."

She nodded.

"I also have agents investigating everyone John hired from outside the area. A response to one inquiry was waiting when I returned from seeing Turnby, but I cannot decide whether it has any bearing on John's death."

"Tell me." She sat on a garden bench.

He paced twice before continuing. "I wondered why the Bridwells believed so many of John's lies—Mrs. Bridwell repeats slanderous gossip at the drop of a hat, and her husband is nearly as vehement. It is not a trait I usually associate with a vicar."

"Some people thrive on scandal." She shrugged.

"Like Miss Hardaway in Ridgefield, or Lady Beatrice in London." He shook his head. "Gossips are found everywhere, but they rarely repeat proven lies. Destroying their own credibility would set them up as laughingstocks and lose their audience for future tales."

"What is your point?"

"Mrs. Bridwell delights in repeating known slander, especially about you." He joined her on the bench. "At first I thought that it was spite born of envy. You are everything she is not—beautiful, talented, kind, and possessed of a social position she can never achieve. Or it might have arisen from guilt—you still look after the poor and ailing, a job she ought to be doing."

Her cheeks heated at the unaccustomed praise. Her eyes fell to the hands twisting in her lap, but she remained silent, unsure how to respond. This was exactly the sort of flattery she had hoped to avoid. Yet warmth suffused her skin.

"But neither of those explains her vehemence. Then there is the vicar. Not only does he rip at your character, but he considers John a reasonable man."

"Hardly surprising. John controlled his living. No one ever criticized John in public, and I doubt anyone discussed him with Bridwell even in private, so he may not have known the truth." She twisted away, presenting her back. "We've been through all this. What purpose is served by repeating it?"

"Why does Bridwell continue his praise even though John is dead?"

"To hold his position. As John's brother you will applaud his loyalty."

"He might think that, I suppose. But I could not keep him here even if I approved of him. My father promised that post to your brother and paid for much of his schooling. The plan was to bring Howard here as a curate until your father retired, then give him the living."

"I know, but that is ancient history. Howard was still at the university when Father died. Even if the post had been offered, he would have turned it down—as you would know if you had been here. He and John were mortal enemies. John was furious that your father had paid all Howard's tuition in a lump sum that the school refused to refund. Howard was better off making his own way from the start."

"But everyone knew Howard was being trained for the post. They loved him as they loved your father."

"Which was reason enough for John to look elsewhere."

"How did he explain it?"

"That was easy enough. He did not want the post to sit vacant while Howard completed his schooling." She had been too mired in grief to question events. The Bridwells had come to officiate at the funeral, then stayed. And it wasn't as if the change had left her homeless—though John would have gloated if it had. She had married Frederick two months earlier.

For the first time, she wondered if John would have tossed her father out with the other servants if he hadn't wished to torment her.

"Did you ever wonder why John chose the Bridwells?" James asked, interrupting her thoughts.

She shook her head. "I assumed the bishop filled the vacancy, though I know John could evict them if they displeased him—which was another reason Howard would never have accepted it. Your father was shortsighted to believe it would have worked."

"Or blind. He could never admit that his heir was wanting." He sighed. "I did some checking. Not only did John request Bridwell, he had to fight to get him here."

"Why?"

"The bishop was ready to remove Bridwell from the clergy."

"What?"

"My secretary visited Bridwell's last posting. He had become entangled with a girl who wound up dead, but the evidence was murky. Bridwell was one of three men who might have killed her. John's testimony exonerated Bridwell and focused attention on another man—who was ultimately hanged."

"So he brought Bridwell here." Fury sharpened her tone.

He nodded. "John swore Bridwell was innocent, then offered this post to allow the town to put the matter to rest. Some had been questioning whether justice had been served, but they accepted his solution. Bridwell was grateful, and John gained a vicar loyal solely to him."

"But why would Bridwell care?"

"I think he was guilty—evidence later showed the other man could not have done it. John probably had proof all along. Blackmail would explain why Bridwell supported him against everyone else in the parish."

"But that would also give him a motive for killing John." She had twisted back to stare at him.

"True. Who would ever suspect a vicar?"

"Then why continue supporting him?"

"Think, Mary. If he changed, people would ask why."

"Of course. And if he continues, you are bound to send him away."

"But I may be wrong on every count. I haven't one shred of evidence."

"Have you spoken to Squire Church about this?"

He shook his head. "Isaac's prejudices aside, every man in the area had reason to hate John. So I must ask myself what Isaac's grievance was. If a vicar had cause to kill—and had already done so—why not a magistrate?"

"I cannot see him killing anyone." Her hand gripped his arm. She had never considered any of her friends as potential murderers. Yet he was right. Everyone had hated John.

"I did not mean to distress you, Mary," James murmured, covering her hand with his. "Do you care so much for him then?" His stomach twisted at the thought. He had not taken Isaac's claim seriously when the man announced that he would take her to wife. Had she formed a *tendre* for him?

"I care for everyone," she said sadly. "It distresses me to think of my friends and neighbors as potential killers. It was easier to think of the culprit in the abstract than to assign him a known face."

"Perhaps I should cease sharing my information with you." He stared into her eyes. Was this a crisis of nerves, or was she protecting someone?

"No. Not knowing would be worse." Her voice was breathless, stirring the fires that she ignited every time they met. Her hand trembled. Those blue eyes were deep pools, swirling with conflicting emotions. But fear was not uppermost today. Nor was anger. He saw curiosity. Desire. Heat. Uncertainty?

"As you wish," he whispered, moving close enough to blur the sight. "We will share." Everything. His lips touched hers. Lightning burst through his head as her hand clenched tighter.

He fought to keep it light, keep it nonthreatening, keep it simple. But his free arm slipped around her shoulders, pulling her closer.

She tensed.

Don't frighten her, he admonished himself, holding part of his mind aloof so he could think. She dragged at his reason like opium, drawing him toward mind-numbing rapture with a promise of sensual pleasure. But the promise was a lie, at least for now.

Her lips softened as he brushed them lightly, then trembled as he angled his mouth across them. But she did not draw back. Her fingers released their grasp to slide around his neck. Her bosom pressed into his chest, each breast the perfect size to fill his hand, each point stabbing new desire into his loins.

He needed relief, craved it beyond even his next ragged breath. He wanted to deepen the kiss, wanted to pull her closer until every curve of her body touched his, wanted to rip—

No, he reminded himself again. This was not the time. He could fantasize later. One wrong move would wipe out every gain he'd made.

But it was already too late. His arm had tightened, imprisoning her against him. She stiffened, fighting free of his grasp.

"No!"

He let her go, knives stabbing his heart at the terror blazing in her eyes.

"Stop!" he ordered as she scrambled to her feet. "I won't touch you again."

"What—" She glanced back, her terror gradually fading when he made no move to rise.

"You cannot rush into the house until you have yourself under control," he reminded her soothingly, though he had to swallow his pounding heart before he could talk. "You have guests."

"Of course." Her mind must be working again, for she was smoothing her gown and checking her hair. He spared a moment to exult that she had lost herself in that kiss.

"Sit down, Mary. Your face is white. If you swoon, I will have to catch you. I don't want to break my word about touching you."

She gingerly resumed her seat, but she was practically falling off the end of the bench.

He sighed. "What just happened?"

"Nothing, my lord. I told you once before that I was not available for dalliance. You should have listened."

"I am not interested in dalliance. I could never dishonor you so." It was true, he realized in shock. His desire was stronger than ever, but he would never be content with merely bedding her. He needed more. Much more.

"Stop," she begged, but her eyes had widened in horror. He cursed himself for losing control of his face, allowing her to see his intentions. "I will leave as soon as my sisters are settled. You have no place in my future or I in yours."

"Leave?" His head swirled.

"Now that Justin is home, I have no reason to stay. My widow's portion will support me quite nicely. For once I will be able to live where and how I choose."

He remained silent. What could he say? He had rushed his fences, pushing her into a decision he could not like. But argument would achieve nothing.

Her reaction to what had been a fairly chaste kiss showed just how rough Frederick must have been with her. He had no further doubts that she feared intimacy.

And the signs had been glaringly obvious—she flinched
from any touch, froze at every compliment, grew fidgety if a
man stood too close, and fled any hint of warmth. He should
have listened harder to that voice warning him to proceed with
caution. She had not been ready for a kiss.

But she was remarkably responsive. The kiss hadn't terrified
her half as much as her reaction to it—which would make her
even more wary.

So he must fall back on light friendship, doing nothing to ag-
itate her until he could win her trust.

But he *would* have her. That kiss had opened his eyes. No
more dithering about the strength of his desire. No more debate
over her place in his life. He loved her. Forever. Her recoil
could not have hurt this deeply if his emotions were not fully
engaged.

He quickly brought his face under control, thankful that she
was nervously shredding the flowers she had clipped instead of
looking at him.

He had a new goal—marriage. But first he must reestablish
their partnership.

"I will not return to the house," he decided aloud. They both
needed time to settle. "But I will be back. We still have John's
murder to solve and questions about Frederick's death to answer. Neither of us can learn enough singly. But I promise I
will never hurt you. Nor will I touch you again without your
consent."

"Stubborn, aren't you?" But only the slightest irritation
twisted her face. "I will tell your friends that you were called
away."

She watched him leave, then wrapped her arms around her
waist and shivered. What was she to do? She had understood
his message, for he had hidden nothing. He wanted her—in his
arms, in his bed. As his wife? That last had been less clear, but
no more acceptable. Why couldn't he have chosen someone
else, someone who wanted what he could offer?

She did not. It wasn't just the marriage bed she feared,
though that was terrifying enough. He was an earl, with endless
social obligations, including visits to court. She was a vicar's

daughter, who had never been more than ten miles from Ridgefield.

Somehow she must dissuade him. He could be relentless in pursuing his goals, as his determination to uncover John's killer proved. It was one trait the twins had shared. But she could never wed again, especially into the peerage. Lords had to produce heirs. She had married Frederick in ignorance and tolerated him only because he had never returned to her bed. If she had to face *that* regularly, she would throw herself into the quarry.

James would not live in London, leaving his wife to run the estate. And how was she to face the gossips? They had raised their brows when she'd married Frederick, for she was unworthy to be a baroness. No one would accept her as a countess.

Are you sure? demanded that insidious voice. *You would not be the first to leap to so high a station. And you enjoyed that, didn't you?*

Heat returned. Yes, she had enjoyed it. Too much. She had never dreamed that kissing could feel so good.

Her lips tingled. She had never been kissed before. George had considered it improper outside of marriage, and Frederick had been too intent on *that* to bother. So she hadn't expected the warmth, the melting desire, the sheer *pleasure* a kiss could bring.

Lies, of course. Like everything else, it was a plot to lure her into bed. But she would not succumb. She must keep her mind on truth and see that he understood the reality of their separate worlds.

Consoling herself that he would eventually admit defeat, she returned to the house, arriving in the drawing room doorway just as Justin finished a toast.

"—and may your futures be blessed." He turned and smiled. "There you are, Mary." His eyes narrowed for a brief moment. Could he tell what she had been doing in the rose garden? He must know that James had arrived with his friends. Heat crept across her face.

"What is the occasion?" she asked to distract his attention. Even the girls held small glasses of wine.

Caroline jumped up, but Edwin touched her arm. "Breathe first," he murmured.

She complied. "I have accepted Edwin's offer of marriage."

"Wonderful!" Mary hugged her closely, suppressing her own fears. Edwin was a good man, she reminded herself. Quiet, studious, and loving. Very like her father. He would never hurt his wife. "Welcome to the family."

"Thank you. I will cherish her." He met her eyes, his own reflecting honesty.

She relaxed. And this explained Justin's presence. Edwin must have spoken with him earlier. She suppressed the stab of pain over being excluded from the discussion. Family decisions were no longer her responsibility.

"Harry has offered for me," said Amelia without warning.

This news wasn't so welcome, and her pain was far worse. Why hadn't Justin at least sought her opinion? He knew almost nothing about the girls' suitors. But she no longer had any authority over the Northrups. And this validated her decision to move far away from Northfield, so she would escape these reminders in the future. She forced her lips into a smile.

"I love her," Harry admitted, meeting her gaze.

"Then I must trust you to treat her well."

"I will." He must have read her doubts, for he continued, "In time, you will believe it."

Justin handed her a glass of wine, repeating his toast. She waited until Justin and Harry were engrossed in conversation before drawing Amelia aside.

"Are you sure this is what you want?" she asked softly. "Harry seems a good man, but his reputation is not what I had hoped for."

"Half the young men in London are known as libertines," she said calmly. "Most settle into marriage. He swears it was no more than sowing wild oats, and he considers fidelity important. I spoke to Justin about that yesterday. He has known many men in his years in the army and confirmed that most engage in affairs in their youth. In his experience, those who conduct liaisons with married women have little respect for vows, but those who eschew matrons are likely to remain faithful. For all

Harry's wildness, I have heard no tales linking him with married ladies."

"Perhaps he will make you happy, then," she admitted grudgingly, though the fact that Justin considered him just like other men appalled her. Only a very few men were different enough to trust. Her father had been one, and she suspected Edwin was another. But she could not argue further. "Think about it. If you discover anything that makes you uncomfortable, call off the betrothal. I do not trust men who have been tempered in London excesses. Town bronze is merely a polite term for unbridled debauchery. Look what it did to Frederick."

"London did not lead Frederick astray, Mary," said Amelia. "Even Lord Ridgeway was not responsible. Frederick was cruel long before he set foot in the city. He was already a wastrel who preyed on the weak when Ridgeway befriended him. It was not a case of a master corrupting his pupil, but a meeting of kindred spirits."

Amelia had voiced this sentiment before, but Mary had never listened. Believing it was tantamount to admitting that her father had sold her to a dissipated profligate. It was more comfortable to curse John for destroying a weak-willed boy, though she must then accept some of the blame herself, for John would not have cared about Frederick if not for her. And Frederick would not have been vulnerable to John's evil if not for her.

Are you sure about that?

She frowned. If her understanding of men was deficient, then she might be making new mistakes. She could not chance alienating Amelia because she had judged Harry wrong.

So what was the truth? Had her father understood Frederick's nature?

Vicar Layton had taken pride in knowing every resident of his parish, and he had been an astute judge of character. If he had knowingly contracted his only daughter to a lecherous wastrel, then he must have believed that she was a fallen woman.

No, claimed the voice. *You are missing something.*

Shaking off the pain, she reviewed the events of that autumn.

Her father had known he was dying, though he had not yet informed his children. Had illness affected his judgment? Fred-

erick had been away at school for several years, so his pecca-
dilloes might have been unknown outside the family—and to
be honest, she had heard nothing against him. A father desperate to secure his daughter's future might have convinced himself that all would be well, despite the groom's tender years.

And Frederick *had* been young. They had wed when he was
barely eighteen. Gentlemen rarely considered setting up their
nurseries so soon. But impending death might have pushed her
father into accepting an alliance he would otherwise have eschewed. Mary had already been twenty, and she had no dowry.
Howard had been a university student with no prospects until
he secured his own living. Where would she have gone once
her father died? She could not have stayed at the vicarage.

But he'd had doubts, she realized, remembering their talk on
the eve of her wedding. He had stressed Frederick's youth and
volatility, warning her that it would take time before he would
grow into a steady companion. He had reminded her not to
chastise him or question his decisions. Taking her place in society would require patience, for her bloodlines had been di-
luted through several generations. The other aristocratic wives
would be watching her. And on and on.

She had listened with barely half an ear, and had completely
missed his points. Because she was older, she had treated Frederick more as a young brother or son than as a husband—just
as she had treated Justin, Amelia, and Caroline. And she had
been so accustomed to running the vicarage that she had immediately taken charge of the Manor, changing routines without regard to tradition or custom.

Her manner may have been high-handed, but she had also
been quick to accept blame for every problem—if she had satisfied him, he would not have left for London; if she had de-
ferred to his judgment, even when he was wrong, he would
have taken charge of Northfield and learned to run it; if his
home had not become a battleground, he would have accepted
her.

But her guilt hadn't stopped there. She had honestly believed
that her willfulness had forced him away, leading to every one
of his subsequent problems—falling in with bad companions,
indulging in all the vices that tempted green young men, squan-

dering his inheritance, whiling away his life like the other wastrels that littered the city. Even John's friendship had been her fault. John only took the youngster under his experienced wing to punish her.

The guilt had suffocated her, fueling the feelings of inadequacy she had suffered since childhood. Her mother had endured a long illness before her death, becoming querulous and finding fault with every effort to attend her. Once she was gone, Mary had assumed her place at the vicarage, but her efforts had never been good enough, a fact her father had pointed out often.

Of course you could not replace your mother, scoffed the voice. *You were ten years old!*

Which was true, she admitted. She had been held up to an impossible standard. No wonder she had felt unworthy.

And the gossip had aggravated that image. As had the gentlemen. First George had abandoned her. Then James. And finally Frederick. Only John had stayed, but he had used every incident to feed the gossip, raising new doubts in her mind and pouring on the guilt. It was all her fault.

No! No more. She was not responsible for any of it. She was innocent of ruining Frederick. His failings were rooted in his childhood. Perhaps he had hidden his true character when he had approached her father to ask for her hand. The previous baron's death had been unexpected—an accident while hunting with friends—so his sudden desire to wed had seemed reasonable. He had needed someone responsible enough to raise his young siblings, and marriage would free him from his guardian.

Now that she thought about it, he had chosen her solely on those grounds. Providing an heir had never been mentioned. Nor had helping him with the estate.

So in his usual fashion, he had solved the immediate problems as quickly as possible, with no thought to the ultimate consequences. Like other young men, he had had no interest in a wife. He had probably not even heard the rumors about her. He had believed that a vicar's daughter of advancing years would make an adequate substitute mother. All he wanted was to rid himself of responsibility and escape to London to resume the life his father's death had interrupted.

So she had had nothing to do with his defection. Her actions had been no better or worse than anyone else's. She was not perfect, but neither was she a pariah. She need look no further than Caro and Amelia for proof that she had accomplished something worthwhile.

The guilt slipped from her shoulders, first in a trickle, then a rush. She was free. Her head felt light for the first time in years. She wanted to laugh, to dance, to run.

She was free.

Amelia was chuckling over one of Harry's stories. She had never looked happier. Would it stay like that?

She hoped so.

The girls would have better marriages than she had experienced. Each had found someone who cared for her. Neither felt pressured to wed out of duty or honor or any of the other reasons people committed matrimony.

Which meant that her own duty was nearly done, the duty for which marriage had contracted her. Once the weddings were over, she would be free of the last shackle.

The jointure Justin had reinstated would more than cover that cottage. A place that was hers alone, that would never be taken from her, where no one could intrude without her permission. It had been her ultimate dream. Security. Peace. Belonging. Only one cloud intruded.

James.

He was not a man to give up without a fight. Even the gulf between their respective positions would not deter him if he was determined to win. So she must convince him that he did not want to pursue this particular war.

Chapter Twelve

James set aside an account book as his friends entered the library. "Are congratulations in order?"

Harry's grin nearly split his face. "They are indeed."

Edwin's smile was dreamier. "You left early."

"Business."

Harry snorted. "If business was that urgent, why did you go with us?"

"Lady Northrup suggested a new approach. The books contain notes on staff discipline. I'm compiling a list of specific grievances people had against John."

"This obsession is getting out of hand," observed Harry, shaking his head. "You are worse than Edwin and his Romans."

"But not as bad as you and your conquests," protested Edwin, laughing. "What will you talk about now that you have given up wenching?"

"Homer," he said instantly, striking a pose of learned pomposity. "The intricacies of the *Odyssey,* the drama of the *Iliad,* the ineptitude of the translators that forces me to slave for months—nay, years—composing my own editions."

"That will certainly endear you to society's hen-witted hostesses," said James with a grin.

"Fashion," decided Harry, adopting the demeanor of a fastidious dandy and twisting his voice into a bored drawl. "The intricacies of the cravat, the drama of choosing the best color and cut of a jacket, the ineptitude of clothiers that forces me to slave for hours—nay, days—finding the perfect thumbs and fingers to make an acceptable pair of gloves." He peered suspiciously at his hands.

"Brummell beat you to that complaint," pointed out Edwin.

"And bores us into a stupor with his endless repetitions of it," added James.

"Are you suggesting I avoid the trite? But society prefers the trite. It does not tax even the simplest mind."

"Surely, you are not implying that Lady Beatrice is simple-minded," said Edwin, pretending absolute shock.

"Never!" Harry glanced behind him with a theatrical shudder. "Sharp as a tack, that lady. And she'll crucify you for thinking otherwise, even in jest. I swear she can hear us even as we speak."

"So what *will* you talk about," asked James.

"We will remain on my estate much of the year. Amelia has interesting ideas about improving it. And when I am in London, I will bore everyone by rhapsodizing on the joys of the married state. Or with politics. My father's last letter hinted that he might give me that seat in Commons after all."

"Hardly boring. You should consider marriage for yourself, James." Edwin grinned.

"Later."

"Why not court Mary?" Harry's prodding remained light-hearted, but a serious note crept into his teasing. "It would hardly interfere with your investigation since she is helping you with it."

"What did I do to deserve this?" James asked, half to himself. "A man steps into parson's mousetrap and immediately demands that all his friends join him. You sound like Lady Hardesty," he added, naming one of London's ubiquitous matchmakers."

"He has a point," put in Edwin lightly. "I've seen the way you look at her—and how she looks at you, for that matter."

"Can you honestly swear you're not thinking about it?" demanded Harry, prodding harder.

"No."

"Well, then—"

"It's not that simple." His tone wiped the grins from their faces. "Lady Northrup has suffered greatly at men's hands—or so I suspect. She has no interest in tying herself to another one."

"I thought Amelia was being coy when she mentioned

Mary's plans to leave," said Harry. "In fact, I assumed that she wanted me to push you a little."

"Not at all."

"Perhaps Caro can suggest something that will help," said Edwin.

"No!"

Both men jumped.

"Stay out of it. And keep the ladies out of it. No prodding; no questions, even innocent ones. She's skittish enough to bolt if she feels threatened, and I truly need her help to find John's killer."

Edwin exchanged glances with Harry, then shrugged. "If that is what you want."

"Absolutely."

"How is the investigation proceeding?" asked Harry.

"The more I learn, the more confusing it gets. But I am convinced that Frederick was somehow connected. Within hours of arriving at Ridgeway, John received a note that lured him to his death. So the motive must be rooted in his previous trip home—which he cut short, fleeing the moment Frederick died. He did not even stay for the funeral."

"I know little of Frederick, but I can ask Amelia about him," said Harry with a shrug. "Or would that bother Mary?"

"She knows I am investigating his death. She has questions about him, too, but she cannot find answers—just as I have trouble learning the truth about John."

"Then I will talk to Caro."

"And I will speak with Amelia. Frederick was a degenerate, which explains why Mary is so unhappy about my betrothal."

"She still is?" He had hoped he'd assuaged some of her fears.

"Justin and Amelia had already accepted my suit, so Mary had no choice, but she distrusts my reputation."

"I take it she has no qualms about you, though?" said James, glancing at Edwin.

"None that I noticed."

James ignored the ensuing discussion of wedding plans. Had he convinced them to leave Mary alone? If she felt pressured, she would run. Or she would dig in her heels so hard that he would never convince her to give him a chance. She was not a woman who changed her mind easily.

Damn Harry's eyes. And Edwin's. It was bad enough that he had rushed his fences with Mary, but he had not realized that his friends could also deduce his intentions. His control must be slipping.

Frustration, of course—beyond the slow progress in finding the killer. And it could only get worse. He had promised not to touch her, eliminating those small contacts that built intimacy—the hand on her back, helping her in and out of carriages, sitting close enough to brush her leg, dancing . . .

Dancing? He swore. He should never have kissed her. Now they were both in trouble.

Sir Richard was hosting an evening of informal dancing. Should he go or stay home? Perhaps watching him dance with others would soften Mary's heart.

But that would not work. Mary was a baroness. Avoiding one of the highest-ranking ladies in the room would cast new aspersions on her head. Yet skipping the gathering would insult Sir Richard and add to the suspicions everyone had of him.

Damn! No matter what he did, someone would suffer.

Kissing her had been a mistake. He had not understood how deeply her fears ran. And revealing his intentions had driven the wedge in farther, creating a host of new complications.

Perhaps he should just explain the problem and let her decide. A simple country dance involved minimal contact, but would satisfy the social niceties. If even a country dance was too much for her, then he would stay home. At least that would not reflect on Mary.

The watcher clenched his fists as Ridgeway exchanged pleasantries with Miss Hardaway. James was sneakier than his brother had been, cloaking his evil in kindness and using generosity to deflect attention from his black heart. When he showed his true face, the pain would be even harsher for being unexpected.

But what could one expect of a French agent? They were trained in trickery, expert at manipulation, and regularly used false charm to wheedle information from unsuspecting innocents.

James surpassed his brother's evil, adding treason to the cruelty, brutality, and debauchery that the twins had practiced for so long.

Hatred gleamed in his dark eyes. The most credulous were already falling under the earl's spell. Some even swore that James had been absent that day.

He knew better. But even if the tales were true, it made no difference. James would have been there, given the opportunity. And who was to determine which twin had lied? No, both were evil. Both deserved death. The wicked must pay for their sins.

Assuming a casual demeanor, he headed for the Lusty Maiden.

"Yes, indeed," Miss Hardaway agreed as James seated her in the confectioner's shop. "Robby is a good boy, despite working for your brother, begging your pardon."

"I am sure he is," he said soothingly. "But you can hardly fault me for checking on John's employees. His judgment was unsound, and I must have a loyal, hardworking staff."

"You need have no fears about Robby. I employ his brother, and I have known the family since childhood. Excellent servants. Mr. and Mrs. Hayes both work at the inn. Each of the children, down to the youngest girl, who just hired on as a kitchen maid at Northfield, is a good worker, honest, and respectful of his betters."

"So when Robby claims that a summons drew John to his death, I should believe him?"

"Absolutely."

"Even though no note was ever found?"

"That boy never told a falsehood in his life. I remember when he was eight. Bobby Barnes and four others swore the ghost of Jeremiah Perkins rose from the churchyard and chased them clear to the inn. But Robby denied it. He had seen nothing and refused to claim otherwise just to cover his friends' fear."

"So John received a note. Do you have any idea who it was from?"

Miss Hardaway waited until cakes and tea were served and they were again alone. "None."

"When was it delivered?"

"Robby doesn't know. Ridgeway found it at half past noon, but no one had been in the library—or no one admitted to it."

"I understand you suspect that the note concerned something illegal."

"Ridgeway would have demanded that anyone legitimate attend him."

He nodded. "Perhaps, but he might have gone out to inspect a problem."

She snorted. "Don't you know your brother better than that? If a problem had arisen, he would have sent Walden. He didn't bother with estate matters."

"True." Leaving the house implied a need for secrecy beyond what even a terrified staff provided. "So the subject was illegitimate, but the gentleman was someone he trusted."

"Perhaps. Robby claims John was unhappy about the summons—furious would describe it better. So it wasn't a meeting he had expected."

"I wonder which of his crimes finally caught up with him," James said lightly, hoping his implied condemnation would encourage her to talk about John's misdeeds.

"It could be anything," she replied primly.

"Such as?"

"Some believe he debauched Sir Tristan's daughter last year."

"That would have been during his previous visit?"

She nodded. "No one could disprove the charge, though Ridgeway was entertaining house guests during most of his stay. And the girl married Mr. Derwyn shortly after the rumors started, putting paid to most of them. They moved to York."

"Unexpectedly?"

She shook her head, her eyes fading into disappointment. "He had accepted a position as steward to Lord Thorne. 'Twas what allowed their marriage. He had courted her for two years."

He must discover the details of the marriage. Derwyn may

not have known the truth until after the ceremony. Sir Tristan could have packed the girl off to avoid further embarrassment or arranged Derwyn's post because she was increasing. Either man might have taken steps to avenge his honor.

Honor was a powerful motivation. He knew two young lords whose escalating animosity was entering its third year. The quarrel had begun over a perceived slight by one to the inamorata of the other. But instead of settling the matter in a duel—which would have been the end of it—the injured lord had insulted the other, who had replied in kind. Each attack had provoked a counterattack. Neither now cared that the girl had long since wed another.

He swallowed a bite of cake. "Does anyone else have a recent grievance?"

"Your tenants. They all believed that he was about to raise the rents again."

He nodded, though he had not heard that particular story. Why had Walden not mentioned it? Or Jem?

Walden had left yesterday, a tepid recommendation in his pocket. James had agonized over the wording for days. Now he wondered if letting him go had been a mistake. Had Walden been responsible for John's death?

He had discounted the notion earlier. Walden must have known what John was doing to the tenants, yet he had not raised a single protest. But a demand to raise rents yet again might have been more than even a spineless coward could tolerate. Weak men rarely struck back at their persecutors, so their rage built. When they finally exploded into action, they could be even more vicious than their quick-tempered friends.

Walden was the one person who could have easily drawn John away from the house. And he could have recovered the note before anyone suspected John was missing. No one would have noticed the steward visiting the library.

"Barnes grumbled for months about the damage John's guests inflicted on the inn," continued Miss Hardaway.

"I know about that, and have taken steps to rebuild the wing. Are there any other tradesmen with grievances?"

"The Ridgeway account was six months in arrears with the chandler—but that was a chronic problem with every merchant." She frowned. "There was an argument in the linen draper's about a year ago."

"John actually visited a shop?" He sounded so incredulous that she smiled.

"No. Now that I think on it, Lord Northrup caused that contretemps. Mrs. Ruddy was attending a sick relative, so when Ruddy's daughter contracted influenza, he asked Rose Moore to watch the shop for a few days. But she wasn't very knowing about the stock. Northrup thought she was disrespectful and knocked her down. Ruddy came down from Alice's sickroom and found what Northrup needed. Gave him a good price, too, just to smooth over his temper."

He couldn't see how the incident related to John, but he would relay it to Mary. Frederick had died shortly thereafter.

Miss Hardaway continued to ramble, relating old gossip, rumors, and speculation, but nothing of interest turned up.

He reviewed her information as he drove back to the Court. The gossip had confirmed his impressions of Robby. The lad had talked more freely after meeting with Forbes, but he knew little more than what Mary had already reported. He had hired on after Frederick's death, so his sole contact with John had been the morning the note appeared. Veiled warnings from the other employees had revealed that John was a man to fear. Other mutterings gave the impression that John and his friends engaged in outrageous practices, but no one ever spoke of specifics for fear of reprisal. Since Robby had witnessed nothing for himself, he wasn't much help.

He sighed. No one else was willing to talk beyond generalities. But the note did help, moving the tenants to the bottom of his list of suspects. Not that their grievances were petty, but John would never have met one away from the Court. Of course, the note might have lied, claiming to be from someone else. He thought it unlikely, though. Few of the tenants could write, and none could write well enough to forge the hand of someone John would trust. Besides, impersonating a friend would require intimate knowledge of John's affairs—information unlikely to come a tenant's way. But a tenant might have taken advantage of finding him out alone.

Unlikely, he decided, recalling the isolation of the ridge. So who were his prime suspects?

Mr. Derwyn lived too far away to be responsible for the attack near the quarry, so he joined the tenants at the bottom of the list.

Sir Tristan was another matter. He was the owner of the estate beyond Brewster's Ridge, the estate reached by that rarely traveled path. The rumors were vague, but the fact that they had carried so far from Sir Tristan's home gave them veracity. So Sir Tristan was a definite suspect.

Walden could both have written and destroyed the note. He was the one man John had met with before his death. If they had argued, John would not have ridden out to meet him, but even a minor incident might have snapped Walden's temper. Or he might have discovered that John meant to turn him off. No evidence supported such a plot, but John may have wanted a more villainous steward.

What about Bridwell? He had a past he wanted to hide. Perhaps John had threatened to expose him or was trying to force him into some new crime. Bridwell could have summoned him on the pretense of accepting his orders.

Or Barnes could have lured him. He might have overheard something incriminating at the inn. And he might have samples of handwriting that would allow him to impersonate one of John's friends. His anger would have been hot when Frederick died, and John's refusal to repair the damage—which bit deeply into Barnes's income—would have kept his temper on the boil for months.

How many of the local gentlemen had John fleeced at cards?

His head ached. He had never thought of himself as naïve. He had traveled the world, witnessed the depredations of war, watched easily inflamed Latin passions explode into mayhem, ignored the torture and butchery that petty Indian princes inflicted on their enemies. But even knowing John since before birth had not prepared him for finding such evil and pain in his own home.

He slowed his team as he entered the woods. Since the attack, driving here had made him nervous, but this was the shortest route from town. Taking the longer road would add miles to the journey and concede victory to his unseen enemy.

Yet he hated these woods. Eyes alert, he scanned the trees, looking for any hint of movement. He had seen nothing the first time, though the culprit must have been fairly close. The difficulty of throwing that rock between the trees would have jumped drastically with even a small increase in distance.

Every rustle made him flinch. But only birds and squirrels roamed today. Their friendly chatter declared that he was alone.

Miss Hardaway was beginning to accept him. Everyone else in town had been polite, but wary—Barnes, Ruddy, Bridwell, the inn's head groom, the chandler, the confectioner. They did not trust him. It might take years before they welcomed him.

He breathed a sigh of relief as he left the trees behind. But his imagination was far from dead. He could feel eyes boring into his back as he carefully skirted the quarry. Rounding the narrowest corner, he flinched, picturing the long fall he would have taken if Mary had not somehow halted his team. His eyes followed the ribbons and measured the width of the road. How had she done it?

He shivered.

His mind needed a rest. For the remainder of the trip, he considered ways to convince Mary to dance with him at Sir Richard's party.

Pulling up before the Court, he handed the phaeton to a groom and headed for the library. But he had hardly settled into his chair when Forbes appeared in the doorway.

"What is it?"

"Matt asks that you come to the stable, my lord."

James frowned, but Matt was his own groom, who had been with him for fifteen years, had accompanied him on his travels, and had no connection to Ridgeway.

He was halfway to the stable before he thought of the other possibility. He had only Forbes's word that Matt had requested this meeting. Was Forbes conspiring with whomever had killed John? The butler had seemed less suspicious since receiving Turnby's endorsement, but it might have been an act.

His eyes darted right and left. A hedge screened the stable yard from the formal gardens. Was someone lurking behind it?

Where was the usual bustle? No grooms exercised horses. No stable boys carried used straw to the refuse pile. No coachmen polished the brass fittings on their conveyances.

Silence thrummed in his ears. Chills crawled up his spine.

Then Matt appeared in the doorway, and the scene returned to normal.

Laughter echoed from beyond the dog run. Peering around a corner, he spotted two stable boys fencing with staves, cheered on by half a dozen grooms. One of the boys tripped, sprawling face first into the mud. Renewed laughter rolled across the yard. The lad's opponent helped him to his feet, then squared off for another round.

Matt touched his arm. "I thought you should see this," he said softly, leading him around the other end of the building. He squatted, pointing to the phaeton.

Red mist welled up to blind him. Someone had cut halfway through the rear axle. Another attempt.

" 'Twere fine when you left," vowed Matt. "I checked her meself. Don't trust the lads here none."

"Why?"

"They none of 'em liked your brother, milord. There's been too much mutterin' 'bout identical twins to my way o' thinking, despite me swearin' you were far away all those years. Don't know if it's more'n mutterin', but I ain't takin' no chances. I keeps a close eye on the horses and equipment."

"I appreciate that. It happened in town, then. Had to. I left it in a corner of the inn's stable yard, but I didn't unhitch the horses because I wasn't planning to stay long."

The inn had been busy, so the ostler had kept his grooms jumping. They would have had no time to admire his rig—or to notice if someone else had been doing so.

Thank God he had driven slowly. Speeding over the quarry road would have made the phaeton bounce, cracking the axle and spilling him out. If it had happened on that narrow corner—which was quite possible, given the condition of that road—he would have gone over the side. People might have noticed the cut on the phaeton's axle, but by then it would have been too late.

He fought down shudders at how close he had come to dying.

Again. But the killer had underestimated the impact of his earlier attempt. Either the man did not expect him to be cautious near the quarry, or he did not know that Mary had recognized his intentions.

Mary.

He could not afford to make assumptions. Would the killer strike Mary to silence any chance she might know?

Later, he decided. It was more important to fit this attack with his other facts.

The culprit had known he was in town that day. Either he had been there on his own business and taken advantage of an unexpected opportunity, or he had followed him there. Which narrowed his list of primary suspects to those in town, those on the estate, or those he had passed on the road.

Had Walden stayed in the area, hiding out in the woods or in an abandoned cottage? There was such a cottage halfway to town. He would check it in the morning for signs of occupancy.

He had passed two tenants, the Adams brothers, and Sir Richard on his way to town, but someone else might have spotted him and hidden until he drove past.

Besides the town's residents, any of whom could have seen him, Isaac had waved before disappearing into the doctor's house—probably not a professional visit; the two had been friends since childhood. Sir Maxwell had come out of the tailor's. Lady Carworth had been chatting with Mrs. Bridwell. And those were only the ones he had noticed. Market day brought dozens of people to town. Others could have seen him and stayed out of his sight.

He returned to the library and poured a glass of brandy. His head hurt.

This second attempt put paid to the notion that someone had wanted to discourage further investigation into John's death. The killer was serious—which meant Mary was also in danger. She had asked as many questions as he had.

Whatever his feelings about the attacks on him, he would not tolerate injury to Mary.

Chapter Thirteen

Mary sank onto the bench in the rose garden and wept. Damn James! Damn him, damn him, damn him! He had destroyed her peaceful retreat.

Amelia had been bursting with happiness that morning as they planned the ball that would celebrate the betrothals. Mary had tried to be supportive, had tried to share her joy—and she had carried it off. But the effort had brought on the headache that was pounding her temples and pressing against the backs of her eyes until they threatened to pop onto the ground.

How could she place Amelia's life in the hands of a libertine? Yet how could she stop it?

The deed was done. Justin had approved. Letters had already been dispatched to Harry's family and the newspapers. Amelia could not back out now without ruining herself.

Mary dabbed at her eyes. Never had she felt more helpless. After eight years of running the estate, making all the decisions, approving every action, she had not even been consulted about so important a decision. Women rarely were, of course, but she was finding the transition to the traditional subordinate role more onerous than she had expected.

It should not have surprised her. Since her earliest childhood, she had assumed more responsibility than was considered seemly. First with her family, then with the Northrups. How quickly life could change. Two weeks had stripped her of everything. Even a role as lady of the manor was denied her here, for the widow of the previous lord had authority over nothing.

New tears flowed. Amelia's life had changed even faster. How could she know Harry well enough to wed him, when she had met him only ten days ago? He could easily keep a genial facade in place that long. Frederick had done so for the entire month between their betrothal and their wedding. John had been adept at hiding his true nature until after he had achieved his goal. Even Edwin might be living a lie.

But she was powerless to break the betrothals, powerless to order investigations into their backgrounds, powerless to protect the girls from harm. The admission filled her with panic. Her life was out of her control, as were the lives of those she loved. And she was powerless to stop it.

Hoping to at least calm her panic, she had sought the peace of her rose garden where the scents of a thousand blooms would soothe away her pain.

But James had stripped her even of peace. The garden no longer offered surcease. He remained there—huge, virile, tempting her down a path that would destroy her.

Why had he accosted her here? Anyplace else would have been better—the house, the stables, out on the road. Instead, he had tainted her one refuge.

Her fists clenched, remembering his touch. Shivers rolled up her arms—but not from fear. Warmth pooled in her womb. Her breasts tightened, growing heavier, prodding her to awareness. His kiss still tingled on her lips.

She swore again, fleeing the garden that no longer offered sanctuary. He must be in league with Satan. How else could he affect her so strongly? He was bigger than Frederick—taller, broader, stronger. Capitulating to his demands would kill her.

Yet she wanted to. Insidious devil that he was, he had made her desire him. The intensity in those dark eyes stopped her breath whenever he pinned her with a glance, coiling heat inside that could burst into flames with the slightest hint of that crooked smile. Even his tension aroused her, for she knew he held himself in check with difficulty. Every gesture made it worse, for she could imagine those long finger stroking her, those beautiful hands cradling her breasts, his lips—

Please, God, no, she pleaded, almost running as she approached the stables.

A laugh floated out to meet her. Lighthearted. Carefree. Trailing into giggles.

Mary rounded a corner and stopped. Sunlight drenched an emerald-green lawn and the stately oak that had stood there for more than a century. Blue sky blazed overhead, dotted with tiny puff clouds. Mary's heart calmed as she gazed on the peaceful scene.

Caro's yellow dress could not have had a more perfect backdrop as she sprawled on the grass amid half a dozen puppies. She giggled as a pink tongue washed her face and another tickled one ear. Two of them pounced on her legs. Another gnawed playfully at her fingers.

Edwin sat in the shade, absently petting the mother as yet another puppy chewed on his boot. His eyes watched Caro, his face revealing such love that Mary caught her breath.

The puppy abandoned his boot to chase its tail, yelping when he caught it. Caro grabbed the hapless fellow, tickling his tummy as Edwin laughed and another of the pups raced after a butterfly.

Mary backed away, loath to intrude. But the image had lightened her heart. Such innocent pleasure was outside her experience—as was Edwin's approval of it. Not even her father would have tolerated chewed boots.

But Edwin did not seem to care, and he had reveled in Caro's fun.

She released a sigh, admitting that Caro's future was secure. And perhaps Amelia would be all right, too. Edwin and James both swore that Harry was honest and caring, though it was impossible to imagine *him* sitting on the ground with a litter of puppies.

She laughed, then laughed again when she realized that her headache was gone.

James frowned as he rode toward Northfield. Harry and Edwin were already there, but he needed to see Mary. And it had to be alone.

The second murder attempt had shaken him badly. It had taken all of a largely sleepless night to bring his emotions under control—a vital step, for he could not afford to break down around Mary. He needed to hold her, to absorb her strength so he could banish his own fears. Only then could he protect her from harm. But she was not ready for that.

Besides, she had needed time before facing him again. Calling yesterday would have pressured her, strengthening her determination to resist him.

But they must talk.

He had stopped at two empty cottages that morning. Neither held any sign of recent occupancy. Both floors were covered in dust, undisturbed by any feet. If Walden remained in the area, he was hiding in a remote location. No one had seen him.

At least Mary was at home and agreed to speak with him. But one glance revealed that she had set even more distance between them than he had feared.

"I will apologize again for my behavior at our last meeting," he said once greetings were out of the way and she had offered him a glass of wine. "Then we will put the incident behind us."

"Very well, my lord," she said coolly.

"It won't happen again," he promised. "Not because I didn't enjoy it, and not because I don't wish to repeat it, but because I respect you too much to cause you distress."

Her eyes widened, though she said nothing.

"There is a problem, however," he continued calmly. "I vowed not to touch you without permission, and I intend to honor that vow. But Sir Richard's dancing party is tomorrow. Your rank is such that refusing to dance with you will cause speculation. So we can either share one set—country dances involve little contact—or I can decline to attend. Your choice."

"But staying away will reflect poorly on you and insult Sir Richard."

"I can live with that."

She bit her lip. "I cannot. One set, my lord."

"Thank you. It will be the highlight of the evening. Harry tells me that you remain concerned about his reputation," he continued, giving her no time to react to his claim. He shifted his eyes to the portrait above the mantel to avoid her white face and clenched hands. She looked so fragile, he wanted to pull her into his arms and promise her safety.

Frederick's father provided a suitable distraction. He had never realized how shifty the baron had looked, his beady narrow-set eyes far too like a fellow he had known in India. Ashwini had been his chief clerk for two years, but he had come to a bad end, helped to the afterlife by a group of street assassins. Somehow, they had known that Ashwini had stolen the packet of gems his office manager had left unattended for a moment.

"I cannot help it," Mary said on a long sigh. "Everything happened so fast. How can any of us know whether he is sincere?"

"Sooner or later, you will have to let yourself trust, Mary." He ignored her glare at the intimate address. Despite his own brief acquaintance, he had forged deep bonds with both of his companions since arriving at Ridgeway. "No one can deny that Harry has enjoyed life. But he is responsible and takes his vows seriously. He inherited a prosperous estate from his grandmother, and has an enviable knack for wise investing—fortunate in a younger son who must provide for his own future. And he loves Amelia deeply."

"He says he does, but how can I believe him? Ten days ago he did not even know she existed."

"Do you think a Season in London would have given them more time to become acquainted?"

She nodded. "Three or four months of attending a variety of activities would certainly reveal more of his character."

"Mary, you don't understand London." This time he met her glare. "I lived there for two years before my father died, and I just spent two months attending Marriage Mart events, so do not imply you know more of London than I."

Not until she acknowledged his expertise did he continue. "A gentleman cannot pay close court to a lady without offering for her, which makes it nearly impossible for two people to become acquainted before committing themselves. Think about it. Sharing a set at a ball will allow them to exchange perhaps a dozen brief comments—none of a profound nature. But sharing a second set raises expectations."

"That is true of country sets, but what of the waltz?" she demanded skeptically.

"Yes, waltzing allows more conversation, but it was only approved at Almack's this past Season and is still frowned upon for young girls. Waltzing twice with the same lady will definitely raise expectations. As will dancing with her several nights in a row. They might drive in the park, but even there, most conversation is with other people. Driving more than once raises expectations, as does including her in theater parties, paying morning calls, taking her to an art exhibit, or nearly anything else. He must pay equal attention to several ladies if he is to avoid linking his name to one. Once those names are linked, he risks both of their reputations if he does not offer for her."

"So how does he choose a wife?" Her forehead was deeply creased.

"After checking her family, her dowry, and her connections, he tries to divine her character from a few superficial meetings and judges her interest through an exchange of flirtatious glances. And he prays that he will discover her faults before he is too involved to cry off. But even a betrothal gives a couple little chance to become acquainted. Living in each other's pocket is frowned upon, as is any contact that might call her virtue into question, so they will continue to be surrounded by other people until after the wedding."

"That sounds awful."

"But true. You must realize that aristocratic marriages are still arranged mostly for financial and dynastic reasons. I knew more about the last horse I bought at auction than about any young lady I met in London. Harry and Amelia have already spent more time together and discussed more serious topics than they could have managed in two or three Seasons, even had they been betrothed. They love each other, something few society couples ever experience. Most know little beyond the superficial until after marriage, so they are lucky if they develop a comfortable friendship."

"I understand that, but love can also cloud perceptions. What happens when he decides that Amelia will discredit him in society? He has lived in London for years, but Amelia knows little of town and has never craved excitement. He is attracted now because she seems so different from his usual flirt, but I fear he will soon grow bored."

"No one can predict the future," he admitted. "But I honestly believe his heart is engaged. He was seriously looking for a wife last Season, having grown tired of languishing in town, but he wants a wife of substance. I have often heard him complain that the girls making their bows were shallow and selfish. Amelia is not."

"True." Mary's voice had relaxed. "Perhaps this will prove good for her. I just hope that she is not overwhelmed by town. One cannot expect him to eschew London in the future."

"No." He could not erase every fear, he conceded. "In fact, his father has offered him a seat in Commons. But Amelia seems a levelheaded young lady whose training will see her through every challenge."

He had deliberately introduced the idea, because Mary had been responsible for that training. He suspected that many of her fears mirrored her own concerns. She did not feel comfortable even in local society, so she assumed that Amelia shared that unease.

"You have a point," she conceded when he dared mention this conjecture. "But not entirely. Neither of the girls is at ease in company. Frederick was not well liked, and my reputation is tarnished. Because I raised them, people question their morals. And gossip being what it is, the rumors will carry far beyond Shropshire. A single incident could ruin her in town."

"But Harry's reputation will protect her," he reminded her.

"Destroy her, more like."

"Mary." He sighed. "London society is not Ridgefield, and men have always been judged by different standards than women, even here." He caught her glare and returned a rueful smile. "I agree that it is unfair, but that is the way of the world."

She nodded.

"John was despicable by any standard, but Harry and other young bucks are beloved by all." He met her gaze. "Yes, he conducted several affairs, but only with ladies of a certain class."

"Courtesans?" She glared.

"Willing companions," he corrected her gently. "Society expects such escapades from single gentlemen. They look askance on those who eschew them, for a gentleman is supposed to bring experience to his marriage bed. Harry never knowingly bedded a married woman, though society would have shrugged if he had, so long as the meetings were discreet."

She gasped.

"I know that your upbringing was different, but the *ton* does not always follow church teachings. All that matters is that Harry is honorable. He does not seduce innocents; he does not fleece greenlings; he does not lie or cheat."

"So a gentleman is welcomed as long as his adultery is discreet and his fleecing confined to men old enough to know better?"

"All too true," he answered before he spotted the twinkle in her eye. He laughed. "You are far more knowing than you let on. Many gentlemen have flexible ideas about what constitutes dishonor. But my friends and I take a literal view. Marriage vows include fidelity. Breaking them is dishonorable. Harry would never do so, which is what you really wanted to know, isn't it?"

She nodded, but he knew there was more, for other fears shadowed her eyes. He ignored her uneasiness about moving into aristocratic society. That could be dealt with later, but this might be a good time to give her something to ponder.

"Harry will be gentle with her, Mary. He would never hurt her, for allowing fear into his bed would reduce the pleasure for both of them."

She snorted, though she tried to cover the sound with a cough.

"I am serious, Mary. Intimacy is beautiful, bringing enjoyment to both parties. It is true that a brutal man can make it painful, but that changes the nature of the contact to assault. Think about it."

"Very well."

"Good. Have you learned anything new since we last spoke?"

"Nothing. But contemplation has forced me to admit that you are probably right about Frederick."

"That he was murdered?"

She nodded. "Justin talked to Squire Church yesterday. The evidence for accident seems conclusive at first glance, but it does not stand up under scrutiny."

"Did he notice marks on the road?"

"He didn't look. He found a man with a broken neck in the

bottom of a quarry, so he decided the fall had killed him. Frederick's clothes were muddy despite landing on bare rock, thus he must have fallen from his horse onto the muddy road. Drunkenness explained how he wandered over the edge."

"But?" She had accepted murder, so there had to be more.

"The fall was a straight drop—no projections to snag him on the way down, for the quarry wall undercuts the road at that point. He did not roll once he landed on his right side, yet his left temple carried a wound." She stared at his head where he had absently shoved the hair back, exposing his own cut. "One could make a case that he struck his head when he fell from his horse, but the tops of both boots were full of mud."

"Somebody pulled him to the edge."

"I believe so, and it must have been the same man who attacked you. Since your only provocation was asking about John's death, the three incidents have to be related."

He nodded. "I also spoke with Isaac, and got a more detailed description of John's injuries. They included a blow to one temple—which was why Isaac assumed John had been overpowered by a larger, stronger assailant."

"But it was a rock, so the motive must relate to something John and Frederick both did. But that is more likely to involve people from London. They came here rarely and never remained long."

"Nonetheless, the culprit is here. John fled after Frederick's death, returning to London. Why would a London killer wait to dispatch him until after he had returned to Ridgeway? Besides, yesterday's attack removes the last doubt."

Mary's heart leaped into her throat. Another attempt? Heat and cold washed over her in waves.

"What happened?" Somehow, she kept her voice steady, though she had to set down her cup lest her hands betray their shaking. She wanted to leap up and examine him for wounds.

"While I was visiting Ridgefield yesterday, someone sawed halfway through the axle of my phaeton. If I had been speeding as gentlemen are wont to do, it would have broken on that curve by the quarry."

She shivered. "How long were you in town?"

"Most of the day."

"That does not help much, then. It was market day. Anyone could have been there."

"And probably was. But the note that drew John to his death must have come from someone he trusted—or someone who impersonated someone he trusted."

"I doubt it." She met his eyes straight on, then nearly lost track of her thoughts as heat again coiled inside. "He would have invited a trusted friend to the Court. I believe he went out because he did *not* trust the man. The note made him so furious that he intended to settle matters his own way, possibly by killing its writer when he reached the meeting site."

He frowned. "It is possible. He was clearly ambushed."

"There is an abandoned shepherd's hut on Brewster's Ridge a quarter mile past where his body was found. Perhaps that was the meeting place." She sighed. "I wish I knew what the note said. Maybe the man was blackmailing him, or had threatened blackmail to draw him out."

"You have a devious mind."

She would have taken offense, but he had spoken absently, still in shock over admitting that John might have plotted murder. Learning such truths about a brother was bad enough. Being a twin must make it worse. Twins were supposed to be close.

"Maybe I'm wrong," she said, more to console him than because she believed it.

"No, it fits too well, and places Sir Tristan at the top of my suspect list."

"Why?"

"Rumor claims that John debauched Sir Tristan's daughter. John was killed midway between Ridgeway and Sir Tristan's estate."

"I never believed the rumors about Julia. John had been gone for two months before they started."

"So you think he was innocent?"

"Of that charge, yes. Why would she hide it so long?"

"Maybe she discovered she was increasing."

"That's a thought. Or perhaps they had an affair, but she claimed rape when her father discovered she was no longer innocent. Or she might have had an affair with someone else, but cited John to protect her lover—everyone knew he had a roving eye and would resort to force if seduction failed. Or her lover might have started the rumors because she spurned him."

He sighed. "You can think of far too many possibilities. A lady should not know so much about the sordid side of life."

"Why? Ignorance makes one vulnerable. If I had been less naïve in my youth, I would have done a better job of avoiding him." She bit off her words, but it was too late to recall them.

"Did John force you?"

His voice had turned dangerous, revealing a fury she could not explain.

"No. He tried to seduce me, but I refused."

"And he just dropped it?"

"He was young enough at the time to retain a few scruples, though I had to strike him before he accepted my reluctance. But he never forgave me for turning him down."

"Thus the lies he spread. How old were you?"

"Sixteen." She shrugged.

Back in 1800. Damnation. "I wish I had known."

"Why? Short of killing him, you could have done nothing without hurting me worse. Don't you understand him yet?"

Pain squeezed his eyes shut. "Yes, I understand him far too well. You bested him, something he would never have forgiven. His original lies hurt you but did not ruin your life. So he drove off your suitor with worse stories, which added credence to his earlier tales. And he ordered the Bridwells to keep the stories alive. Did he have a hand in arranging your marriage?"

"No. Frederick's guardian suggested that. He wanted the lot of them off his hands as quickly as possible. John did not learn of it until later. Then he took Frederick under his wing."

"Frederick and John would have become friends and allies anyway," he pointed out. "They were too much alike."

"Enough. There is another problem with Sir Tristan," she said, ruthlessly returning to business, though she should have realized ten years ago that John had driven George away. It was so obvious. "The killer struck down Frederick as well. But no rumor connects him with Julia."

"Perhaps not, but it would not have been the first time they'd shared a victim." He snapped his mouth shut, proving that he had not meant to reveal that.

"I don't need protection. After seven years as his wife, nothing surprises me." She sighed. "But you are ignoring the killer's choice of weapons. Rocks and knives are hardly aristocratic tools. Wouldn't Sir Tristan have used a pistol if he wished to dispatch John?"

"A pistol would call dueling to mind, casting suspicion on gentlemen with recent grievances. Surely he is smart enough to choose weapons that would point to the lower classes."

"Then why kill John on a lane leading to his own estate?"

He frowned. "Perhaps he didn't think of that since the murder was actually on Ridgeway land."

"Don't blind yourself as Squire Church does," she warned. "If you have to twist the evidence to make it fit a theory, then the theory is invalid. It is more likely that the killer chose the spot because the rumors supplied a ready scapegoat. So who else do you suspect?"

He frowned, but allowed her to move on. "Walden. He could have easily lured John away from the house—inspecting an estate problem, for example. And he would be able to destroy the note if John had not already done so."

"True, but he was a meek man. Why would he have harmed Frederick?"

"Perhaps it was an accident. He couldn't express his rage at John, but it might have burst out at another target. He might have met Frederick near the quarry and found himself in a quarrel. If John learned the truth, he would have sought revenge. Or more likely, John would have used his knowledge to blackmail Walden into some other crime. Seeing endless repercussions over an unintentional death, Walden would have had to eliminate John."

"Interesting theory. You also have a remarkable imagination. So why did John leave after Frederick's death?"

He frowned. "Coincidence?"

"Unlikely. What about your tenants?"

"I had discounted them, for few of them can write and none well enough to impersonate a friend. But if someone was blackmailing him, then they will have to go back on the list."

"But what had he done locally that might attract blackmail? He was rarely here. A blackmailer was more likely to come from elsewhere."

He muttered what sounded like imprecations. "Perhaps John killed Frederick. That would explain his flight. And if someone saw him, they might consider blackmail."

"Which puts everyone on the list, not just the tenants."

"That is true anyway. There is not a resident for miles who doesn't have a motive."

"True. But which of them has the strength and accuracy to knock three men senseless with rocks?"

"Ouch!"

She raised her brows.

"I had not considered that particular skill, but it is crucial. I will have to inquire about who throws well. Yesterday's incident eliminates no one, for anyone in town would have had access to my phaeton. It was parked in an out-of-the-way corner of the inn's stable yard."

"Speaking of the inn, what about Barnes? Both John and Frederick were there the night the fire started. And Barnes is both a champion quoits player and an accurate thrower. I saw him pick off a rabbit at twenty paces one day."

"And he could tamper with my phaeton without drawing attention."

She frowned. "Not really. He is rarely in the stable yard, so draws the eyes of every groom when he appears."

Another theory gone. "Then there is Bridwell."

"Did he have a complaint against Frederick?"

"I don't know, but he has a big one against me. I sent notice to the bishop yesterday that I wished to replace Bridwell with your brother. If he heard about the letter, he could easily guess at its contents."

Howard would be pleased to have his own living, for it would allow him to wed. But James's voice deflected her thoughts, flowing over her like velvet and raising desire. *Intimacy is beautiful. . . .* Warmth and yearning choked her breast. She wanted his arms around her, his lips on hers, his—

Don't trust him! It's a trick! But the yearning increased, reminding her that life was empty, nights were long, and she had no one who could share her thoughts. Once the girls wed, she would have no one at all.

His words no longer made sense. She was falling into the rich depths of his eyes. His voice wove spells that bound her, paralyzed her, froze her thoughts. The warmth burst into flames, consuming her body. Not until he moved did she escape.

"I will let you know if I learn anything new," he promised, standing.

She automatically rose. "Thank you." What else could she say? She had no idea what he proposed to do.

Her hand reached out, without thought. Smiling, he raised it to his lips, then bade her farewell. But his fingers lightly caressed her palm before he released her, weakening her knees. By the time she stiffened them, he was gone.

James kept his face solemn until he was away from the Manor, then he laughed. He had her. She was firmly hooked. All he had to do now was reel her in.

He shifted in the saddle. He would have stayed longer, but caution had sent him away. In another minute, he would have swept her into his arms—and would have terrified her into locking the doors against him.

She cared. She wanted him as much as he wanted her, but the fear still lurked. Desire had shoved it aside for one glorious moment, but he had not yet won the battle. It was that naked yearning that had eroded his control. Without her fear to hold him at bay, he didn't trust himself.

He groaned.

He might be frustrated out of his mind right now, but he had to keep it slow. At least she had granted him a dance.

He pulled his mind away from long legs and a generous bosom, unclenching his stomach muscles in his effort to relax. She had thought of possibilities he had not considered, giving him yet more paths to follow. Investigating those would keep him occupied.

The man stared into the fire, cursing his failure. The cut had been too shallow.

Sawing that axle had been risky, for he had been in a public place in broad daylight. The specter of eyes boring into his back had made his hands shake. And his fear of exposure had made him flee before testing his work.

And so he had failed.

It was time to end it. Long past time. He could no longer rely on an accident. This last effort would raise suspicions anyway. He doubted Ridgeway would consider the cut a prank.

So no more chances. Their next encounter would be decisive. And he had little to fear. No one connected him with John's death. No one suspected that Northrup's accident had been well-deserved retribution. Ridgeway's demise would cause talk, but it should not affect him.

Soon it would be over. Soon he could find peace. Soon . . .

Sir Richard and Lady Redfield considered themselves the luckiest of hosts. Not only were they holding the first formal gathering since word had spread of the Northrup betrothals, but they had no marriageable daughters, so they were not bemoaning the loss of the most eligible gentlemen to appear in Ridgefield in some time. Pity the poor women who were sponsoring elaborate entertainments but now had no chance of snaring a match. Few considered Ridgeway a viable choice. Of course, there was still Northrup. Three-and-twenty wasn't *that* young. Seven years of military life had aged him.

Mary smiled as Lucy Granger batted her lashes at Justin. The girl was on her best behavior tonight, determined to erase the memory of her last public appearance.

Lady Redfield did not call her modest gathering a ball. Instead, she had patterned her evening after the informal waltzing parties that were all the rage in London. A full quarter of the sets were waltzes, though she included many other steps in deference to country sensibilities.

Mary had made a point of disapproving the waltz since the first military man returning from the Continent had described it. Allowing a gentleman to hold her in his arms was a repugnant idea, but tonight she perversely wished to participate. James danced divinely, and *his* arms would have been welcome.

Or so that insidious voice insisted. She couldn't get rid of the plaguey thing, proving that James had already seduced her conscience. Would her body be next?

"Scandalous!" hissed Miss Hardaway from the next chair. "I never thought to see your charges waltzing."

"Nor I, but I could hardly refuse them permission to dance with their betrotheds, and Justin had already agreed."

"Of course a man would agree," said Miss Hardaway. "My sister in Southampton tells me scandalous tales about officers."

"Who is betrothed?" interrupted Miss Sharpe. "Why was I not told?"

"She never remembers anything." Miss Hardaway sounded pleased.

"Amelia has accepted Mr. Crenshaw, and Caroline is to wed Sir Edwin," Mary explained. "Those are the gentlemen who are dancing with them right now."

"How delighted you must be." Miss Sharpe actually clapped her hands.

"Quite."

"You should have remembered," said Miss Hardaway chidingly. "I've already told you three times."

But Mary knew the gossip didn't mind. Miss Sharpe's failing memory provided a perpetual audience for her tales.

She wrenched her eyes from the dancers. James was twirling Miss Lawton around the room. The girl was an exquisite beauty despite her minimal breeding. He seemed enchanted.

One hand had closed into a fist, so she deliberately relaxed it.

Miss Hardaway repeated the latest gossip, with Miss Sharpe's shrieks of surprise and wails of sorrow punctuating each story. Mary listened without comment, but nothing could explain why the sabotage to James's phaeton had gone unnoticed.

James led her out for their country dance. By the time they had completed one pattern, she was grateful it was not a waltz. Every touch of his hand burned through her gloves. Every brush of his body weakened her knees until she feared she would collapse. Warmth burned her cheeks, posting her thoughts for all to read.

"You seem overheated. Shall we find some lemonade?" he asked when the set concluded. "And perhaps a corner where we can talk privately for just a moment?"

She nodded, praying that he would attribute her flush to an unusually warm evening. But he was too good at reading her mind for her to believe it.

"Have you learned something new?" she asked when they had retired to Lady Redfield's morning room.

"Not exactly, but I did some thinking after leaving you yesterday. If I hadn't been so furious over the attack, I would have realized it sooner. Only someone who lived in town could have cut that axle."

"Why?" She concentrated on her lemonade, ignoring his shoulders, which stretched even wider under an elegant wine-colored jacket trimmed in black velvet. Tonight's cravat jewel was a ruby.

"To inflict the damage, the culprit had to crawl underneath my phaeton—and probably lie on the ground. But that corner was rather muddy. Who would risk it unless they had clean clothes nearby?"

"A very good argument. Who knew you would be in town that day?"

"No one. It was a decision I made after leaving the Court. I had originally intended to call on Isaac."

"So the attack was spontaneous. Could Barnes have reached that corner without being spotted by one of the grooms?"

"Not unless something distracted the entire stable staff."

She sighed. "Miss Hardaway was recounting gossip just now, but none of the tales would have done so." The words were almost random because he was staring at her mouth. She ought to walk over and look out the window, but her feet seemed stuck to the floor.

"What was the most exciting story?" he asked, then slowly licked his lips.

What? Mesmerized by the seductive passage of his tongue, she had no idea what he'd said. Had he asked her a question? She couldn't move, couldn't think, couldn't escape the heat pouring through her body. The corners of his mouth twitched upward.

"I want to kiss you, Mary."

She clenched both hands around her glass to keep from stroking his chest. The ruby pulsed in the candlelight, inviting her touch, promising fiery pleasure and ecstasy beyond imagining.

"I am asking permission," he continued softly, sliding close to lift her chin with the tip of one finger. "You need not fear me, now or ever. I would never hurt you."

She raised her eyes, but saw only longing in his. There was none of the cruel calculation she had once spotted when Frederick looked at a new maid.

"Please, Mary?" He offered his hand.

Fear curled in her stomach, but she could not deny him. Slowly she set down the glass and laid a hand in his. Gently he drew it to his lips, pressing a kiss to her wrist where he had flicked open two buttons on her glove. His other hand stroked down the side of her neck and across her shoulder.

Despite her high-necked gown, she shivered.

"One kiss?"

She nodded, expecting a repeat of the kiss in the garden. But it wasn't.

He brushed his lips across her mouth, exhaling gently. It was she who turned back for more, who demanded a second touch, then a third.

He nibbled experimentally, making her lips tingle with excitement. She increased the pressure. Her hand slipped around his neck as she stretched on tiptoe to better reach his mouth. The movement brought her against his body, sending sparks stabbing through each breast. Rubbing against his chest created delightful sensations.

He groaned.

His tongue swirled lightly, slipping behind her lips to tease and beg. Fire burst along her veins; every muscle trembled. Whimpering for more, she opened her mouth.

Dear God. He thrust inside, conquering even as he playfully invited participation. The yearning grew until she could barely contain it. Heat collected in a wet pool between her legs.

A stab of fear quickly fled, for he was not constraining her.

One hand rested lightly on her hip. The other moved slowly up her back, leaving warmth in its wake.

He was trembling and taut as a bow string. And hard. *That* part of him strained against her. Another spurt of fear coursed through her mind. Would he lose control and attack?

But again the fear drained away. He used no coercion, instead enticing her with pleasure and sultry promises. She could not pull back. The yearning was too powerful. His touch felt too good. And he would not hurt her.

Merciful heavens, I trust him!

It was James who finally eased away. "That is enough for now," he murmured, his voice husky. "More than enough. But I will leave you with one last thought. Lovemaking is life's greatest joy. It can be wild and frenzied or soft and sweet. But it should never frighten or inflict pain. You know what I want, but I swear on my honor as a gentleman that I will never hurt you."

With that, he slipped out of the room.

Mary collapsed on a couch. What was she to do? And not just about his desire. He had made it clear that he had more honorable intentions than merely bedding her.

How could she give herself to any man? It would put her in his power, giving him control of her life.

Yet how could she live alone after knowing him? She wanted him. If he had pressed, she would have gone to him without pause. His touch had banished the fear—for the moment. Was it a trick?

She was caught on the horns of dilemma. Her plans were made. But leaving sounded less desirable than ever before. That idyllic cottage no longer looked so peaceful.

It looked lonely.

Chapter Fourteen

James stared at the note. It was succinct, but unsigned.

I know who killed your brother, but if he sees us together, he will kill me, too. Meet me in the old mill at dusk.

He frowned.

How had it gotten onto his desk? Forbes denied accepting delivery, as did the footmen. On the other hand, there were so many ways in and out of the Court, anyone could have slipped in.

So who had written it?

Not the miller. Tate had died well before John's murder—which made the mill an ideal place for a clandestine meeting.

Or for a trap.

Yet he could not ignore such tantalizing bait. Exposing the killer would resolve many of his problems. On the other hand, the man had already made two attempts on his life, so he had to be careful.

The most important precaution would be avoiding an ambush. To that end, he would arrive early and hide until the informant appeared. If the man was one of his suspects, he would remain hidden, talking from the safety of his shelter.

But even that wasn't enough. He had no idea how obsessed the killer was or what he had planned. His actions had been inconsistent. Frederick had been knocked senseless and pushed over a cliff. But John had been bound, tortured, then stabbed repeatedly. Was such rage directed personally at John, or had it built up after six months of brooding over the killer's grievance?

More importantly, how angry was he now? So far, the attempts had been more like Frederick, but each failure would have increased his frustration. Would he explode into another murderous frenzy? One well-placed rock would leave him at the man's mercy. So he must take Harry and Edwin along.

Thus he needed hiding places for three men. He hadn't been inside the building for more than twenty years—and it could have changed drastically since Tate's death. If the grinding stones had been removed—common practice when abandoning a mill—he might be facing an empty room.

Slipping the note into his pocket, he called for his horse. He would pay a quick visit to the mill. If the interior offered no concealment, he must devise an alternate plan.

The mill was several miles down the valley, reached most quickly by cutting through Northfield's woods. Since Harry and Edwin were visiting the Manor, he did not expect to run into anyone, so he was surprised when Northrup approached. The baron looked less than pleased to encounter him.

"Would you prefer that I not use the shortcut?" he asked.

Northrup's face flushed. "Of course not. You are welcome to ride here anytime. After all, we often cut through your woods to reach town."

James nodded. "Then what is troubling you?"

"I was heading for Ridgeway. I must ask your intentions toward Mary." He sounded apologetic, his youth making the question almost impudent.

"I mean her no harm."

"Perhaps, but you could harm her nonetheless. She is vulnerable just now."

"Why? She was not attached to Frederick, is accustomed to being in charge, and is quite definite in her opinions."

"True, but her life is in turmoil. Whatever his failings, Frederick's death means tremendous change for her." Northrup met his eyes squarely. "I will not pretend he was a good man, for I knew him too well. Escaping him was one of my reasons for buying colors."

"So Lady Northrup said."

"By vulnerable, I meant that she faces many adjustments. As good as her stewardship has been, I must oversee my own property. Those who have condemned her for taking on a man's job hail my actions as proof of her incompetence, reviving all the malicious gossip that has plagued her for years—much of it started by your brother. Your attentions are making it worse, for most people believe you had an affair with her ten years ago. Why else would an earl's son befriend a vicar's daughter? Some think you left because she tried to force you into marriage to make up for losing George."

"False. Every word of it."

"I believe you, though few will. Which is why you should cease calling on her. Rumors already claim that you have resumed the affair. Several people noted your absence from the party last night. She has borne more than her share of insults in past years. I won't have her hurt again."

"Nor I, but I will not allow petty gossip to dictate my behavior."

"A pretty vow, but it disregards the effect on Mary."

"I will not hurt her, but neither will I be blackmailed into avoiding her."

"Why?"

"Three reasons. The first is practical—she is helping me investigate John's murder, and has discovered information I would not have found on my own. The second is perverse—I refuse to give the Bridwells even a temporary victory; they will be leaving soon, and I will see that everyone learns why they knowingly repeated lies."

Northrup's eyes widened, so he explained Bridwell's background before continuing. "My third reason is personal—I have every intention of wedding Mary, but she would refuse me if I offered just now. She is still scarred by Frederick's abuse."

He nodded. "And has not forgotten your brother's attack."

"I know he tried to seduce her when she was sixteen, but Mary said nothing about an attack. What do you know of it?"

"I was there." He sighed. "I was hiding in the woods to escape punishment for fighting with Frederick. Since I was up a tree, they did not see me."

James nodded in encouragement as Northrup paused.

"John stopped her as she returned from visiting one of the tenants—right about there, actually." He nodded toward a small clearing twenty feet away. "He first claimed to be you, but she laughed and told him he was a miserable liar. That did not sit well."

"It wouldn't."

"He tried to talk her into a kiss, but she refused, citing an urgent errand. When she backed away from a caress, he pressed her. So she compared him unflatteringly to you. That's when his mood shifted from flirtatious to nasty."

"I am not surprised." Cold clenched his heart. John had needed to be better than everyone—especially his twin. But Mary would not have known that at so tender an age.

"I had seen that same change often enough in Father to know what it meant. When he made his next grab, I started down, thinking maybe I could help her. But she took care of him herself, planting a vicious knee in his privates and cracking him in the temple with her basket. It must have contained something heavy, because he dropped like a rock. She fled. Since my help was no longer needed, I stayed in the tree, fearful of attracting his attention. By the time he recovered enough to leave, she was long gone. The rumors started that very day, accusing her of loose behavior."

And not just because she had bested him, James realized, though that would have been unforgivable on its own. She had seen through his impersonation in an instant—the only one who had done so. Thus he had to discredit her lest she expose his imposture. And he would have made sure his twin's reputation was worse than his own so no one would ever again compare them unfavorably.

"Some of the rumors were about me?"

He nodded. "Those came later. The first tales claimed she had thrown herself at John, enticing him into a lusty affair. Two years passed before the ones about you started."

"All false."

"I know. Anyone who considered the tales impartially must realize that they are suspicious."

"Yet few ever question gossip, which is why I must reveal John's lies and Bridwell's collusion."

Northrup frowned. "Then I must also ask about a tale I heard in India."

What was this? he wondered sharply. He had had more than

one confrontation with East India officials who disapproved of
his trading. The last one had led to a rumor claiming that he had
arranged Ashwini's death to deprive a valued customer of those
gems. False, of course, as even the customer had agreed—he'd
probably been behind the theft himself. Now he suspected that
Rigby had taken advantage of every opportunity to tarnish his
reputation abroad.

"When I first arrived in India, I heard tales about many Englishmen. Because your name was familiar, those concerning
you stuck in my mind."

"They would."

"One claimed that you fathered a boy on your mistress, but
when she demanded that you take them back to England and
acknowledge him, you struck out in anger and killed them
both."

"That is one I have not heard before." It took an effort to control his voice. "It must have started after I left."

"Perhaps."

"It is a very twisted version of the truth. There was a mistress
and there was a child, though neither was mine." He named an
army officer.

Northrup's eyes darkened. "I begin to see. He was a credit
neither to the regiment nor to humanity."

"Was?"

"He died in battle, to no one's regret."

"He tossed the girl out when she disclosed her condition. Her
family refused her a roof, so I took her on as a maid. When I
decided to return to England, I made arrangements for her and
the child to emigrate, but they succumbed to cholera a month
before they were to sail."

Northrup nodded. "I will mention that to Mary—I related the
original tale on returning home." He ignored James's grimace.
"And if you truly care for her, you have my blessing. But don't
hurt her."

He left, continuing toward town.

James relaxed his fists. Poor Mary. She had been ill-used for
years. If only he had identified his attachment earlier, he would
have taken her with him into exile. His love had sprung up long
before his return. The seeds had been sown ten years ago, but

he hadn't been thinking in those terms. And anger and grief had clouded his mind even further.

Somehow he would make it up to her. As soon as he finished this business—which he hoped would be today—he could concentrate on calming her remaining fears.

A tenant passed, doffing his cap, then a farmer and the midwife. As he rounded the next corner, he again jumped. This path seemed as crowded as Park Row during the fashionable hour. Mary pulled her horse to a stop and smiled. Who was chaperoning her sisters?

"Harry and Edwin took the girls for a carriage ride," she answered.

He must have asked the question aloud. "My apologies. I did not mean to impugn your manners, but I just passed Northrup, so I was surprised to see you."

"Were you coming to Northfield?"

"Not this time. I was heading for the mill."

"Have you found a new miller?"

"I can hardly do so without checking the condition of the building. John had authorized no repairs in ten years." But his evasion did not fool her. She could read his mind as easily as he could read hers.

"But that is not your purpose today." She frowned.

"This was on my desk when I awoke this morning." He handed her the note.

"It's a trap," she announced immediately.

"Probably, which is why I must look over the building now. I will take Harry and Edwin tonight."

She nodded thoughtfully, again reading the note. "I've seen this hand before."

"Could it be Walden's?"

"No."

Disappointment forced out a sigh. He had really wanted it to be Walden, who was not a native and had been one of John's minions. "How about Bridwell?"

She shook her head. "His wife writes all their correspondence."

"Another good suspect gone."

"Unless this really is genuine," she pointed out.

"Do you think it might be?"

"No, but stranger things have happened."

He slipped the note back in his pocket. "At least this limits the sender to someone whose hand you have seen—on invitations, perhaps, or on accounts."

"I have probably seen every bit of writing in the area at one time or another, but I've seen this hand quite recently. I just don't remember where at the moment. Perhaps the files will jog my memory. We keep all the receipts, and I still have the responses to our dinner."

"I will call on my way back from the mill—if you will be home by then," he added, remembering that she had been headed away from Northfield.

"Certainly. I was just on my way to Ridgeway. My maid heard something you should know."

"About John's death?"

"I doubt it has any bearing on that, though the tale reflects poorly on him."

"As does everything else I learn about him."

"This one concerns Tom Ruddy's daughter Alice."

"The linen draper?"

She nodded. "Alice died of influenza about a year ago. I paid little attention at the time because I was still in shock over Frederick's accident."

"How long had it been?"

"A few days, maybe a week. I don't really recall. But Alice was a pretty girl who enjoyed flirting—all very innocent; her reputation was spotless. Her only failing was that she was a bit credulous."

"How old was she?"

"Fifteen."

He flinched, afraid he knew where this was going.

"Her death was unfortunate, but not uncommon. Half a dozen people died of influenza last year, and many more suffered."

"But that was hardly John's doing."

"Of course not. But she had gone to Ridgeway a few days earlier, hoping to get a position as a maid. The rumor claims that she not only failed to get the job, but lost her virtue in the process."

How much truth was in the tale? he wondered. Everyone knew Mrs. Washburn never hired young girls. It was her defense against John's lechery. Even the most credulous girl should have known her chances of being hired were nonexistent.

But her claim may have covered her real purpose. John could charm the birds off the trees when he put his mind to it. He never used force until he had failed to gain cooperation. He would have enjoyed seducing the girl, luring her into his lair with either the promise of a job or a tour of the house. Ridgeway contained enough treasures to captivate a simple girl. And too many innocents enjoyed the danger of flirting with a libertine.

She would have stood no chance of escape.

"Thank you for telling me," he said aloud. "I've no doubt the tale is true. And judging from others I've heard, she would have suffered greatly at his hands. Perhaps it is a mercy she contracted influenza. One of his other victims tried to drown herself in the lake."

Mary blanched. Only then did he realize that he had spoken. *Ass!* he berated himself, tempted to beat his head against a tree. How was he to calm Mary's fears after confirming that intimacy was so frightening that girls would rather kill themselves than live with the memory.

"Most men are not like that," he said, forcing calm into his voice. "Which is why John's behavior was so appalling."

"I know," she said, but he could see that she was far from convinced. "I will try to remember where I've seen that hand. Stop at Northfield on your way home. Perhaps we will both know more by then."

She turned down another path and left him.

Mary cursed herself even as she cantered toward the safety of the house. But she had needed to escape his company. The heat in his eyes had made her—just for a moment—long to fling herself into his arms and his bed.

Fool!

He was far more dangerous than his brother, for his kindness weakened her defenses.

Hurling stronger invective at her own stupidity, she dismounted and strode into the house. She had nearly fallen into the same trap as Alice Ruddy—calling at a bachelor establishment. The servants would have repeated the tale, confirming every rumor about her. The resulting scandal could have damaged Caro and Amelia.

Idiot! She didn't even have an excuse. The tale about Alice had no bearing on his investigation. The girl had been dead for a year, so there was certainly no urgency about it. Her real reason for calling was pathetic—she had wanted to see him. If she had needed further confirmation of the danger he posed, she need look no further.

It was time to find that cottage. Staying here was clearly unbalancing her mind. Perhaps Devon would be suitable. Lady Carworth had visited cousins there two years ago, returning with tales of the salubrious climate and a new fascination with sea bathing. Devon was sufficiently removed from both Shropshire and Lincolnshire that she would never see him again. This odd yearning would surely subside once he was out of sight.

Are you sure? The voice taunted her, reminding her of his words only last night. He had sounded so sincere when he vowed never to hurt her. The idea that lovemaking could be enjoyable was insidiously enticing. Why would touches and kisses build such desire if the reality of intimacy was always pain?

But she pushed the thought aside. Experience was more trustworthy than tempting promises made by a gentleman who cheerfully admitted he wanted her. She had a huge advantage over the naïve girls who went in ignorance to their marriage beds. She had lived through the reality. Barely.

As soon as they identified John's killer, she would find that cottage. In fact, she needn't wait that long. Once she matched that hand, she would write to their man of business and instruct him to seek out an appropriate property.

Pulling out the current month's receipts, she started sorting. Was the proposed meeting real or a trap? Her mind toyed with possibilities while her fingers turned over papers.

Butcher . . . thatch for a tenant cottage . . . blacksmith services . . .

If it was a trap, the killer must have given up on staging accidents. He no longer cared if people recognized murder. Did he plan to leave the area, or was he the last person anyone would suspect? Could it be Isaac? He was the one man who had no known grievance. And he had a champion throwing arm.

Candles . . . harness . . . two rams . . .

James was not stupid. He had been asking questions, poking into the past, prodding the magistrate. The accidents had put him on his guard. So the killer must know that he would bring company to the meeting—and probably weapons. She shivered.

Coal . . . repairs to Wilson's barn . . . subscription fee to the circulating library . . .

The meeting had to be a trap. The mill was isolated, uninhabited, dangerous. It was surrounded by woods, reachable only by a winding lane that branched from the distant road.

Seed . . . hay . . . a dozen buckets . . .

What would he do? It would depend on his identity, but he had to make certain that James died this time. Failure would bring the authorities down on his head. If the killer was a gentleman, he might use a gun. A tenant would have no access to a gun and little skill with weapons. But the note had not been written by a tenant. And the killer had revealed deadly aim with his rocks.

Dresses for the girls . . . ten scythes . . . fabric for servants' clothing . . .

Trap!

She screamed.

Receipts rained onto the floor.

They had not considered a third possibility. The killer was wily. He would never allow James to set up a counter-trap. Knowing an intelligent man would check out the meeting site if given the opportunity, he would already be in position.

She was trembling so hard, she had trouble removing her muff pistols from the gun cabinet. Gulping air, she shakily loaded each one.

Please God, let me be wrong.

The simple operation seemed to take forever, but she could

not rush. A poorly loaded pistol was useless and would endanger her. Sweat was trickling down her temples by the time she was done. Making sure that each trigger was locked into its handle so the guns would not accidentally discharge, she jammed them into a pocket and raced to the stables.

Another eternity passed while a groom saddled her horse. She kept her face placid and her hands relaxed. If she was wrong, she did not want to alert the culprit of her suspicions.

But she knew she was right. James was in danger. She could feel it in the pain exploding through her head—or was it his?

Kicking Acorn to a gallop, she jumped a hedge and raced toward the mill.

Fabric for servants' clothing. Usually Mrs. Ruddy wrote out the accounts, but sometimes her husband did it. As he had done this month.

Ruddy was strong, though considerably shorter than the twins. But that hadn't mattered. He had one of the best throwing arms in the district. He and Barnes had vied for years at quoits, and Ruddy prided himself on his accuracy.

The pounding in her head grew worse, dragging her heart into a matching rhythm.

She could understand why he had hated John—Alice had probably been raped. She could even accept that Frederick had participated, which explained his accident. But what grudge could Ruddy have against James? Unless James had been hiding information, he had never once suspected the merchant.

Be careful. She repeated the admonition, slowing to a walk as she approached the mill. James's horse was tethered near the door. No other was in sight, but she could take no chances. Dismounting, she led Acorn into the cover of the woods.

Ruddy's mule was tied to a tree.

Chapter Fifteen

James tethered his horse to a post, pausing to examine the mill's exterior. The stone walls seemed strong, though the roof sagged dangerously in the middle and the few small windows were shuttered. He cautiously circled the building. Weeds grew thick across the path. The attached cottage appeared gloomy and desolate, with a flower garden long since gone feral. After his wife had died, Tate had done little to keep it up.

He shook his head. The sluice gates that controlled the flow through the millrace had rotted. Though Tate had died less than a year ago, debris was already building up in the race. Surprisingly, enough water still flowed to keep the wheel turning. This stream rushed faster than most, flushing the race after each storm.

Climbing the few steps to the platform that surrounded the wheel, he assessed the deterioration. The platform itself was reasonably sturdy, though several boards showed signs of incipient rot. The wheel was another matter. Many of the paddles had broken, making its rotation far from smooth. The uneven rhythm rasped nerves already stretched with tension.

A system of pulleys had once hauled bags of grain through the wide upper window. Now they dangled from broken spars, held in place only by a single length of frayed rope. A pigeon strutted along the window ledge, its beady eye quizzing him as arrogantly as Brummell's glass.

But he was not here to evaluate the condition of the mill, he reminded himself sharply. Casting a last wary glance upward, he jumped down and completed his circuit.

The door hung drunkenly on one hinge, revealing a thick

layer of undisturbed dust on the floor. He relaxed. No one had entered in some time.

He pushed the door wider, its creak drowned by the jerky thumping of the wheel. It reverberated through the mill, explaining why Tate had always been half deaf.

Finding a new miller would be difficult. He could see dry rot in several beams. Water damage proved that the roof leaked. A hole gaped in the floor of the tiny office.

The mill had never been formally abandoned, he realized as his eyes adjusted to an interior lit only by the open door and a few shafts of sunlight sneaking through cracks in the shutters. The massive grinding stones had been uncoupled from the drive shaft, of course, but their bulk still filled the center of the room. Gears and chutes cast grotesque shadows.

The floor shook as he stepped closer. The drive shaft turned with the wheel, sending shivers through the mill. Would the floor give way, dumping him and tons of stone into the cellar?

The image drove his feet toward a wall, farther from the stones. The killer might have set the stage for another accident. If the floor gave way, he would be badly hurt and easy to finish off. Who would suspect murder? The mill was a logical place for him to visit, for he had to find a new miller.

He shivered.

More shadows loomed as he moved farther from the door. The three of them could hide nearly anywhere tonight—so long as they wore dark clothing, he admitted, catching glimpses of white. Bird droppings. The spots were widely scattered down here, but mounds of them must fill the granary upstairs. Birds would have found a way in and picked the place bare.

Even light colors stood out. A branch gleamed in the corner, stripped of bark from tumbling in the river, its wood bleached by the sun. A glance down revealed the blaze of his cambric shirt, visible in the slightly darker V of his gold striped waistcoat.

So they must wear black. And walk carefully. Dusk would hide multiple footprints once they were past the doorway—provided the informant carried no lantern.

He frowned. Perhaps Harry and Edwin should enter through the miller's cottage.

His eyes suspiciously probed the shadows. The unrelenting thump and creak of the wheel reverberated in his head, drowning other sounds and making him edgy. He glanced over one shoulder. Anyone could sneak up on him without warning.

The building needed more repairs than he had expected, so perhaps he should tear it down. He had heard speculation in London that steam engines would soon replace water wheels for power generation. If water mills went the way of cottage spinning, there would be little point in repairing this one. Replacing it with new methods would give his dependents a head start on the future.

But that was not why he was here today. Skirting the edges of the milling room, he assessed hiding places. Rotting grain sacks were heaped beside a stack of lumber. Someone had used the site as a dump—probably Tate himself. Ginger beer bottles littered the floor, though the brown earthenware containers only drew his attention when he stepped on one, turning an ankle. Tate had been uncommonly fond of ginger beer, he recalled as his finger traced the potter's mark—*Bourne of Denby*. He tossed it atop a pile of refuse in the corner, where it joined a carriage wheel, broken chairs, a barrel with rotting staves, and a rusting plow. The junk would offer concealment for a small army.

The steps leading to the granary were blocked by yet another trash pile. Had Tate ceased operating the mill before his death? Perhaps the man had suffered a lengthy illness.

But Tate did not matter at the moment. He turned toward the living quarters. As soon as he checked that entrance, he would find Harry and Edwin so they could plot their strategy for this evening.

He was passing the millstones, when stars exploded through his head. *Trap!* screamed his mind as darkness descended.

Tom Ruddy dropped his club to the floor and smiled, the whites of his mad eyes gleaming in the darkness.

James blinked, trying to focus. Where was he?

The soft glow of a single candle barely penetrated the darkness, deepening the shadows beyond its meager circle. The floor pulsed under his side, matching the uneven beat of the mill wheel.

Thump . . . thump thump . . .

Dust tickled his nose, but when he tried to brush it away, his hands would not move. They were bound behind his back.

"So yer awake, yer bloody lordship."

Tom Ruddy lounged on the fringes of the candlelight.

Memory surged back with a vengeance. How long had he been unconscious? Had darkness fallen? He couldn't move his head enough to see if sunlight still sifted through the shutters. All he could sense was the wheel.

Thump thump . . . thump . . .

He refocused on Ruddy. "So it was you."

"You sound surprised. You shoulda known I'd pay you back for my lovely Alice." His voice wavered with grief—and madness.

"I never met your daughter," he said slowly, fighting down panic. "I only heard of her death last week. Influenza, wasn't it?"

Thump . . . thump thump . . .

"As if you didn't know! None of them lies, now. Yer brother said the same thing, but I know better. You killed her. I found her broken body where you tossed her in the quarry. Put it about she'd died of influenza so's that bloody Mrs. Bridwell would keep her poisoned tongue off my darling, but I know what happened. She lived long enough to tell me who done her in."

Thump thump . . . thump . . . thump . . . thump thump . . .

Water splashed and dripped outside, taunting the dryness of his mouth. His heart had lodged firmly in his throat, pounding in the same uneven rhythm as the wheel and constraining his voice. "Then you'll know I had nothing to do with it. I've not been near Ridgeway in ten years."

"So ye say, just like ye always did, but we seen through ye in the end. Ye bloody twins—teasing and playing yer silly games, standin' in for each other so's you could claim to be elsewhere. It won't work this time. I don't care which of you was with Northrup that day. I'll kill you both to avenge my

Allie's murder. But first I'll make ye suffer like she did. Tell me what you done to her."

The knife sliced through his jacket sleeve. The wheel squealed, rasping his nerves.

"I wasn't there."

Ruddy's eyes flashed as he sliced through the shirtsleeve and into the flesh beneath. "Tell me."

James gritted his teeth to suppress any cry of pain. He needed to think, but panic and a second cut to his leg clouded his mind.

Thump . . . thump thump . . . thump . . .

The wheel beat against his ears. How was he to break through Ruddy's madness to convince him he was innocent?

"Why do you want to know?"

"Tell me! Confess! Maybe you'll spend eternity in a cooler corner of hell."

"I wasn't there!"

The wheel screeched—or was it him, screaming? Ruddy refused to listen, shouting and raging over the attack on Alice, demanding an admission of guilt.

Thump thump thump thump . . .

Rushing water clogged his ears, speeding the wheel, speeding his heart. Pain exploded through his stomach, blows landed on his ribs, fire burned down his thigh. And every jerking shudder of the wheel vibrated through the floor, magnifying his suffering.

This was far worse than the attack from those Italian brigands that had crippled Luigi. They had only wanted money and were content with beating him senseless once they got it. This could only end in death.

Thump thump . . . thump . . .

"Stop!" Mary's voice split the darkness, drowning the wheel.

His heart froze. What in Hades was she doing here?

Ruddy paused, his arm poised to strike.

"Drop the knife," she ordered, stepping into the flickering candlelight. One hand nearly obscured a tiny pistol, but her expression rivaled the furies. Blue ice flashed in her eyes. Her voice sliced the air like tempered steel. And despite the pistol's diminutive size, its barrel yawned as wide as a cannon.

Hope kindled in his breast—and joy. But they were immediately swamped by terror. Ruddy was insane. What would he do to Mary?

"Drop it," she repeated coldly.

"Not bloody likely," swore Ruddy. The knife descended.

"Run," shouted James at the same moment. He couldn't bear to have her witness his death. "I lo—"

An explosion obliterated his words.

"Aaah!" screeched Ruddy, grabbing his leg. The knife twisted, slamming against James's side, then bounced free to clatter onto the floor a foot from his face. Ruddy fell behind him.

James gasped, rolling to dodge Ruddy's kick. Stars danced through his head with the change of position, but he fought down the darkness. Mary might need help.

"Don't move, Mr. Ruddy," she snapped, the steel clear in her voice. She pulled out a second pistol, cocking it to drop the trigger into place. "The next shot will hit your heart. If that doesn't kill you, I'll try again. Muff pistols are wonderful weapons. Half a dozen will fit in a pocket."

Ruddy froze. Mary was now only six feet away. He had no doubt she would make good her words.

"Are you all right?" She glanced briefly at James.

"I'll live." Thanks to her, but he couldn't say that yet. The situation was still precarious. Terror swirled through her eyes. He doubted she had even a third pistol. How long until Ruddy deduced that?

"Can you slide away from him?" She stooped to pick up the knife, keeping her eyes on Ruddy and the pistol steady.

He didn't waste energy answering. Searing pain burned through the cuts on his arm and leg, and sharper stabs radiated from kicks to his groin, ribs, and spine, but he humped across the floor until he was out of Ruddy's reach. Only then did he gingerly sit up.

Keeping the pistol steady, she sawed through the rope that bound his hands, nicking him twice, but he remained silent. The moment the cord parted, he grabbed the knife and freed his legs.

Ruddy was whimpering, still clutching his thigh. Mary's bullet had passed clear through, leaving a gaping hole in the back. Blood pooled on the floor.

Fighting down nausea and light-headedness, he tied Ruddy's arms and legs, then collapsed with his head between his knees.

"Lord Ridgeway was telling the truth," Mary declared, uncocking the pistol and returning it to her pocket. "John often impersonated his brother, but I've never known James to do so. John was a liar. You should have realized that. Everyone else does."

"Ha!" snorted Ruddy.

"It's true. I've caught John impersonating James more than once. As has Cotter, Turnby, and several others. Didn't you know that James left England ten years ago and did not return for five years? Even then, he stayed away from Ridgeway, for John had thrown him out following their father's funeral."

She ripped a strip from her petticoat as she talked, first bandaging James's cuts, then giving him the rest so he could stop Ruddy's bleeding.

"I was in London when John attacked your daughter," James said as he worked. "If you need proof, ask the Regent. On the night your daughter died, I was at Carlton House with two thousand others, celebrating the prince's elevation to his new office."

"Ha!" snorted Ruddy again. "Why would the prince invite a younger son and not the earl?"

"You aren't the only one who had grievances against my brother," said James sadly. "Refusing John an invitation to the most prestigious event of the Season was a cut direct from Crown to subject."

"Oh, no!" Mary's soft gasp drew the men's attention. "Frederick was also cut that night. No wonder they came home without warning."

"And no wonder they were looking for trouble," James finished for her. "Inviting me emphasized the cut, proving that even John's title brought him no power and no respect in higher circles."

"So they would have sought to prove their power here." Her voice cracked.

"The inn fire. Wilson's farm." He should have seen it sooner, he realized in despair. But he had not connected the dates.

"But why attack my Alice?" demanded Ruddy.

"I heard she went to Ridgeway to ask for a position," said Mary. "Perhaps she wanted a peek at the house, or maybe she sought a glimpse of the earl. She would not have realized that she was putting herself in danger."

"My Alice was a good girl," insisted Ruddy.

"I'm sure she was," agreed James. "But that would not have stopped my brother."

"Or my husband," added Mary.

"Especially when they were spoiling for trouble. Her fate would have been the same if she were a saint."

Ruddy crumpled, a broken man. "I wronged you, my lord. You're right that he was a liar. He told me straight out, even through pain, that it was you. He swore he'd not been here. He swore he'd been in London celebrating with the Regent. I didn't believe him at first—and things had gone too far to let him go anyway—but the words ate at me. I couldn't take a chance. Alice deserved better."

"How did Alice die?" asked James.

"They ravished her." Tears trickled down Ruddy's cheeks. "Both of them. She lost count of how many times, but she was desperate to escape, so when they left her alone, she tried to run. But she was so weak, she stumbled and hit her head on the corner of a table. When they found her, they thought she was dead. Ridgeway was furious at Northrup for leaving her, so he made Northrup dispose of the body. She tried to tell them she was alive, but she couldn't make her voice work. Northrup took her out to the quarry and dumped her."

"How did she survive that?" demanded James.

"It were the nearest end, which isn't so steep as up by the road. I musta happened on her almost immediately."

He didn't ask what Ruddy had been doing on Ridgeway land. If he hadn't been looking for Alice, he had undoubtedly been poaching.

"She lived long enough to tell you the tale?" asked Mary softly.

Ruddy nodded. "Poor Alice. Her hair was soaked in blood,

and her face was so pale. I figured God helped her survive that long so's I could avenge her death."

"I doubt it, but you'll have to make peace with God yourself."

"She died almost immediately. I carried her home and let on that she had influenza. Enough others were afflicted that no one questioned it. My wife was attending her mother's deathbed, and I hoped to spare her the pain of knowing how Allie died." His voice suddenly hardened. "I'd hardly got her settled when Northrup showed up, raising a ruckus in the shop. He called my Allie a lazy slut for not being there—as if he didn't know where she was. I couldn't shirk my duty after that." His eyes closed, shutting his pain inside.

"What now?" Mary asked James quietly.

"If I turn him over to Isaac, he'll hang. Whatever the provocation, he killed two lords."

"And came far too close to killing a third," she added with a shudder.

His arm slid around her shoulders. Reaction was setting in. Now that the danger was past, she was ready to collapse.

"Can you hold up a little longer?" he asked.

She nodded, but tremors belied her bravado. He seated her on the lumber stack, pushing her head down to her knees. His own head was also spinning. He needed to conclude this business quickly and get her away—get them both away.

"I cannot condone murder, whatever your reasons or however evil the victims were," he said, prodding Ruddy until his eyes opened so he was sure the man could hear him.

"I understand."

"Probably not. If I could arrange for you to be transported, I would do it, but I can't." He paused a moment in thought. "No, having you confess to theft won't work. I have to tell everyone what happened—to prove I will not treat them as John did and to remove the stigma John's lies caused innocent parties like Lady Northrup."

Mary was staring, as was Ruddy.

"I'm going to give you a chance, Ruddy. You cannot remain in England. But neither can I condone John's actions." He leaned wearily against a post. "You will write a full confession, which I will turn over to Squire Church. In return, I will pay passage to America for you and your wife. You will have to leave immediately if you hope to be out of the country before the authorities start looking for you. If they catch you, you will hang. And once you leave the ship, you're on your own. But don't ever try to return. Killing a lord—even one like John—is a grievous offense."

Ruddy was almost incoherent in his thanks.

"Enough." He wasn't being quite as altruistic as Ruddy thought. It was even odds whether the man would survive that wound, and he didn't want Mary to suffer if he died. She had been through too much already. "I will leave you here while I escort Lady Northrup home. My valet and groom will collect you in an hour or two, take you to town, and supervise your confession. When it is complete to their satisfaction, they will give you the passage money."

Without another word, he helped Mary from the building.

Mary waited nervously in her sitting room. Caroline and Amelia had been shocked when James brought her home, riding before him on his horse with Acorn trailing behind. They had been more shocked to see his tattered coat and bloody bandages. But she had insisted that they keep to their plans to deliver a basket to an ailing tenant.

Justin had been appalled when he'd arrived half an hour later. And his disclosures left her head spinning.

James was innocent of every calumny heaped on him in India. Taking in another man's mistress and arranging for her care was exactly what she would have expected of her former friend. A similar tale probably underlay that orphanage in Italy.

He had vowed to return as soon as he had made arrangements for Ruddy. Now she anxiously awaited his call, wondering how badly he was hurt. She had been too dizzy to ask earlier, but Ruddy had been kicking him when she'd arrived. Was anything broken?

Yet her fears for his health were not her only concern. She was also fighting an acute case of embarrassment. He had half carried her out of the mill, supported her head when the realization that she had shot a man had spun her stomach out of control, hurling her breakfast into a bush, then cradled her gently before him on his horse. How could he excuse such gauche behavior?

And he must have sensed her reaction to that ride home. Despite being only half conscious, her body had quivered with desire. His chest had been hard, his arms like iron bands as they pressed her close. His heat had enveloped her, countering the lingering cold. His breath had whispered through her ears, sounding almost like endearments. She had nearly protested when he had lifted her down and released her.

How could she yearn for a man's touch? Yet how could she not yearn for his touch? She loved him—far more deeply than that youthful infatuation.

Her terror when she had realized that he was walking into a trap had confirmed it. Seeing him tied and bloody with Ruddy looming over him with a knife had banished her last doubt. His leniency proved that he was a vastly different man than John had been. Their kisses had promised something she had never experienced before—pleasure. Now she could only pray that he was truthful about the rest.

"Lord Ridgeway," announced Trimble from the doorway.

"Send him in."

"You look better," James said the moment Trimble left. And she did. While still pale, her face had a modicum of color, and her hands were no longer shaking.

"So do you. How badly did he cut you?"

"Scratches." He didn't mention the ribs. At least one was cracked, but it would heal. He hesitantly joined her on the couch, needing to touch her, needing to assure himself that she was alive and well. "I wish I could thank you for coming after me, but I can't. You might have been killed."

"You would have been." She looked away. "When I realized he was using the letter to draw you into a trap, I had to follow. I could not have lived with myself if my inaction had let you die."

His heart lightened at her intensity. "I'm grateful, of course. But seeing you so close to a madman nearly drove me insane. I didn't realize you were such a good shot."

"I'm not." She laughed a little hysterically. "I was aiming for his heart the first time, but I missed."

She was shaking again, so he draped his arm around her shoulders and pulled her close. "It's over," he crooned, lifting her into his lap. "It's over, and we're both safe."

Her control broke. Turning into his shoulder, she cried until his own eyes were wet.

"Shush, love. It's all right." One hand stroked down her back, soothing, comforting. He fought to keep the gesture light. He hated tears. Most were wiles women employed to get their own way, though these were real enough. She needed the release, so he could only endure the pain that stabbed him with every sob.

But eventually, they eased. One of her hands crept around his neck as her head burrowed under his ear.

"Feel better?" he murmured.

"Mm-hmm." He couldn't see her face, but her rosy neck showed that she was thinking again, and probably embarrassed about breaking down.

He recalled his vow to never touch her. It had slipped his mind at the mill, but unless he wanted to destroy her limited trust, he had better do so now.

"Should I set you down, or may I hold you?"

No response.

He had tensed to lift her away when her fingers crawled into his hair and clung. "No need. I feel safe here."

Safe. His heart swelled. No other vow could make him feel better. His hand stroked her hair, then tilted her head back so he could look into her face.

"Mary, you will always be safe with me. I love you."

"Is that enough?" she murmured uncertainly.

"More than enough. Listen to your instincts. They won't lie. They know that I will never harm you."

She frowned.

"Think, love. How else were you able to tell us apart, even when John was hiding behind my identity?"

"You were safe—always." She relaxed.

"Always," he repeated. "And listen to your heart. Doesn't it recognize that we belong together?"

She smiled, then closed the small gap that separated their mouths. And he was home. Keeping it light was impossible. But she didn't protest.

Mary sank into the kiss, drowning in sensation. Their lips brushed, then pressed firmly together as his tongue slipped inside. It rasped gently against hers, curling, twisting, enticing hers into a dance that grew more frenzied by the second. Her breasts tightened painfully, but it was a welcome pain, an urgent pain that demanded further contact. When his hand closed around one, she thought she would die of ecstasy.

"Dear God, Mary," he groaned. "I want you; I need you; marry me."

He was more than ready to carry this further, she realized as he pulled her closer, bumping her hip into his groin. But even the thought of what that entailed no longer frightened her. She would always be safe with him. Loved. Honored. Cherished. Yet she still hesitated.

"Are you thinking clearly?" she asked, pulling back to look into his eyes. "You know I will never fit into your world."

He was panting, so it took him a moment to find his voice. "That is the first truly foolish thing I've ever heard you say. You have never failed to meet any challenge you faced. After stopping a team of panicked horses and rescuing me from a killer, holding your own in London drawing rooms will be child's play."

"Maybe."

"Definitely. I wasn't going to pressure you," he admitted. "But after today, I can no longer be patient. I love you. I want to spend my life with you—and only you. Will you accept my hand in marriage?"

"I love you, James. I would be honored."

"I will never hurt you," he promised again. "If you need time, you can have it, but I would like to wed as soon as possible."

"So would I." She reached up to brush the hair from his forehead. "I realized today that my other fears paled against the fear of losing you. I trust you—for everything. I always have."

"Thank God." He pulled her close for another kiss.

This time it was a tap on the door that pulled them apart.

Justin entered, followed by Trimble carrying a tray holding wine and three glasses. Mary scrambled to her feet.

"I take it congratulations are in order," said Justin, focusing on Mary while James straightened his cravat and smoothed his jacket. "Will we be holding three weddings this autumn?"

Mary met James's eyes. "We will post banns immediately and be wed in three weeks."

"By Mary's brother," added James. "It will be his first official act as Ridgefield's new vicar."

Her eyes misted.

"The girls will be delighted," declared Justin, handing each a glass of wine. He raised his own in a toast. "May your love bring you happiness and good fortune for the rest of your days. And may those days prove long and fruitful."

"Amen," murmured Mary.

"To us," added James.

They drank. And when James again lost himself in Mary's eyes, Justin slipped away, leaving them to celebrate in private.